I0743590

# GHOST CITY GIRL

BY

# SIMON PAUL WILSON

# Dedication

To Corey

May your love of reading and writing never fade

# GHOST CITY GIRL

# ONE

*Good morning, good morning, good morning!*

*It is 6am on Monday the first of December, and you are listening to Osaka Sector Radio Seven, the most popular station in the whole of Nihon City, broadcasting live to bring you up to the minute news, weather reports and the very best in popular music. Osaka Weather Control has forecast another cold day ahead, with temperatures falling as low as minus twenty and an eighty percent chance of snowfall. UV and toxicity are expected to stay safe at levels three and four, respectively. Reports from the DPA warn of a point-two percent possibility of paranormal activity. Citizens are advised to stay clear of border zones numbered twelve through twenty-two at this time.*

*Now for today's main headlines: Police are still searching for two high-school students who went missing four days ago in the Kyoto Sector. Ami Yoshimura and Yumi Onuki, both fifteen, were last seen attending a lightball match at Kyoto Sector number one high school. An official announcement, made yesterday, states that the matter is being investigated. Whether there is any connection between the disappearance of the two students and the return of Red Raku, last year's most prolific serial killer, has yet to be confirmed.*

*In global news, talks between Europia and the NUK have broken down after allegations of...*

"Off."

The apartment's radio-alarm deactivates, plunging my bedroom into silence. I close my eyes and think about going back to sleep, just for an hour or so. One more hour of sleep would be heaven. Sadly, I know this is impossible. Mother is sure to be awake and making her way towards the living room at this very moment, shuffling through the house like a zombie. It is only a matter of time before she calls for me.

I pull the covers over my head and think about how cool it would be if Mother really was a zombie. I would be happy if she was undead.

A zombie would have more of a life than Mother ever will.

Since getting more rest is out of the question, I throw back the sheets and swing myself out of bed. The ambient temperature in my room has dropped dramatically, causing me to shiver. My thin pyjamas offer little in the way of warmth. They do look cute, though.

"Lights."

A thin neon tube flickers on, illuminating my room in a shade of yellow that makes my skin look jaundiced. I slide my cold feet into a pair of slippers and stand up.

The apartment's sensors pick up my movement and initiate morning protocols. The dulcet tones of a traditional English butler fill the room.

"Good morning, Kichi."

"Good morning, Perkins. Increase room temperature by five degrees, please."

"Certainly, Ms. Kichi," Perkins replies. "Now, what can I get you for breakfast on this fine December morning?"

"The usual please, Perkins."

"Of course. One bowl of inferno noodles will be waiting for you in auto-serve hatch three. Can I prepare you a beverage?"

"Iced tea. Blueberry."

"Certainly. Your drink is now ready for you in auto-serve hatch two."

"Thank you, Perkins."

"It is my pleasure, Ms. Kichi."

I put my dressing gown on and open the curtains. The video-window shows a pastoral field, complete with grazing cows. The cows look content as they munch happily on fresh green grass. A simple life. Another dream I cannot hope for.

One of the cows turns to look at me and blinks its huge eyes. She looks so cute. I wonder what real beef must have tasted like.

"Ki-chi. Mo-ther. Plug."

I cannot help sighing heavily at the sound of Mother's voice. She has reached her destination and needs my help. So begins my day.

"Ki-chi. Plug. Mo-ther."

Every day she forgets more and more vocabulary. Soon she will be unable to say my name. It is only a matter of time before she forgets how to speak entirely. What will she do then? Just sit and wait for me?

"Ki-chi..."

"I'm coming," I shout. "Wait a moment."

"Plug..."

I wish she was undead.
I wish so much.

Mother sits on the sofa. She doesn't acknowledge me as I enter the living room. I doubt she even knows I am there. The only thing she is focusing on is the blank TV screen that occupies most of the north-facing wall. Nothing else matters. That screen is her life. Her god.

"Morning, Mother."

She doesn't look at me. I stand directly in front of her and look down at the cadaver that was once Yuki Honda. I slowly repeat my greeting, accentuating each syllable. Mother stares straight through me and says one word:

"Plug."

I walk around to the back of the sofa and pick up the two long cables that trail from the rTV box on the wall. Both the red and blue cables end at large, vicious-looking jacks. This is where she needs my help. I fold back the two flaps of prosthetic skin located at the corner of each of her eyes, exposing two deep hungry-looking sockets. I slide the jacks into place with two sickening clicks.

Mother is now plugged in.

The screen bursts into life as soon as the connections are made. The spiraling rTV logo fills the wall and a range of menus fly onto the screen, allowing Mother to choose what she wants to watch and who she wants to be. She no longer needs me. It is time to leave.

I sit at the kitchen table and dive into my bowl of inferno noodles. The spices numb my lips and burn my tongue. Still, I manage to devour the whole bowl before draining my iced tea in one long refreshing gulp. I notice the remnants of Mother's breakfast sitting by the sink: an empty bottle of vito-water and an open packet of three-in-one meal tablets. From within the living room, I can hear her enjoying her so-called life. First, there is a childish giggle, then comes a slight moan of pleasure. Yeah, it's definitely time to leave the house.

"Perkins. Play classic selection one. Volume setting seven."

"Very good, Miss."

My mood lifts the second a killer Otoboke Beaver track starts playing. I shower, brush my teeth, dry my hair and then go about selecting what clothes to wear. I know it's going to be cold out, so I end up dressing in a thermo bra and long-pants, a long-sleeved t-shirt, a black hooded top, two pairs of green and red striped socks, a pair of green combat trousers and a black combat parka. After putting my hair in bunches, I am finally ready to escape the apartment.

I don't bother to tell Perkins to kill the music, preferring not to hear what is happening in the living room. I make my way to the front door, put on my favourite pair of army boots and then stand in position. After taking a full body and retina scan, Perkins asks for my password.

"Lemons."

I wait a few seconds for the password to be accepted and my voice to be recognised.

"Goodbye, Ms. Kichi," says Perkins. "Enjoy your day."

One by one, the thirty-seven locks are released and my front door slides open. The door hisses shut the second I am past the threshold. I can still hear the locks sliding into place as I walk down the corridor and turn the corner.

The corridors of apartment block 7A twist and turn like a maze. Even after living here for more than ten years, I still manage to get lost now and again if I don't pay attention. The other thing about the apartment block is that it stinks. A pungent mixture of onions, garlic, fish, urine, vomit and incense clings to the walls despite regular disinfecting. I dread to imagine what the lower levels would be like.

It is now seven-forty and the apartment block is coming to life, its residents ready to face another day full of nothing but cold. An old man stands in the open doorway of Apt 77796 and says hello. I look to the floor and quicken my step. A naked pensioner is not the kind of thing I like to see first thing in the morning.

I finally reach the lifts to find only two of the ten are in working order. No big surprise there. I press the green up arrow on both operating panels and wait. Thankfully, during this time in the morning, there are not many people heading up or out. Most of the tenants here work late shifts or don't work at all. We morning commuters are in the minority. The strip-light above me suddenly sparks and fizzles, making me jump. I reach into my parka pocket in search of some nico-gum. Sadly, I don't find any.

"Good morning, Kichi. Are you going to work today?"

Ms. Pang joins me at the lifts. As usual, she is dressed entirely in a vivid shade of purple. Her hair, eyes and lips follow the same colour scheme as her clothes. Ms. Pang is from Hong Kong City, but has lived here in Nihon for the last eight years or so. I'm not sure what she does exactly. She has never told me and I have never really thought to ask.

"Not today," I tell her. "I'm off shift until Thursday."

"Lucky you," she says. "I wish I could have a few days off. I'm so busy at the office at the moment. There's even talk of overtime."

"Oh."

"I don't think I have had one full day off this month. Terrible."

"Yes. I guess so."

"Still, the money is good, so I can't really complain. Such a pity I rarely have time to spend any of it."

"Yes, that's a shame."

"Oh well, maybe I can have some time off soon. You never know, it may happen, right?"

"Yes, you never know."

"Dreams. That's what life is all about, Kichi."

"I suppose it is."

Our conversation is interrupted by the arrival of one of the lifts. We wait as the metal doors squeak and shudder open, allowing Ms. Pang and me to enter. I am happy to see the lift is virtually empty, only around a hundred people or so stand inside. This is good. I hate it when it is filled to capacity. The doors close with a loud clang and the lift continues its steady ascent to the top levels.

"Have you seen young Ryuu lately?" asks Ms. Pang in lowered tones. "I haven't seen him for a few days."

"Exorcism," I whisper. "He died."

"Died?"

"Yes. He drowned."

"Drowned?"

"Yeah."

"Poor boy. What a way to leave this world."

"Yeah. It's kind of nasty."

"Poor Ryuu. He was a nice young man. Pleasant."

"Yes. Yes, he was."

We continue the rest of the journey in silence. I lean against the cold metal wall and close my eyes. I think about Ryuu, how terrible his last moments must have been and how I knew almost nothing about him.

The lift reaches its final destination. The doors screech open, allowing daylight and freezing air to flood the metal compartment we stand in. Many of us audibly gasp at the sudden drop in temperature. The lift starts to empty, some of the passengers look like frightened caged animals, the way they squint and shiver as they shuffle forward. I pull up the hood of my parka and turn to say goodbye to Ms. Pang.

"Goodbye, Kichi," she smiles, fixing a pair of purple shades into place. "Have a nice day."

"Thanks, you too."

"I am sure I won't," she laughs. "But thanks anyway."

Smiling, I stride boldly forward into the cold heart of Osaka Sector.

Finally, I am free.

# TWO

It takes me twenty minutes to get to platform seven.

The walkways that spider-web across the city, connecting Osaka central at level one hundred, are teeming with citizens on their way to work or to the malls, everyone desperate to arrive at their destination as fast as possible so as to escape the bitter cold. Not me, though. I take my time, allowing the cold wind to snap and bite at me like a savage beast. I like the cold. The cold is real.

There are fewer people at P7 at this time of the morning, maybe around a thousand or so. Many of them have come here for the view, photographing the distant floating mushrooms that are platforms five and six, and the towers of the government sector. Personally, I think the government buildings look a little creepy. They stretch up into the clouds like skeletal fingers reaching up to snuff out the sun. Not my idea of a cool photo.

I am not here for the view. I am purely here for the snow.

Delicate flakes descend from the sky, only to melt the instant they meet the platform's heated floor. Those that miss P7, spiral down towards the lower city and out of sight, their beauty soon to be tarnished and destroyed by pollution as they journey ever-closer towards level one.

By the time I am ready to leave the platform, I am powdered white from head to toe. I take a photo of myself on my phone before heading cheerily onwards towards apartment block 8C.

The lifts for 8C are almost in sight when I spot two nil-by-mouths working their way through the crowds. My breath catches in my throat as I realise they are heading in my direction. Inside my parka pockets, I cross my fingers and pray they haven't seen me. A girl of my age is exactly the sort of person they are after. An ideal candidate to swell their ever-depleting ranks. The thought of spending time 'communicating' with their sort is not one I relish, especially out in the open as the cold has now managed to fight its way through my many layers, making certain parts of my body tingle. I cast my eyes to the floor and hope my hood can conceal my youthful face.

Sadly, I am too late. I notice one of them point in my direction.

They are upon me in seconds, blocking my path, forcing me to either commune with them or to take to my heels and flee in the other direction. Some passersby glance towards me with looks of sympathy, others with sheer relief that it wasn't them. I look up from beneath my hood and take a good long look at the two people before me. Both of the nil-by-mouths are tall and thin, their tight black shirts and trousers accentuate their skeletal frames, making them look almost as emaciated as mother. By rights, the pair of them should be shivering in their bulky black boots, but they remain seemingly impervious to the cold. The steel surgical masks that are nailed to their faces have crude smiles painted upon them in bright yellow. Their eyes flash greedily at the prospect of fresh blood as the female thrusts her com-pad towards me. The pad displays a language menu. I begrudgingly choose Nihon common speak. The nil-by-mouths look at my selection before shoving the pad back in my face.

"GOOD MORNING, CITIZEN AND SISTER. WE ARE THE SILENT MINORITY. WOULD YOU PLEASE JOIN OUR CAUSE?"

I shake my head. The pad is taken away and the female taps furiously at the touch-screen before returning it for me to read.

"WE OFFER YOU A PLACE WITHIN OUR COMMUNITY. WE WILL EMBRACE YOU INTO OUR HEARTS. TOGETHER WE WILL MAKE A STAND AGAINST THOSE WHO CONTROL US. DO YOU ACCEPT?"

"I'm sorry," I say. "I don't think I'm a good candidate. I love eating and talking too much."

Tap, tap, tap, go her fingers on the com-pad.

"WE CAN SHOW YOU THE WAY.

WE CAN LEAD YOU INTO THE LIGHT.

WE CAN SHOW YOU THE TRUTH.

JOIN US, SISTER."

"Look, I'm really sorry," I say. "It's really cold out here and I need to be somewhere."

Tap, tap, tap.

"WE ARE SORRY ALSO.

WE TRIED TO SAVE YOU.
NOW YOU WILL SURELY GO TO HELL."
Tap, tap, tap.
"HAVE A NICE DAY, CITIZEN."
And with that, our conversation is over. The two spindly ghouls brush past me in search of a more suitable target.

I hate nil-by-mouths. I always seem to run into them and whenever I do, they always manage to freak me out.

Now, that's quite an achievement in a city this weird.
I will go to hell?
I have news for you: I'm already there.
We all are.

Thirty minutes later, I arrive at my destination.

I press the doorbell of apt 86524 and wait, stamping my feet to try to regain some warmth. The intercom emits a shriek of feedback that makes me jump for the second time today.

"Who is it?"

"It's me. Kichi."

The door silently slides open, allowing me to enter Mr. Tanaka's apartment.

"Come through to the living room," he shouts. "I have just made a fresh pot of tea."

The door closes behind me and I count slowly down from five. At zero, I mimic Mr. Tanaka as he shouts for me to take off my shoes and put on a pair of slippers.

"No problem, Mr. Tanaka," I shout back as I undo my bootlaces.

"I should hope not. Now get a move on before the tea gets cold."

I take off my boots, slide my feet into a pair of thermo-slippers and shuffle into the living room.

"Ah, there you are," says Mr. Tanaka. "I was wondering where you had got to."

I am sure Mr. Tanaka is shrinking. He seems to grow a little smaller with every visit. The only things that seem to increase in size are his eyebrows and hair, both of which are thick, white and totally out of control.

"Well, don't just stand there," he says. "Sit down. Make yourself comfortable."

As usual, there are piles of magazines, newspapers, old books and photograph albums on the sofa. I clear enough space so I can sit while Mr. Tanaka pours two cups of steaming hot tea. The second I sit down, a cup is offered to me. I accept it with pleasure. Settling back into the sofa, I take a sip and congratulate him on another excellent brew.

"Of course it is," he says with a wry smile. "I have been making tea for almost a hundred years now. It should be nothing less than perfect."

I take another sip as the old man drains his cup and refills it.

"You're late," he says, scowling at me from a face full of wrinkles. "What kept you?"

"It's snowing," I say. "I stopped to admire the view from P7. Then I got held up by a couple of nil-by-mouths on a recruitment drive."

Mr. Tanaka starts to laugh.

"It's not funny!" I protest with a smile. "They told me I was gonna go to Hell!"

"Did you tell them you were already there?"

"Didn't have the chance." I huff. "They walked off after they said that. I thought it, though."

"You should have shouted it after them. That's what I would've done!"

I laugh and tell him I am not so brave.

"Rubbish!" he says, topping up my cup. "You are one of the bravest people I know. You just need to open your eyes and take a good look at yourself, my girl."

I strongly disagree with him on this point. I am not brave at all. Overly curious and a little sarcastic at times, but definitely a coward of the highest order.

Cut me open and I bleed yellow.

We sit in silence, content to just drink tea and relax.

After a while, Mr. Tanaka lets out a melodramatic sigh and asks if I want cake.

I nod.

The old man pulls the remote control for the TV from out of his trouser pocket and points it towards the blank wall-mounted screen.

The screen flickers for a moment and then dies.

Should anyone be watching or listening to us, the next few hours will now consist of me and Mr. Tanaka talking about mundane, non-sensitive news matters as we enjoy tea and cake.

The TV may be dead, but the scrambler is working perfectly.

We now have total privacy.

"So," says Mr. Tanaka, his eyes full of mischief. "Same topic as usual?"

I nod and grin like an idiot. It's either that or I start clapping.

"Please," I say. "Tell me more about what happened to Tokyo. Tell me about the ghosts."

# THREE

I first met Mr. Tanaka around a year ago.

My father had just walked out on us, due to my mother's addiction to rTV. Not wanting to spend all my time locked in my room, I had taken to wandering around the platforms and walkways all day, only returning home when I absolutely needed to.

It was not a happy time. My father's departure hit me hard, much harder than I could have ever imagined. I would often stand on P7 and wish for a power failure so the energy barriers would deactivate and I would be free to jump to my death.

Better splattered across the streets of level one than constantly asking myself that one question:

'Why didn't my father take me with him?'

Well, one day, I got my opportunity.

The 'We Remember Tokyo' group detonated a bomb close to the government towers, knocking out the power to more than half of the city for just under two minutes.

This was more than enough time.

I remember watching as citizens ran to the edge of P7 and leapt without a second thought.

I will never forget the looks on their faces.

There was no sadness or fear.

There was only joy.

It was as I started to run that someone grabbed my arm and pulled me back. Seconds later, there was a crackling sound and a flash of light as the barrier was reactivated. The air was filled with the sounds of sobbing and horrified screams, police sirens and security announcements. Over all this noise, I heard four words that were spoken so softly they were almost a whisper.

"Are you all right?"

The person holding me relaxed his grip a little and repeated his question.

"Are you all right?"

I spun around angrily to see who had saved my life. I was met with the face of an old man . He was smiling at me. It had been a long, long time since anyone had shown me anything remotely resembling affection.

"You didn't really want to do that," he stated. "I'm sure you didn't."

I remained completely silent. It was as if I had forgotten how to speak.

"I'm sure your life isn't that bad," he continued. "You are so young. You have so much to live for. I know it."

He reached out with his hand to wipe away tears I didn't know I was crying.

"Come with me," he said, taking my hand. "I think you need a cup of tea."

Later that day, the news reported close to seven hundred people had taken their own lives during the two-minute power failure.

Government officials claimed the WRT had released several canisters of a psychotropic gas into the air before detonating their bomb. They said the gas had the ability to induce and magnify suicidal tendencies within five percent of people breathing it in. Other people said it was a disturbing revelation of the mindset of modern Osaka citizens.

These views were soon silenced, of course.

Several days later, the whole Osaka Sector was put on white alert by the DPA after paranormal activity increased by one thousand percent.

I spent the next four days locked inside my apartment, praying that whatever was happening out on the streets would not find its way to my bedroom.

The first thing I did after the curfew was lifted, was go back to drink tea with Mr. Tanaka.

It was on that visit that he first told me about Tokyo and the ghosts.

I've been visiting him on my days off ever since.

Some people may say having a best friend who is old enough to be my great-grandfather is a little weird.

Personally, I couldn't care less about them. Mr. Tanaka is the coolest person ever.

He knows about Tokyo and the ghosts, secrets the DPA have kept hidden from the public for decades.

And now, thanks to him, I know too.

I have always loved ghost stories. Partly because of the thrill of talking about topics that are forbidden, but mostly because I love being scared. Before meeting Mr.

Tanaka, I had only heard a few tales about ghosts. Compared to the stories I know now, these were pretty tame. But still, each story always ended with a line that made the hairs at the back of my neck stand on end and covered my arms with goosebumps.

I absolutely adore this feeling.

Like the subzero temperatures of the city, it reminds me I am alive.

I leave Mr. Tanaka's apartment just after five. I would have been more than happy to have stayed a few hours longer, but the old man had insisted that we call it a day.

"And besides," he had growled. "I need a nap!"

I slowly amble my way towards the lifts of apartment block 8C. The corridors here smell different compared to where I live. My nose tells me that most of the residents here must spend ninety-percent of their day cooking spicy food. By the time I reach the lifts, all I can think of is diving into a huge bowl of inferno noodles. I shake this thought from my head and focus instead on Mr. Tanaka's stories.

Yurei.

Onryo.

These words are now playing on a loop in my head. I close my eyes and focus. My imagination slowly turns those two words into vivid images of terrifying beauty.

I snap my eyes open and quickly turn my thoughts back to filling my grumbling stomach.

I will go back to those images later.

Tonight, it is my mission to scare myself stupid.

Today must be my lucky day.

The moment I step out onto level one hundred, I spy an empty hover cab about to take off. I run as fast as my heavy boots will allow in its direction, praying that no one beats me to it. I make it to the cab without competition and slam my right palm against the passenger door panel. The door slides open and I dive inside, quite literally. Sadly, I manage to completely miss the seats and land with a heavy thud on the cab's floor. Not the most graceful of entries, but at least the ride is mine.

"Thank you for choosing Osaka Cabs," says the auto-pilot as the door closes. "Please state your destination."

"Bar Street, North P5," I reply from the carpet.

"Destination recognized. Thank you. Flight path set. The total cost of this journey will be three thousand Nihon credits. Do you wish to continue?"

Three thousand creds?

Has the world gone insane?

I reach up from my horizontal position and lazily slap my right hand against the pay screen.

"Thank you, citizen. Please wait."

I close my eyes and wait while my palm is scanned and my bank account accessed.

"Thank you, Ms. Honda," says the cab. "Payment accepted. Please be seated."

I drag myself up from out of the foot well and take a seat.

"Thank you. Please fasten your seatbelt."

This auto-pilot has some serious attitude. I feel more like a naughty child than a paying customer. With a huff of displeasure, I strap myself in as told.

"Thank you, Ms. Honda," says the auto-pilot. "Have a safe and pleasant journey."

Without any further demands, the cab slowly rises and starts to make its way towards P5.

I sit back and gaze out of the window. It's not yet six, but night is slouching its way towards the city, dragging behind it a purple-black sky. The towering buildings below welcome the oncoming darkness with displays of red and gold neon.

And all the while, the snow continues to fall.

I press my face against the cold glass of the window and stare down at the city I call home.

It looks so beautiful.

It is such a shame it's so screwed up.

The cab lands at a u-shaped area specifically made for hover cabs to either drop off or collect passengers. Looking out of the side window, I see that as soon as each cab lands and its passengers have got out, they are immediately filled and on their way again. I take a few moments to watch this never-ending cycle of activity before taking my part in the process. As soon as my cab door opens, a fat guy in a green and black striped suit tries to clamber inside, oblivious to the fact that I am trying to get out. I manage to squeeze past him without too much body contact and stumble out onto the street. After straightening my parka, I turn to see the man glaring angrily at me through the cab's window. What I have done to deserve such a death stare is beyond me. I twist my face into a cheesy grin and give him a cheery wave.

His face turns the same shade of red as my underwear.

My grin turns genuine as I turn and disappear down the bar street.

Apparently, there are at least seventy bar streets in Osaka Sector. Personally, I'm not interested in looking for any of the others, as everyone says P5's is the best. That, and the fact it is super close to my apartment.

Situated at level ninety-nine and canopied by the platform above, P5's bar street offers some respite from the freezing cold weather. Although still early, the circular street is already starting to come alive. Most people have come here straight out of work in search of food. It won't be until about ten that the bars, clubs and love hotels will find their customers. I will be long gone from here by then.

I start to wind my way through the crowds, keeping a careful eye out for nil-by-mouths. Tonight, the street is at its busiest. It feels like the whole of Osaka has chosen to eat out and have descended on this place like a herd of flesh-eating zombies. I push my way past the hungry mobs of people peering at menus displayed in windows of sushi joints or haggling with street food vendors, ignoring the shouted invitations to dine at all-you-can-eat noodle bars and the discount flyers which are thrust in my face as I make towards my restaurant of choice.

The further down the street I go, the more chaotic it becomes. Businessmen in sharp black suits brush shoulders with Nu-Harajuku girls being pursued by giggling fanboys, spiky-haired emo-punks push their way past pretty office girls while tourists from other cities point their cameras at anything that moves.

This sea of people just gets deeper and deeper.

Thankfully, the bright green door of WasabiDogs is within sight. I take a deep breath, put my head down and make a break for it. A few minor collisions later, and I arrive at the doorway to culinary heaven.

Just as I'm about to push the door open, I hear screaming.

# FOUR

The street is crawling with police.

Buddha only knows how they arrived on the scene so fast. We, being myself and Hiro, the owner of Wasabi-Dogs, watch as they swarm down bar street like an army of angry radiation ants.

Rad ants with protective glyph armour and pulse guns, that is.

Hiro's twenty other customers sit away from the window, preferring instead to watch the 'action' unfold live on the TV at the back of the restaurant, nibbling nervously at their wasabi-loaded dinners.

Outside, those citizens not lucky enough to have found shelter before the security protocols had kicked in are bustled down the street at gunpoint. It may look exciting on TV, but the looks of terror on the evacuees' faces show otherwise.

"That could have been you," says Hiro, as if reading my mind. "You owe me one."

It had been Hiro who had pulled me into the safety of his restaurant. Like an idiot, I had turned around to see where the screaming had come from, much like everyone else on the street. Hiro spotted me standing at the door, threw it open, and dragged me inside by my hood. Although he half-choked me in the process, any complaints I had vanished the second WasabiDogs' spirit barriers activated. Talking about ghosts and vengeful spirits with Mister Tanaka may be one thing, but the possibility of meeting one of them in real life is an entirely different matter.

With this in mind, I thank Hiro for being my hero.

"No problems," he says. "Have you eaten?"

"Nope," I reply. "Haven't had time."

"You want the usual?"

I nod my head with hungry enthusiasm.

Hiro pats me on the back and leaves me to stare out of the window.

The evacuation of P5's bar street is almost complete. The remaining citizens who are left are like me, safely held captive behind spirit barriers.

I am sure I am not alone in hoping a ghost alarm doesn't sound.

If it does, we are all in trouble.

The reporter on TV is a young woman who has obviously been told to keep a cheerful disposition, in order to reduce panic. The smile on her face is so wide, it looks painful to maintain. It is hard to believe that anyone could be taken in by her fakeness, with the exception of Mother, perhaps.

'As you can see, the evacuation is well under way and, so far, without any fatalities...'

Hiro places a box containing a king-size wasabi dog in front of me. Dinner is finally served.

"Bon appétit," he says.

'...whether the incident is of a supernatural nature has yet to be confirmed...'

I open the box and have to blow my scalded fingers immediately afterwards.

"Be careful," he laughs. "It's hot."

"No kidding," I say, wafting away the thick cloud of steam that rises from the open container.

'...one eye witness stated that there is a body in-volved.'

The camera cuts to a young woman, perhaps eighteen or nineteen. She's wearing a bright yellow puffer jacket that is zipped up to her chin and a pink fluffy hat. Just looking at her makes me feel cold.

'I heard someone found a body...'

The grin she wears is not as big as that of the reporter, but it has an unnerving quality that draws my attention.

'I heard it was cut up really bad...'

When she says 'really', her eyes seem to flash with ex-citement.

'... the face was all messed up...'

I can't take my eyes off this girl.

There is something about her...

Something familiar.

The image of the girl disappears as the news flicks back to the overly-happy reporter and her permanent smile.

"Do you think it's ghosts?" asks Hiro.

I turn away from the news and take a good, long look at my friend.

It is hard to believe he is three years older than me. He looks more like fifty-five than twenty-five. His hair started to thin at seventeen. He blamed his hair loss on bad genes on his father's side. Personally, I blame it on his father having a fatal heart attack and Hiro then having to drop out of university to take over the running of WasabiDogs.

"What do you think?" he asks. "Ghosts or murder?"

I tentatively touch my wasabi dog with the tip of my finger. It now feels cool enough to handle.

"Murder," I say, picking up my dinner. "I think a ghost alarm would have sounded by now if it wasn't."

"I hope it's a murder. Then we can all relax a little."

"Yeah, I guess so."

Hiro turns to the TV and puts his hands together in prayer.

"Please be a murder."

The world is truly a strange place.

Here I am, casually discussing how a murder could be a positive thing over a meal containing no natural ingredients whatsoever.

I bite into my wasabi dog and instantly burst into tears.

"Is it that good?" asks Hiro with a smile.

I nod and give him a thumbs-up.

It is awesome.

At nine o'clock, the beaming news reporter cheerfully confirms that a body had been found on P5's bar street and that the police are officially treating the incident as non-supernatural. Most of Hiro's customers give a sigh of relief. Hiro punches the air in celebration.

"Yes!" he says. "Murder."

A few minutes later, the spirit barriers deactivate as the police march out of the street as quickly as they arrived.

'Life' has returned to normal. The "normal" that I'm used to, anyway.

Time for me to go home.

I get up from my seat at the counter and stretch. Something in my back pops, making me wince with pain.

"You heading home?" asks Hiro.

"Yeah," I say. "I need to see to Mother."

"She still into rTV?"

"Yes."

"Sorry to hear that."

"Yeah, so am I."

"You want another dog for the road?"

I shake my head as I zip up my parka.

"No thanks. I'm good. Do you have any nico-gum?"

Hiro nods and produces a fresh pack from under the counter.

"You're lucky," he says, throwing me the gum. "That's the last pack."

I tear open the cellophane wrapping, eager to have my much delayed fix of nicotine. I shake out two pieces of gum into my hand and pop them into my mouth. After a few seconds of frenzied chewing, the nicotine rush hits. A feeling of bliss washes over me.

"How much do I owe you?" I ask Hiro.

"Nothing," he says, waving a hand. "Forget about it."

"Thanks," I say. "Guess you really are my hero."

Hiro just smiles and leaves to attend to a 'real' customer.

One of these days, he will actually make me pay.

Perhaps.

I arrive home just after ten.

Mother is still plugged in. She stares blankly at the equally blank screen in front of her. The half-smile on her skeletal face shows she has satisfied her cravings for today.

"Hello, Mother. I'm home."

Mother looks at me with the eyes of a dead fish.

I walk behind her, carefully pull the plugs from her head sockets and put the prosthetic skin covers back in place.

Mother does not move.

She remains firmly glued to her seat as I wind up the cables and return them to their housing. Not once does she take her eyes off that screen.

I turn off the lights and leave her in darkness. She will move when she is ready. If at all.

"Perkins?"

"Yes, Ms. Kichi?"

"Please play file RR seventy-four on my bedroom video-window."

"Certainly, Miss."

Something has been nagging at me since leaving WasabiDogs.

Something concerning the girl from the news report, the one whose eyes flashed as she spoke about the state of the body.

The video-window flickers for a second as Perkins loads the requested file. I sit on the edge of my bed and take off my parka as the news recording starts to play.

'A citywide search is now underway for a sixteen year-old student who went...'

"Forward to next clip."

'Osaka Sector police have confirmed that the missing student...'

"Forward next clip."

'Two teenage...'

"Forward."

'Identical twin sisters...'

"Forward."

'A Nihon-wide search is now underway for sixteen year-old high school student, Raku Nakamura...'

The news report plays video footage of a slim young woman walking in a park. Her shoulder length hair is dyed the brightest shade of red. She smiles as she gets closer to the camera, her eyes sparkle.

"Pause."

There she is.

The same smile, same look in her eyes.

The same girl.

Raku Nakamura.

'...now known to be the serial killer, Red Raku.'

# FIVE

I wake up ten minutes before my alarm.

After confirming my suspicion that the girl at bar street last night was Red Raku, I completely forgot to focus on the stories Mr. Tanaka told me. Instead of scaring myself silly with dreams of Yurei and Onryo, I dreamt I woke up one morning with red hair.

I throw back the sheets and am pleased to find that Mother has not altered the temperature settings.

"Good morning, Ms. Kichi," says Perkins as the lights flicker on. "You are early to rise this morning. Shall I disable your alarm?"

"Yes please, Perkins."

"Very good, Miss. Do you require breakfast?"

"In a minute," I say. "Could you check news reports from the last twenty-four hours for any mention of Red Raku?"

"Certainly, Ms. Kichi. Searching news files now."

It only takes Perkins a few seconds to do his job.

"My search has found seven related news items. Do you wish to watch these reports now?"

"Save the results to file RR Ninety, please. I'll watch them in the kitchen. Usual breakfast and beverage."

"Of course, Ms. Kichi."

Thermo-slippers on, I stumble out of my bedroom and towards a breakfast of spicy noodles, iced blueberry tea and brutal serial murders.

Mother stands at the kitchen sink, an empty glass held in one bony hand and an open packet of meal tablets in the other. I take my inferno noodles and iced tea from their auto-serve hatches and place them on the table. Mother remains frozen. A living statue of a woman near death.

"Good morning, Mother," I say. "Are you OK?"

There is a long moment of silence before she finally answers.

"Ki-Chi..."

I walk to the sink and stand next to her. Her long hair hangs limp and lifeless, covering her face. The only thing she wears is a thin, white nightdress.

My Mother, the Onryo.

I open a drawer and take out a pair of plastic chopsticks.

"Are you OK?" I repeat.

"Ki-Chi..."

"Yes, Mother. I'm Kichi. Kichi Honda. Your daughter."

"Mo-ther..."

I close the drawer and sigh.

I know what is coming next.

"Plug..."

After I have finished plugging Mother in, I quickly return to my bedroom to collect a pair of earpods. I then head back to the kitchen and sit down before my cooling noodles. I jam the pods firmly into my ears and turn on the table's video-pad. The pad rises from the centre of the table and rotates its fifteen inch screen to face me.

"Play file RR Ninety please, Perkins."

"Certainly, Ms. Kichi."

I plunge my chopsticks into my inferno noodles and finally start breakfast. Although not really hot in temperature, the spices are still potent.

Of the seven news items, three of them focus on the police finding the bodies of two girls who went missing in the Kyoto Sector and the possibility of Red Raku being responsible.

The next two officially name the girls and confirm them as Red Raku's latest victims.

The sixth talks about the unidentified body found on P5's bar street and likelihood of it being related to the murders committed by Red Raku.

The final is an official statement from the Osaka government, telling citizens not to panic, as the chances of Red Raku slipping into Osaka Sector were very slim indeed.

Ridiculous as it may sound, it really does appear I am the only citizen in Osaka Sector with eyes.

Today is my last day off from work.

Tomorrow, I will be back to the grind and the same old same old.

Still, it gets me out of the house and more importantly, pays the bills.

I check the weather report and find that today will be even colder and with a hell of a lot more snow. This suits me fine. I dress in almost the same clothes as yesterday, except for the addition of one item: a red t-shirt that bears the words 'PLEASE DON'T KILL ME, RED RAKU' in all variations of Nihon speak. These were all the rage when Raku started her bloody campaign just over two years ago. Although there is no evidence to say whether these shirts actually work, I figure it is better to be safe than sorry.

I leave the apartment and head to the lifts. Upon arriving, I see Ms. Pang has made it there before me. The vision in purple waves at me and beckons me over.

"Did you see the news last night?" she half whispers.

"Yeah..." I reply, wondering where the conversation may lead.

Could it be that she too saw Red Raku on the news report from bar street?

"Do you think she's here? Red Raku, I mean."

Obviously, she did not. Looks like I am still alone on this one.

"Maybe..." I say. "What do you think?"

"Well, the government said there was no way she could slip past the sector's border control. But..."

"But what?"

"I'm not so sure," she says, her voice dropping to an even quieter level. "The body they found. They said the face was badly mutilated and her eyes had been removed. Do you see what I'm saying? It fits Raku's style exactly."

"I don't remember hearing that," I say. "Was that on the news?"

"I'm sure it was," says Ms. Pang, putting on her purple shades.

Perhaps I missed a news report. I will have to double-check later.

A lift arrives, putting an end to our conversation. Me, Ms. Pang and around another thirty residents, wait for the doors to open before shuffling onboard. Like yesterday, the lift is all but empty. Today's weather must be keeping some citizens indoors.

"So, what are you doing today?" asks Ms. Pang as the lift doors close. "Anything exciting?"

"Visiting a friend," I reply.

"Oh, that will be nice."

"Yeah."

"Must be nice to catch up with friends. I seldom have time."

"Yes. It's nice."

"To be honest, I don't really have that many friends here. Except for you, of course."

I take a sideways glance at Ms. Pang.

"Me?"

"Sure!" she says with a warm smile. "I think we've waited for the lifts together enough times to qualify as friends, don't you think?"

"I suppose so. Yes."

"Wonderful. Friends it is."

"OK."

My new friend falls silent for a few moments. I follow suit.

"We should go shopping together," she says suddenly. "The next time we're both free. What do you think?"

"Sure," I say, although not really so sure about the idea.

"We could have lunch too."

"OK."

"Do you like spicy food?"

Now she has me.

"Yes. Absolutely," I say, perhaps a little too quickly.

"Wonderful. I know just the place."

She reaches into her coat pocket and pulls out a business card, which she then offers me. Naturally, the colour of the card is purple.

"Give me a call next time you are free," she says. "I think we both deserve some fun."

She is not wrong there.

I take the card and slip it into one of my parka pockets, just as the lift comes to a timely stop at level one hundred.

"Well," says my new best friend. "Here we go again."

Every single one of us gasps, swears, or both as the lift doors open and the cold air attacks us with sharp teeth and pounding fists.

Ms. Pang wishes me a good day and quickly totters away on her high heels to wherever it is she goes to do whatever it is she does. Seeing as we are now the best of friends, perhaps it is time I asked her about her demanding job. I make a mental note to ask her the next time we meet. I am pretty sure I will forget, though.

I face almost an hour's walk in the freezing cold to reach Mr. Tanaka's. My appreciation of the snow's beauty has been replaced with a fear of being frozen to death. There will be no stopping to admire the view today. Pulling up my hood, I take a deep breath and then set off into the canvas of blinding white.

I arrive at Mr. Tanaka's apartment dead on time and without any hassle from nil-by-mouths. This is good. The cold in my fingers, toes and nose is not.

"Is it cold outside?" says the old man, looking genuinely unaware of the sub-zero temperatures currently freezing the Osaka Sector.

"Freezing," I tell him, stamping my feet and blowing on my fingers to emphasise the point.

"Take your coat off," he orders. "You're not outside now. I'll turn up the heating a little."

I do as told, hanging my parka on a coat stand by the living room door. Mr. Tanaka frowns when he sees my t-shirt.

"Why on earth are you wearing that?"

"Haven't you seen the news?" I ask, clearing space on the sofa so I can sit down. "Red Raku's back."

"Yes, yes. But she's not in Osaka Sector, is she?"

I pause. Mr. Tanaka gives a knowing smile.

"Sit yourself down," he says. "Let's have some tea and cake."

# SIX

I finish my second cup of tea and let out a heavy sigh.

Mr. Tanaka looks at me, both of his bushy white eyebrows raised.

"You're absolutely sure? You're certain it was Red Raku?"

"Absolutely certain. It was definitely her."

"I see."

Now it is the old man's turn to sigh.

"I don't know which is the more worrying," he says. "Red Raku's return, or your obsession with her."

"It's not an obsession!" I protest. "Just an interest, that's all."

"Girls of your age should be interested in more mundane things than keeping diaries about serial killers. Things like..."

"Ghosts?"

Mr. Tanaka laughs and wags a gnarled finger at me.

"Point taken. You're a sharp one today, Ms. Kichi."

My host fills my cup for a third time and his own for a fifth.

"So, do you believe that will work?" he asks, pointing at my shirt.

"I don't know," I shrug. "Maybe."

"Do you realistically see Red Raku showing mercy because of a politely-written plea on a t-shirt?"

"Maybe not."

"I think definitely not. I imagine all of her victims begged for their lives and found their cries falling upon extremely deaf ears."

I look down at my shirt and ponder its pointlessness.

"I just feel safer wearing it," I say.

The old man smiles warmly.

"I'm sure you'll stay safe, my girl. T-shirt or not."

We settle into a comfortable silence as we both sip our tea. I turn to look at the scrambler and its dead screen. I can't help but think of Mother and the screen she is glued to.

"So," says Mr. Tanaka, shaking me from my thoughts. "Seeing as you're now the resident expert on Red Raku, have you noticed any distinct behavioral patterns?"

"Two things," I say. "First is the age range of her victims. She likes them young, usually either teenagers or citizens in their early twenties."

"Usually?"

"OK, always."

"How old were her youngest victims?"

"Thirteen. The oldest was twenty-three. You know, maybe there's something important about the numbers, but I can't see it."

"And the second thing?"

"The way she kills them."

Mr. Tanaka leans forward in his chair.

"And how does she kill them?"

I let out a long deep breath. My heart starts to beat just a little bit faster. I am unsure if this is due to a feeling of horror or excitement. Perhaps it is a mixture of both.

"She uses a knife, stabs them to death," I tell him. "Not just once or twice, more like a hundred times, maybe more. Some of the bodies they found were almost in pieces. She cuts out their eyes, too. Reports say she takes them with her, keeps them as trophies. But you know all this though, right? It was all on the news reports."

Mr. Tanaka slowly nods his head.

"Have you heard anything else? Any rumours?"

"Some say she cuts words into her victim's skin."

"Yes, I heard that, too. Do you know what words exactly?"

"Not really. The person who told me had just heard the rumour, not the details."

The old man slowly gets to his feet and stretches, his hands reach up for the ceiling. I hear his spine click and pop several times. It sounds so painful that it makes me wince. Mr. Tanaka just laughs.

"Starting to feel my age," he says. "Still, there's life in this old dog yet."

"Glad to hear it," I say.

"Wait there a minute," he says. "I need to fetch something from my study."

And with that, he shuffles off out of the living room.

I finish what is left of my tea and discover that even when cold, Mr. Tanaka's tea still tastes delicious. I have no idea what his secret is, and I am damn sure he would never tell me, regardless of how close we are. That secret will be one he will take to the grave.

I cradle the empty cup in my hands and close my eyes. It feels good to actually relax on a sofa in a living room. It has been years since I have had the opportunity to enjoy this simple pleasure in my own home. Sharing the sofa with Mother is something I will never do. Not unless she manages to kick her addiction.

That will never happen, though.

Mother is too far gone.

"Are you asleep?"

I open my eyes and have to blink a few times to regain focus.

"Sorry," I say. "I think I must have dozed off."

"You most certainly did," says Mr. Tanaka. "I could hear you snoring from the other room."

"I do not snore!"

"How do you know? Have you ever heard yourself?"

"No, but I'm pretty sure I don't."

"Take it from me," he laughs. "You definitely do!"

I give up on arguing, letting my friend claim victory. He sits back down in his favourite chair, places a heavy looking book on his lap and lovingly pats its cover.

"Do you know what this Friday is?"

I give Mr. Tanaka a blank look.

"The end of the week?"

"Anything else?"

"Not that I know of. Is it a special day?"

"You could say that."

I watch as he opens the book and starts to leaf through its pages, patiently waiting for him to explain what makes this coming Friday worth mentioning.

I begin to feel he has forgotten about the conversation we were having, his attention is now solely focused on that thick book. After several silent minutes have passed, he finally continues.

"This Friday marks the one hundredth anniversary of Tokyo's fall," he says, turning another page. "One hundred years since the ghost quake."

"I didn't know that," I say. "I mean, I knew it was this year, but I wasn't sure when."

"Nor would I expect you to know. That kind of knowledge is strictly forbidden. I sincerely doubt that even the WRT are aware of the special significance of this Friday. I can't imagine what would happen if they did."

The old man stops and looks at me for a moment.

I know exactly what he is thinking.

That day at P5 when the barriers failed.

The day I almost said goodbye to everything.

Mr. Tanaka returns his gaze to his book. He slowly runs a steady finger down one yellowing page, silently mouthing the words as he reads to himself.

"Have I ever mentioned anything to you about the Blood Daughter?" he asks, still without eye contact.

"No," I say. "Never."

"I will not say her name in old Nihongo. Mentioning Yurei and Onryo may be one thing, but the Blood Daughter..."

His sentence trails off, unfinished. The room is now filled with a silence as thick as New London fog.

He turns over the page and narrows his eyes to a point where they look closed. His bony finger now moves up and down the page at speed. He no longer mouths the words he reads.

His head suddenly snaps up, his eyes as large as rice bowls. "Let's have some fresh tea," he says with a wide smile. "Then I'll tell you a little about her..."

"The Blood Daughter is an ancient and extremely powerful Onryo. There are some who firmly believe her to be the very first of that terrible kind. Personally, I am not so sure, but that's just my humble opinion. As you know by now, most tales of vengeful spirits usually concern a girl or woman who was greatly wronged during her life and them taking their own life or being brutally murdered. Not the happiest of stories, I'm sure you agree."

I nod my head in total agreement. The number of 'happy' stories Mr. Tanaka has told me can be counted on the fingers of one hand. Honestly though, I am not too bothered about that. I feel the more gruesome, the better.

Mr. Tanaka resumes his story. I position myself on the edge of the sofa and listen.

"In life, the Blood Daughter was a young woman named Ai. All the stories say she was a pleasant girl with a natural beauty. But inside her was something dark and twisted, an evil that bloomed like a poisonous flower as she grew older. By the time she was thirteen, she had already murdered three people. Her parents were well aware of her crimes, but covered up her sins. She was their only daughter, after all, regardless of the evil things she had done. Luckily for Ai, her father was a fairly wealthy man and had some influence over the town where they lived. Even so long ago, money and corruption were the best of friends."

He pauses to take a sip of tea.

"The three murders had become thirteen by the time Ai reached her seventeenth birthday. Six boys and seven girls had met their ends at the hands of the beautiful Ai. The story says she slit the throats of several of her victims, the others she bludgeoned to death with heavy rocks or hammers. The thirteenth and final victim happened to be the son of a rich merchant who had recently made the town his home. Despite their best efforts to hide their daughter's involvement, her parents found that money could only soak up so much spilled blood. And unfortunately for Ai, she had spilled so very, very much."

He stops again for more tea and to clear his throat.

"A group of villagers came for her in the dead of night, dragged her screaming from her home and out into the woods. The story says that what they did to her was truly terrible. The exact details of her murder are never mentioned. I've searched many times over the years for a complete version of this tale, but have always come up empty-handed. I believe Ai's final moments will forever remain a mystery. But what followed is well-documented indeed. She placed a curse on the whole village. Within a week of her death, the place where she had lived her life had become a ghost town, if you can pardon the expression."

"How did they die?" I ask.

Mr. Tanaka shrugs. I had a feeling he might not know.

"Again, no details. Sorry."

"Not your fault. Is there more to the story?"

The old man takes a slow sip of his tea, looks down at the book on his lap and then towards the scrambler.

"This book says when Ai arrived in Hell, she became the Blood Daughter," he says, turning back to look at me.

The expression on his face is now one of total seriousness.

A sudden wave of intense cold runs through my body, making me shiver. If he is attempting to creep me out, he has totally succeeded.

"The Blood Daughter was born from the darkness and hatred that lived inside Ai. In Hell, all that malevolence was amplified beyond measure. For a being of such power, the curse she placed upon the village was more like an act of petty revenge. The true horror of her vengeance would last for thousands of years."

My arms are now covered with gooseflesh.

Never before has he told a story this dark and with such feeling.

I love it.

"It's said there was some kind of ritual performed to keep the Blood Daughter placated. Should it ever come to pass that it wasn't completed, she would be released from Hell to share her version of goodness with the whole of mankind."

He stops talking and opens the book once more, flicking through the pages until he is almost halfway through the book.

"There you are," he says, jabbing a finger at the page.

He turns the book around for me to see.

"Can you imagine anything that looks like this ever being good?"

I return from the bathroom and retake my seat opposite Mr. Tanaka.

"How are you feeling?" he asks in a concerned tone.

"I'm OK," I reply. "The picture just made me jump, that's all. I totally forgot my cup was still full. Sorry about that."

"Never mind the sofa," he chuckles. "I'm sure both it and your trousers will dry soon."

The book sits open on the table between us. Thankfully, my tea-throwing fit of fright did not damage the book in any way.

I take another look at the picture.

Although nothing more than a crude charcoal sketch, the image is truly the stuff of nightmares.

The Blood Daughter stares back at me, all writhing tendrils of hair and eyes that weep tears of blood. Her crooked smile makes Red Raku's seem positively angelic.

A thought suddenly hits me.

"What's this got to do with Red Raku?"

"Clever girl!" says Mr. Tanaka. "Top marks for remembering."

He turns the page, removing that creepy drawing from sight.

I am not sad to see it go.

"Can you read this?" he asks, pointing to a group of characters written in the old language.

I shake my head and slump back in my chair.

"Not to worry," he says. "There are not that many who can now."

"What's it say?"

"They're the details of the ritual. The steps one must follow to ensure the Blood Daughter remains in Hell."

I creep back to the edge of the wet sofa.

"I'm not going to translate all of it," he says. "The basic information is all you need to know."

His finger hovers next to the first line of characters.

"Their eyes are removed, so as not to see the coming evil."

His finger moves to the second line.

"They shall be cut until enough blood has been spilled."

Then the third and final line.

"Then Earth shall be Hell and the daughter of blood will smile."

Mr. Tanaka closes the book and sits back in his chair.

"Any of that sound familiar to you?"

# SEVEN

I used to go to high school with a girl called Raku Nakamura.

Me and Raku used to sit next to each other in art and maths classes.

To say we were the best of friends would be a bit of an exaggeration, but we were happy to chat with each other at school and would often hang out at a nearby ice cream parlour before going home.

When our time at high school came to an end, we promised each other we would do our best to keep in touch.

After a year of having all my messages ignored, I gave up on trying.

When Red Raku's true identity was officially made public, my old friend contacted me out of the blue, just to say she was not the Raku from the news report.

"We just have the same name!" she had cheerfully informed me. "How spooky is that?"

I told her it was not spooky in the slightest. The chances of there being only one person in the whole wide world with the name 'Raku Nakamura' were very, very slim. I went on to say that anyone being surprised by this would have to be very, very stupid.

"I don't understand why you're being so mean," she had said. "I thought you would've been relieved to know it wasn't me killing all those people!"

As politely as I could, I told my 'friend' that the news report had made it clear that Red Raku was from Okinawa Sector. Anyone with half a brain would be aware of this. Knowing the person on the other end of the phone was born and raised in Osaka Sector had taken her off my suspects list, not that she was ever on it.

I ended the phone call by saying the reason why I was being 'mean' was because this was the first time I had heard from her in years, despite me sending many messages in the past, and that an apology for ignoring these messages would have been a better way to start the call.

After cutting the connection, the sound of my parents arguing came flooding into my bedroom. This was back when my dad still lived with us and Mother could still string a coherent sentence together.

In hindsight, perhaps this was the real reason why I acted like I did. I sometimes think about that call and wonder if I could have handled it a little better.

Then I think what would have happened if Red Raku had not started hacking people to pieces.

Would she have still called me that day?

The answer to that has two letters and starts with a big fat 'N'.

It is just after  seven when I leave Mr. Tanaka's.

Leaving behind the warmth of his living room, I walk outside into a heavy snowstorm. Bloated clouds spew out a never-ending barrage of snowdrops the size of boiled synth-eggs, pummeling anyone stupid enough to be out and about.

I am one of those stupid people.

My original plan had been to go to WasabiDogs for dinner, but that was before I saw how bad the weather was. Heading straight home now seems like a much better idea. I pull up my hood, lower my head and take the walkway that leads to P7.

While walking, I think back to what Mr. Tanaka told me about the Blood Daughter and the ritual to keep her from escaping Hell. More importantly, I think about Red Raku and how she is mirroring said ritual.

Is it just coincidence that her killing style matches the procedure to stop an evil spirit from slaughtering everyone on the planet?

Maybe it is. The only way to be certain of this would be to ask her.

I pity anyone foolish enough to try.

Mr. Tanaka's biggest question was how she could have heard the story.

"To be influenced means to know," he said.

So let us say she knows. What we should ask next is 'how'.

Like the old man said, this kind of information is strictly forbidden, not the sort of thing an average citizen would be able to find easily.

Does this mean she has books of her own?

Or is someone telling her the stories?
Does Red Raku have her own version of Mr. Tanaka?

The snowstorm eases up by the time I arrive at P7.

Heavy clouds still fill the night sky, blocking out both the moon and stars, but now only a fine powder falls upon Osaka Sector. I stop for a moment to watch those tiny delicate flakes dance under P7's night lamps. Their movements are beautiful, hauntingly so.

Even though I am wearing a smile, a deep melancholy feeling grows in my heart. I pull back my hood, close my eyes and turn my face to the sky, allowing the snow to fall on my face.

I count fifty flakes before pulling up my hood and heading for the walkway that will take me to apartment block 7A.

The entrance to the walkway is blocked. A large crowd of citizens stand motionless, whispering to each other and pointing down the walkway, some are also taking photos. I reach the blockade and ask what is happening.

"A nil-by-mouth," says a woman in a white parka. "Just standing there on the walkway."

Although I loathe nil-by-mouths, I am confused why everyone has frozen. Everyone knows that standing still will only make you a bigger target.

"It's coming closer!" shouts a man.

Everyone suddenly takes several panicked steps back, forcing me to do the same or be knocked to the floor.

"Look at that!" says another man. "I just got an awesome photo!"

My curiosity is now piqued.

I squeeze my way to the front of the crowd so I can see what has got everyone so spooked.

The woman in the white parka was wrong.

She said there was a nil-by-mouth, as in there being only one.

In fact, there are five of them.

The nearest one is a few meters away, the other four some distance behind. Further back still stands another line of cowering citizens.

The closest nil-by-mouth stands with its back towards us, slowly swings its head from left to right, as if looking for something.

The other four remain motionless, watching.

We all take another step back when it suddenly turns to face us.

I can now see that this one is a young male. His hair is cut brutally short, accentuating the size of his ears. The metal plate that covers his mouth has a smile painted across it in bright yellow, just like all members of the Silent Minority.

This one though, is different.

Firstly, this one feels the cold.

I can see him shivering violently in his thin black clothing. The way his body twitches and convulses make it look like he is performing some kind of macabre dance under strobe light.

And then, there is the expression of fear.

The grin he wears may be nailed permanently in place, but the look in his eyes is both heartbreaking and horrific to see.

There is a loud gasp from the citizens behind me as the nil-by-mouth jerks forward two steps and then falls heavily to his knees. I flinch as I imagine how much that must have hurt.

The com-pad he was holding falls from his grasp, clattering to the floor before him. With a shaking hand, he reaches over to his only form of communication and starts to tap at the screen.

"What's it doing?" asks a man. "I can't see."

"Messing with his pad," says another.

"He's writing something," I say. "That's how they speak."

The nil-by-mouth stops what he is doing and slowly lifts his head to look at his audience, his eyes as big as those of the cow on my video-window.

It is then that I notice the tears.

"He's crying...."

Buddha knows why, but something tells me to go to him.

Citizens give another startled gasp as I take my first step forward.

"What's she doing?" I hear them ask.

Good question.

Wish I had an answer.

I carry on walking. It feels like I am on autopilot or possessed. The next thing I know is I am crouching down in front of him with no fear at all.

When did I get so brave?

Looking at the shivering wreck before me, I feel nothing but pity. His entire body shakes with cold, each tremor larger than the last.

He looks at me with tear-filled eyes and points to his com-pad.

I pick it up and get to my feet.

Written on the nil-by-mouth's com-pad are two words, repeated in every known Nihon dialect.

"What's it say?" shouts someone from the watching mob.

I wipe away a tear and turn towards them, holding the pad up high.

"Help me."

Mr. Tanaka told me nil-by-mouths first appeared after Tokyo was sealed off from the rest of the world.

When the government announced there would be no efforts made to rescue any of the twelve million citizens trapped in that sector, the rest of the population rose up in anger.

Their rage soon disappeared when the first of the ghosts made their way past the barriers.

The government acted swiftly to deal with the spirits that had managed to break through and then strengthened the walls, assuring the public that such a breach could never happen again. The masses thanked the government for keeping them safe, prayed for those that were not and then went on with their lives.

There were some, though, who did not give up on Tokyo.

One day, a group of citizens wearing white surgical masks, marched to the government buildings in Osaka and sat down outside.

None of them spoke.

They just sat there in silent protest.

Mr. Tanaka said the police moved them away countless times, but these citizens were persistent and kept on coming right back. After a few days, the police gave up and let them carry on with their mute vigil.

The hunger strike lasted for over sixty days.

The next protest took place a month later.

The Silent Minority had been born.

I have often thought about why someone would decide to become a nil-by-mouth. What would it take to make an ordinary citizen think that nailing a sheet of metal to their face and starving to death could be a good thing? For a start, those nails have got to hurt and the process of dying of hunger cannot be pleasant.

I can understand the anger those citizens must have felt a hundred years ago. How could everyone just wash their hands of Tokyo like that and then carry on as if nothing had ever happened? To witness apathy on such a scale must have been terrible to see.

But like I said, that was a century ago. Things are different now.

Apathy rules.

No one talks about what happened to Tokyo, mostly because no one really knows. That information has been redacted from the tomes of history.

Deleted.

Mr. Tanaka reckons that not even the nil-by-mouths know the details of their true origins.

"They're just another religious cult now," he said. "Toothless zombies without bite or purpose. Idiots."

I remember laughing when he called them idiots.

Looking down at the poor creature at my feet, laughing seems like such a heartless thing to do.

I kneel down and place the com-pad back in front of the quivering nil-by-mouth. It may be my imagination, but his skin appears to be turning blue. I always thought that was a myth, turning blue with cold. The nil-by-mouth looks at me with his vacant eyes and then at his pad. I feel like I should say something, so I do.

"How can I help?" I ask.

He starts to slowly tap his answer onto his pad. I move a little to the right so I can read his reply easier.

"I NEED TO MAKE A CHOICE."

"What choice?"

It takes him a few minutes to type his answer.

"HEAVEN OR HELL.

HELP ME.

PLEASE."

"I don't understand," I say. "How can I help?"

The nil-by-mouth looks at me for a moment. His eyes are now red from crying. Tears stream down his face and over his painted grin. He returns his gaze back to his pad and starts tapping at the screen again.

"IS YOUR LIFE GOOD?

ARE YOU HAPPY?"

It is now me who takes a while to answer.

"Yeah," I lie. "Life is good. Everything's cool."

He points to his second question, tapping the screen with a trembling digit.

"Yeah," I say. "I'm happy."

"YOU LIE," is his eventual reply.

The com-pad's screen suddenly glows a bright white. His damning words are erased and replaced with two red boxes. Both of the boxes contain characters I am unable to read. The nil-by-mouth studies them for a moment before selecting the first box. The screen goes blank the instant his selection has been made.

I look up to find myself surrounded. The other four nil-by-mouths have decided to join our little chat. I hate the way they can move so quickly and so damn quietly. I nervously get to my feet. The tallest of the group flashes her pad at me.

"YOU SPEAK NIHON COMMON?"

"Yes," I say. I can feel all of my compassion and tenderness fading as a 'real' conversation with a nil-by-mouth begins.

"THANK YOU, CITIZEN."

"What for?" I ask. "What did I do?"

Tap, tap, tap.

"YOU HAVE HELPED OUR BROTHER TO SEE THE ERROR OF HIS WAYS.

HE HAS RETURNED TO THE LIGHT.
RETURNED TO US.
THIS IS THANKS TO YOU."

I should take this opportunity to get the hell out of here, to walk away and head back to the safety of home, to be as far away from these weirdos as possible. Instead, I keep on asking questions.

"But I didn't do anything! How did I help him see the error of his ways? What error did he make in the first place?"

The tall female turns to the three that stand and nods her head. Two of them lift their kneeling comrade to his feet. He looks as if he is drifting in and out of consciousness. As the female starts tapping on her pad, a black hover car silently rises from beside the walkway and lands with a hiss and jets of steam. I watch as they half carry, half drag him towards the waiting vehicle.

The female shoves her pad in my face, blocking my view. I really wish they would learn some manners.

"OUR NEW BROTHER HAD A MOMENT OF WEAKNESS. HE DARED BREAK ONE OF THE FOUR COMMANDMENTS. HE HAD TO BE PUNISHED. HE HAD TO SEE WHERE HIS WEAKNESS WOULD LEAD HIM. YOU SHOWED HIM THAT LIFE IS POINTLESS. YOU REMINDED HIM THAT HE WOULD DIE ALONE AND BE DAMNED. HE THEN CHOSE TO RETURN TO US. THANK YOU, CITIZEN."

"How did I do that?" I can feel my anger rising. It scares me. "All I did was talk for a few minutes!"

Tap, tap, tap.

"WHAT DID HE ASK YOU?"

"He asked if I was happy."

Tap, tap.

"AND YOU SAID?"

"I said I was."

I swear I see her painted smile grow larger. Her eyes convey a sick sort of satisfaction from our interaction.

"THERE IS THE ANSWER.

THERE IS THE LIE."

She starts to turn her back on me. A part of me wants to grab the skinny freak, spin her round and slap her. I have never felt so angry, so frustrated. I take a deep breath and after exhaling, fire off one last question.

"What did he do? What mistake did he make?"

She stops, taps something onto her pad and turns to show me.

"HE FELT HUNGER."

I watch their hover car leave.

As soon as it has cleared the walkway, the crowds start moving again. It is like the play button has been pressed, releasing them from their freeze-frames. Citizens pass me from both directions. None of them stop to talk to me, to ask what happened. A few of them look, but not one of them summons up the courage to ask me anything. I can hear them talking to each other about how they hope their dinners have not been spoiled or which restaurant they should go to.

Apathy does not just rule here, it is God.

I think about that young nil-by-mouth and the 'crime' he committed, trying to make sense of what just took place.

A nil-by-mouth felt hunger, so they marched him through Osaka Sector until he was almost dead from hunger and cold.

They pushed him to his limits, just to see if he would see the great mistake he had made.

Then, when death was almost upon him, they gave him one last chance to return to their twisted family.

So what would have happened if I had not been on that walkway?

Would he have made a different choice?

Would the others have just stood there and watched him die?

What if I had told him life sucks?

A guy about my age, dressed for a Siberian winter, smiles at me as he passes and glances upwards.

"Beautiful night."

I look up at the sky. He is totally right. The snow clouds have all gone, revealing a blue-black sky that glitters with tiny white stars.

"Yeah," I say. "Beautiful."

Finally, some truth.

I arrive at my apartment door and slump against its cold metal surface. It has been a very long day. I press my left hand against the palm reader and wait for recognition.

"Good evening, Ms. Kichi," says Perkins. "Opening door now."

As the thirty-seven locks open, I think about how nice it would be not to find Mother still plugged in.

What I would give for the door to open and to have Mother greet me like a normal human being.

To ask how my day has been or if I would like something to eat or drink, to notice my hair has grown or ask if I am dating anyone.

To treat me like her daughter.

I am snapped back to reality when I hear someone cough behind me.

I plunge my left hand into my parka pocket and feel for my can of riot mist.

"Don't worry," says a muffled voice. "I'm not gonna rob or kill you."

Like I am going to believe that.

I find the riot mist and clench my fist around it, my thumb on the trigger. I slowly turn round, ready to give whoever it is a face full of pain, should they try anything.

A man stands leaning against the corridor wall. He wears clothes that are not too different from my own: a heavy black parka, combat trousers and boots. His hair is shoulder-length and streaked with grey. The lines around his eyes also tell me this man must be around forty or so. A dark green surgical mask keeps the rest of his face a mystery.

What is it with people hiding their mouths?

"Your name is Kichi, yes?" he says. "Kichi Honda?"

Although muffled, his voice is deep and as smooth as mocolate.

I can imagine he could make many girls go weak at the knees, just by speaking.

"Yes," I say. "I'm Kichi Honda."

My thumb caresses the trigger of the riot mist.

"I saw you just now," he says. "On the walkway."

"OK..."

"You were talking to that boy, the nil-by-mouth."

"Yes. I was."

"Why?"

I shrug my shoulders.

"Why not?" I ask.

The man shakes his head and quietly laughs into his facemask.

"There aren't many who'd offer assistance to a nil-by-mouth."

"Maybe I'm a nice person."

He laughs again, louder this time.

"Then you're definitely in the minority, if you pardon the pun."

"Excuse me, Ms. Kichi," interrupts Perkins. "Is there a problem? You have not entered the apartment yet."

"It's OK, Perkins," I say. "I'll be in soon."

"Very good, Miss."

The man shifts position slightly and folds his arms.

"Nice security system you have there," he says. "Must have cost a lot. Still, better to be safe than sorry, right?"

The hand holding the can of riot mist is now sweating. I am worried that should anything happen, the can will slip from my grip before I have time to spray him.

What does this guy want?

"Did the nil-by-mouth thank you?" he asks.

"Thank me for what?"

"For talking to him. Did he thank you?"

I shake my head.

"No, he didn't"

"Then let me thank you instead," he says. "Thank you."

I am now utterly confused. My poor brain is melting. This day has been far too weird.

"Why are you thanking me?" I ask.

He unfolds his arms and moves away from the wall. I instinctively take a step back, almost spraying the inside of my pocket with riot mist.

"Because that's what I would've done," he says. "But I wasn't fortunate enough to meet someone as kind as you."

He reaches up to his face and pulls his mask down.

I stumble backwards, pressing myself against my apartment door.

"After being left for dead, I had to resort to drastic measures to ensure I continued living."

I now know who this man is.

The hideous scarring around his mouth tells me everything.

The man covers his face once more and winks an eye.

"Be seeing you, Kichi Honda."

With that, he turns away from me and walks down the corridor. I do not stop hugging the door until he has turned the corner.

I explode into my apartment, slamming the door shut behind me.

"Activate locks!" I shout.

"Very good, Ms. Kichi," says Perkins.

Once the locks have all slid into place, I let out a deep breath and kick my boots off. I can undo the laces tomorrow.

"Would you care for a drink, Ms. Kichi?" asks Perkins as I walk towards the living room. "Or a snack, perhaps?"

"Caramel sake. Make it a double. And Inferno noodles."

"Certainly, Ms. Kichi. Your food and beverage await you in auto-serve hatches two and three."

I walk into the living room to find Mother worshiping a dead screen.

I position myself directly in front of her.

"Hi, Mother," I say. "Guess who I just met."

Mother looks straight through me, as per usual.

"I just met Hitoshi the hungry ghost."

# EIGHT

Hitoshi Takashi is something of an urban legend.

Most citizens have heard something about the nil-by-mouth who tore off his metal faceplate and now lives at the bottom level of Osaka Sector. The rumours as to why he ripped off his mask range from totally sick to absurdly comical, the most common story being the one about him mutilating himself outside an all-night burger joint, due to him being unable to fight his desire for a king-size 'whatever' meal. I guess this is where the 'hungry' part of his nickname comes from. The reason for the 'ghost' part is because no one has ever actually seen him. Most citizens have a friend of a friend who has seen him on the street or spotted him standing outside a restaurant, but they have never seen him with their own eyes.

Like the one about the boy in the auto-serve hatch or the girl who received midnight video-calls from Tokyo. We tell these tales, but never experience them ourselves.

Now, I can say I actually met Hitoshi Takashi, the hungry ghost.

He spoke to me. He even showed me his scars.

And he knew my name.

Half of me wonders how he could possibly know that.

The other half prefers to just bask in the coolness of it all.

I cling to that feeling of cool throughout my supper and right up to me going to bed. By the time I have slipped under the covers, my face aches from all the smugness.

Wednesday starts as every other day does: I get up, plug Mother in, have breakfast, shower, get dressed and then leave the apartment.

I am a slave to routine.

Today is different, though. Today, I have to go back to work.

I arrive at the lifts a little later than usual. Much to my displeasure, there must be at least a hundred citizens already waiting. This means the lifts are going to be full to capacity. Not a good thing. I pop a stick of nico-gum in my mouth and find my place at the back of the queue. After a few minutes pass, a hand taps me on the shoulder. I turn to see Ms. Pang smiling at me.

"How are you today, Kichi?" she asks. "All ready to return to work?"

"Yeah," I reply. "Well, as ready as I can be."

"I know what you mean," she says. "It's always difficult to go back to work after some time off."

As per usual, our conversation is interrupted by an arriving lift. Everyone stumbles forward into the cold metal box that will deliver us to the outside world. Once inside, I see that my earlier assumption was right; the lift is almost three-quarters of the way full. The doors close with an echoing clang. I cross my fingers and hope for a swift ascent.

"So Kichi," whispers Ms. Pang. "Any news? Gossip?"

Hitoshi Takashi's unmasked face instantly pops into my head.

"Nothing new with me," I say.

Lies seem to be coming so easily these days.

"Oh," says Ms. Pang. "That's a shame."

For a brief moment, I swear I see a look of confusion on her face.

A nonchalant shrug of her shoulders restores her smile.

"Well, if anything should happen, be sure to save it for when we have lunch. You still have my card, right?"

"Yep," I say, patting my pocket. "Still got it."

"Wonderful," she beams. "I am so looking forward to it."

The lift comes to a jolting stop at ninety-eight. The doors slide open, allowing a horde of citizens to march inside. The vast compartment now feels full to the brim. I press myself up against the wall as the feeling of claustrophobia rises within me.

Thank Buddha, there are only two more levels to go.

I close my eyes and try to focus on my breathing. My subconscious decides to display the face of Hitoshi Takashi in the darkness behind my screwed up eyelids.

"Be seeing you, Kichi Honda," he silently mouths.

I can feel the movement of the lift as it edges ever closer to level one hundred.

"Be seeing you..."

His masked face disappears and is replaced by Red Raku's.

Damn it. I forgot to wear my t-shirt.

The lift comes to a stop and I hear the doors hiss open. I snap my eyes open and start to squeeze my way out of the packed compartment. Once outside, I carry on walking until I am well clear of the exodus. I stop and take another round of deep breaths. The cold air freezes my lungs, numbing me like an injection of anesthetic. Another stick of nico-gum finishes the job. Normal service has now been resumed.

I see Ms. Pang heading in my direction. I smile as cheerily as possible and walk to meet her.

"You feeling OK?" she asks.

"Yeah, I'm fine," I reply. "I just get a little freaked out when the lifts are totally full."

"I understand. My older brother was the same, except more so. It got so bad that he had to buy an apartment right next to the entrance of his apartment block. Cost him almost a century's salary!"

She shakes her head and laughs quietly to herself.

"Anyway, I better be off. You're sure you're OK?"

I give her two thumbs up and tell her I am cool.

"Good, good. Have a great day and see you soon."

"Yeah, see you."

"And don't forget about our lunch appointment," she says before dashing off. "I'm waiting for all your gossip!"

As I watch her disappear into the crowd, I wonder what 'gossip' I could possibly share.

I arrive at work, dead on time and with zero enthusiasm. After only thirty minutes, I pray for Red Raku to come find me and put a bloody end to my miserable existence.

I work at a mall, directly underneath platform seven. The P7 mall is one of the biggest in Osaka Sector, selling everything under the sun and millions of other things that nobody really needs or wants.

My official job title is Customer Greeter. This means I say hello to people as they enter. When I first started, I used to thank people for coming as they left, but was told by my manager that it was someone else's job.

As my brain starts to dissolve like tofu in boiling water, I try hard to tell myself I am lucky to have this position. The unemployment level in Osaka is at around seventy percent and rising. Most hard labour and factory work is now done by bots and droids. As machines can work fifty times faster than the average citizen, and work for free, the need for real people has taken a drastic nosedive.

While most citizens are blissfully out of work, content to survive on what the government gives them, there are still some of us who need as many credits as they can get. Even the most menial of jobs can seem like a blessing to people who want more from life or have dependents.

I however, do not feel blessed.

As I greet my seven hundredth customer, I think of Mother 'enjoying' herself at home.

My life sucks. Big time.

At break, I go to the staff canteen and order chili-fried rice from the auto-serve machines. I take a seat next to a girl called Miho, the person whose job I was jeopardising by thanking shoppers as they left the mall.

"How's your day?" she asks, shoveling a pile of noodles into her mouth.

Miho is one of these people with a super overactive metabolism. The amount of food she eats is far beyond ridiculous. She never seems to stop. Every time I see her away from her post, she is pushing something into that greedy little mouth of hers. By rights, she should be the size of a repro-elephant. Instead, she is as slim as they come, looking more like an advert for diet pills than the eating machine she really is.

The thing about her that really makes me mad though, is she is just so damn nice.

"Same old, same old," I reply. "You?"

"As yesterday was and how tomorrow will be. How were your days off?"

"Not bad."

"Do anything nice?"

"Visited a friend and had tea and cake."

"Cool. I went on a date with Akira."

I suppress a flinch of jealousy. Akira works as an aisle attendant, helping customers find what they are looking for or reach for those difficult to get to items. He is one of those guys who make girls fawn over him or become giggling imbeciles. I am one of the latter.

"How did it go?" I ask.

"Pretty good," says Miho as she finishes her noodles and starts to help with my rice. "He's kind of quiet though."

"How do you mean?"

"Well, he took me to eat at that new sushi place on platform two. He never said a word for the whole of the cab ride there and not very much during dinner. It was a little uncomfortable."

"Did you help him eat his dinner?"

Miho bursts out laughing. Thankfully, she covers her mouth, saving me from being sprayed with partially chewed rice.

"Of course not! I was on my very best behaviour."

"So what happened after dinner?"

Miho leans forward, her eyes wide with excitement.

"Well, we went for a walk."

"And?"

"And...he held my hand."

"No way!" I say, with as much sarcasm as possible. "Did you wear protection?"

"Get lost, Kichi," she says with a smile and a one finger gesture. "I thought it was really sweet."

"Sorry," I say. "Just joking."

"Jealous, you mean."

I return the finger I was given, but not the smile.

"Ha!" says Miho. "I knew it!"

My shift comes to an end at six o'clock. I run to the staff changing room and quickly take off my red skirt suit uniform, ridding myself of any association with my soul-destroying job. Once back in my own clothes, I feel my mood start to lift a little. I don't loiter to catch up with Miho or catch a glimpse of Akira. All I want to do is get out of this place and as soon as humanly possible.

I take the employees' exit out of the mall. The evening air is as cold as ever. A stark contrast to the slightly uncomfortable warmth I have just come from. I zip up my parka and pull my hood into place.

The back exit leads to a lift that goes up one level to platform seven and a small waiting area for hover cabs. Usually, there is either a very long queue or not a single cab in sight. Tonight is different. Firstly, there is no queue. Somehow, I managed to be the first of the morning shift out of the building.

Secondly, there is a cab waiting.

Thank you, Buddha. Thank you so much for making me lucky with cabs.

Without a second's hesitation, I am at the cab door, waiting for my palm print to be accepted. When the doors open, I leisurely climb inside and take a seat.

"Thank you for choosing Osaka Cabs," says the autopilot as the door closes. "Where would you like to go?"

"Bar Street, North P5," I reply.

This cab's autopilot is much more relaxed than last time. This one makes me feel like a valued customer and doesn't get on my back when I neglect to fasten my seat belt. As the cab lifts off, I see a steady stream of employees leaving the mall. I relax back in my seat. The grin on my face may be smug, but it feels so good.

My journey is almost over when I hear the noise.

A mechanical howling rises up from the bowels of Osaka Sector, up past level one hundred and into the sky. The baleful sound floods the hover cab and rings in my ears, rising in pitch until it is a shrill and painful scream.

I have been dreading this terrible sound all my life.

The ghost siren.

Something has breached the walls.

Something has escaped from Sector Thirteen.

I lean over to the window and look towards the eastern skyline. I am unsure whether it is just my imagination, but the horizon seems to glow a bright red. I turn to look west and only see a pitch black sky.

It is when I look back towards Sector Thirteen that I see the light, a ball of pure white in the distant sky. And it is growing.

Within seconds, it expands to the size of the moon.

Then it explodes.

The interior of the hover cab is filled with a blinding white light that strips me of my sight. I rub my eyes and blink furiously, but with no results.

Then, the shockwave comes.

I am flung from my seat and slammed against the roof. When I fall, I do not hit the floor. My head strikes the cold glass of one of the cabs windows. The left side of my face pulses with pain. Blood runs from somewhere above my eye and into my mouth.

Although partially blind, I am still able to sense two things.

Firstly, the vehicle I am in is now on its side.

Secondly, it is falling out of the sky.

# NINE

There are three basic instructions for if the ghost siren sounds.

One: If at home, activate all security barriers and wait for further instructions.

Two: If in a public area, immediately make your way to a safe zone and wait for further instructions.

Three: If in a private vehicle, land at the nearest opportunity, activate the vehicles security barriers and wait for further instructions. If travelling in any kind of public transport, please wait for the vehicle to land and wait for further instructions.

There are no instructions for what to do if you are inside a hover-cab that is falling out of the sky.

Aside from the sirens' eerie wail, the only other sound I can hear is my heart beating rapidly. That most vital of organs pounds so violently in my ears, it makes my head hurt. Not that this really matters. A slight headache is now the least of my worries.

I wonder just how long it will be before the cab collides with something. The chances of it reaching level one without smashing into a walkway or platform are quite slim. Then again, if the cab crashes onto a platform, my chances of survival could be a lot higher. Maybe I will break a few bones, if not all of them, but at least I won't be pizza.

Pizza.

If I survive this, I will order wasabi pizza to celebrate.

If I survive.

I wonder what Mother will do if I die.

Will anyone tell her I am dead?

Will she even care?

Please, Buddha and Kannon. Please don't let me die like this.

From my crumpled position, I feel around the interior of the cab for the pay-screen. Upon finding it, I feebly slap at the screen.

"Hello?"

Nothing.

I try again, this time with more strength.

"Hey! Cab! Can you hear me?"

The cab does not reply. I press my hand firmly against the screen and try again.

"Hey! Citizen about to die here! Help me!"

Nothing again.

If I could press my hand any firmer against the screen, I would meld with it.

"Citizen Honda to cab, can you hear me? Don't mean to trouble you, but we seem to be falling out of the sky. Can you kickstart the DAMN BACKUP ENGINES OR SOMETHING?!"

The cab suddenly rotates. I am flung against the ceiling for a second time, before landing face first on the back seat. Through the warm leather, I feel a slight vibration of power.

"Attention, Citizen Honda," says the auto-pilot. "Ghost siren protocols have been activated. This car will now land at the nearest safe zone. Please fasten your seat belt and wait for further instructions."

Thank you, Buddha.

Thank you, Kannon.

Thank you, Osaka Cabs.

Tears of pure relief start to fall from my sightless eyes.

Tonight's pizza will be the best meal of my entire life.

I feel the cab land and its engines die.

Wherever I am, I have made it there safely. I wipe my eyes on my parka sleeve and blink a dozen or so times. Although hazy and blurred, my vision seems to show signs of returning. This is good news. Although a pair of cyber-implants would be cool, the price would be well beyond my very humble salary.

"Citizen Honda," says the auto-pilot. "This Osaka cab has now landed. For your security and comfort, all doors have been locked and security barriers activated. Please wait for further instructions."

"Thanks."

"Would you care to watch a movie while you wait? This cab has a selection of the latest blockbusters from around the world."

"No thanks, I'm having a little trouble seeing at the moment."

"Systems indicate that interior lights are functioning correctly. Is this information incorrect?"

"No. The lights are fine. I was blinded for a while. I'm OK now. Well, sort of."

"You are injured?"

"Yep. I also bashed my head."

"Understood. Do you wish to be taken to a hospital, once the all clear has been given?"

"Let's see," I say, laughing at my choice of words.

I settle back in my seat and reach up to touch my head wound. I wince as my fingertips find the gash above my left eye. I fumble in my pocket and pull out a pack of synth-skin plasters. After tearing off the packaging, I gingerly press the largest plaster against my head. This action results in some pathetic whimpering on my part. Once done, I lean back in my seat and close my eyes.

It suddenly dawns on me how quiet it has become.

"Has the ghost siren stopped?" I ask.

"Yes, Citizen Honda. We are now waiting for clearance to resume our journey."

"Cool," I say. "That's good. Awesome."

My words sound like they come from a million miles away.

Unconsciousness wraps its strong arms around me and bear hugs me into oblivion.

I open my eyes and am happy to find I can almost see again. Although still not crystal clear, it is so much better than being blind. Also, the throbbing of my head has subsided a little. I decide not to touch the injured area, just in case my exploring fingers discover a world of hurt.

"Hello, Citizen Honda," says the auto-pilot. "You are awake."

"Yep. How long was I out?"

"Four hours," the auto-pilot replies.

"Four hours?"

"That is correct."

"Have we been given the all clear yet?"

"Yes, Citizen Honda," the auto-pilot replies. "The all clear was given thirty-eight minutes ago."

"So, we can get moving again?"

"I regret to inform you that this Osaka cab has suffered some damage to its flight engines. The chances of taking off successfully are around point five percent. A distress call has been sent to Osaka Sector police."

"So, we just sit tight and wait to be rescued?"

"That is correct."

I glance towards the passenger windows and notice they are both blacked out. Presumably, this is something to do with the cab's security systems.

"I can't see outside," I say. "Where are we?"

"Level one."

"Level *one*?"

"Level one."

My heart starts to accelerate as my panic levels rise. My mind is now filled with every last story, legend and whisper concerning the bottom level of Osaka Sector.

None of these tales are remotely happy or shiny.

"When did you send the distress signal? When will the police be here? Are they on their way?"

My desperate questions are met with a very strange answer.

"Level one."

As calmly as possible, I repeat my questions.

I get the same worrying reply.

"Level one."

"Please tell me the police are coming."

"Level one. Level one. Level one."

It now feels like I am having a conversation with Mother.

"Level One. One. One. One. One."

The auto-pilot falls into silence. Obviously, not only are the engines damaged. Whatever that explosion of light was, it did some serious harm to the cab when it hit us. I guess I am extremely lucky the cab managed to land safely, even if it did take me down to level one.

Buddha and Kannon heard my prayers after all.

I am reflecting upon my good fortune, when I notice the windows.

They are no longer opaque.

I dive to the floor of the cab. The sudden movement makes my head pound and I have to bite my lip to stop myself screaming.

Then, the interior light goes out.

Kichi Honda, welcome back to darkness.

After several deep breaths, I take a quick peek out of the side and back windows. As soon as I have enough information, I duck down out of sight and check the doors to see if the manual locks are still working.

Happily, they are.

I then reach into my pocket and pull out my phone.

"Voice call," I whisper. "Police."

After a few seconds, my call is connected.

"Osaka Sector police," says a female voice, a little too loud for my liking. "Please state your name and identification number."

"Kichi Honda," I say quietly. "Identification number seven seven five seven three seven seven."

"Please state the nature of your emergency, Citizen Honda."

"I was in a hover cab accident. My cab lost power and we fell out of the sky. Luckily, the power came back on and we managed to land. But then the cab died and I'm kind of stuck on level one..."

"Ah, yes," she interrupts. "We received a distress call from your cab."

"Awesome. So, when are you coming to get me?"

"A patrol car will be with you as soon as possible. The report here says you were injured. Is this correct? Do you require medical assistance?"

"No, I'm OK, I think. I just banged my head, that's all. When will the patrol be here?"

"The patrol car will be with you as soon as possible. Can you give me any information regarding your current location? Are you in any immediate danger?"

"I'm in an alleyway. There's not much light. The buildings on either side look like they are all boarded over. Behind me is a street. I can see some lights at the end. Look, when's the patrol car coming? I'm really scared here."

I am not joking.

I have never been so scared.

"A patrol car will be with you as soon as all priority A incidents have been dealt with. I estimate this should be no longer than thirty minutes. In the meantime, please keep calm. If your situation should worsen, please don't hesitate to contact us. Thank you for calling, Citizen Honda."

The officer then ends the call.

Thirty more minutes?

Dear Buddha and Kannon. Sorry to bother you again, but I really need your help.

For all I know, the stories about level one may be just that.

There is a very good chance the citizens who live at the bottom of Osaka Sector are cheerful and hardworking, just unlucky to have been left behind as progress thrust the city ever higher. Perhaps they cling to the hope that, one day, they will be able to finally afford the clearance to travel past level twenty.

Yes. It is totally possible the citizens who live in the polluted bowels of the city are as pleasant as they come, and are not all cannibals, rapists, organ thieves or murderers.

I glance at my watch. The luminous green digits tell me I have been waiting for ten minutes.

Come on, come on, come on.

I decide to take another look outside, even though my heart tells me this is a foolish thing to do and to remain cowering in the shadows would be a wiser move.

My curiosity has a much louder voice though.

Slowly rising from the cab floor, I peer out of the left side window and straight into another pair of eyes.

The first thing I do is scream.

The second thing I do is dive back down out of view.

Screaming may have been a mistake, but trying to hide again is just pure dumb. There can be no doubt that the person outside has seen me. The faint tapping at the window confirms this. I screw both eyes shut and try to steady my breathing.

The tapping at the window does not stop. Whoever is out there really wants to get my attention. To be honest though, they are very polite with their knocking. Instead of them violently hammering at the door or ripping it off its hinges, all they do is gently tap, like a nil-by-mouth on its com-pad.

After several long minutes, the knocking stops.

I check my phone. There are still twelve minutes left until I am rescued. That is if the police arrive on time, or if they arrive at all.

I put my phone back in my pocket and pull out my trusty can of riot mist. Letting my curiosity lead me once again, I hazard another quick look outside.

This time I do not scream or attempt to hide.

This time, I freeze.

I am now face to face with a girl. If it were not for the glass separating us, I reckon our noses would be touching. As if realising this, she quickly moves back a little and smiles. Not a sinister or evil expression, but one of real warmth. At least, that is how it feels to me.

Perhaps this is how she snares her victims. Maybe she lures people in by appearing all sweet and innocent, and the next thing they know, they are in a bath of ice with half their organs missing.

The girl cocks her head to one side, her sweet smile still firmly in place. If she is trying to look cute, she is most definitely succeeding. She then ups the ante by waving a hand.

I feel compelled to wave back. So I do.

The girl's smile grows even wider. She stops waving and presses her fingertips against the glass.

Again, I follow suit. I also feel the beginnings of a smile creeping across my face.

What is it with this girl?

Why is she having this effect on me?

Only a matter of minutes ago, I was scared out of my wits. Now, I feel totally relaxed. I would even go as far as saying happy.

The girl takes her hand away from the window and loses the smile. Her expression is now one of sadness. Perhaps even fear.

When she points at the door, I know she wants me to unlock it.

I know she wants me to open the door and let her in.

And that is exactly what I do.

# TEN

The girl climbs into the cab and slowly pulls the door closed.

After taking off a heavy-looking backpack, she calmly sits down and turns to look at me. I sit on the floor with my spine firmly pressed against the other door, my knees tucked to my chest and my can of riot mist pointed in her direction. Whatever madness had taken over me has passed. Now, I am in the grip of panic and am ready to give this stranger a face full of agony.

"What is that?" she asks, both politely and innocently. "Is it a weapon?"

Although I understand her well enough, her accent is a little strange. Kind of like old traditional Nihon speak, but not.

I do not answer her. I just try to steady my shaking hand and keep my aim on her face.

The girl slowly shakes her head.

"Many people carry weapons here. But I have better."

And with that, she smiles.

I smile too.

The can of riot mist falls from my relaxed fingers.

"I am sorry," she says, turning to look out of the side window. "Please forgive me."

Now it is my turn to shake my head.

What the hell just happened there?

"It is cold outside," she says, as if speaking to herself. "No one has a heart."

I do not know what she means or how to reply, so I keep quiet and just listen.

"This city is alive with dead people. It is so sad. No one cares about their life. No one can help me."

She looks back towards me and smiles again. I hug my legs even tighter to my chest and screw my eyes shut.

"Do not be afraid," she says. "I will not hurt you. I promise."

Her words sound sweet and honest, but I refuse to believe any of it.

"You are not like the others here. You are different. You are dead, but alive. Like me. We are the same."

I warily open one eye.

"What do you mean?" I ask.

"Your world is empty, but you are still full of life."

"How do you know that?"

"I saw it in your eyes. I felt it when our fingers touched. We are the same. You can help me."

"Help you?"

The girl nods.

"Help you with what?"

"You must help me find someone," she says. "It is very important we find him. There is little time."

"Who are you looking for?"

"The man who failed."

"The man who failed?"

"Yes. We must find him. There is little time."

"Why?"

"Because she is coming," she whispers.

"Who is coming?"

Her reply makes me wish I had kept my mouth shut.

"The Blood Daughter."

For several long minutes, I sit and stare at this strange girl. She simply smiles back at me, as if unaware of what she has just said and the effect those words have had upon me.

In the gloom of the cab, I study my odd companion. I would guess she was around thirteen or fourteen. Any older than that, and I would be very surprised. Her black hair reaches down to her shoulders and is matted together in places, forming clumps as thick as octopus tentacles. Her clothes are also dark and look like a cross between the robes of a Zen monk and a pair of pyjamas.

If this is a new style, it is one I have never seen before.

I am just about to break the silence, when the girl does it for me.

"What is your name?"

"Kichi," I reply. "Kichi Honda."

"My name is Miaka."

"Miaka."

"Kichi Honda, you know the Blood Daughter."

This is very much a statement and not a question.

"Yes," I say. "Well, I don't know her, but I know the story..."

"No story," she sternly interrupts. "The Blood Daughter is real."

"Sorry?"

"She is real. She is coming."

"Coming?"

"Yes."

"What do you mean?"

"How do you know the Blood Daughter?"

What is it with this girl and avoiding giving answers? And why do we have to go back to that topic?

I sigh heavily before answering.

"A friend told me. He's got a book that's got the story in it. And a real freaky picture too."

"Your friend?"

"Yep."

"Your friend can help us."

There she goes with another statement.

Thing is, she may well be right. If there is anyone who could help with things like this, Mr. Tanaka is certainly the man.

"Maybe he can," I say.

"We must go there now."

I cannot help but laugh.

"We can't go there now! We're stuck on level one!"

When I see Miaka's puzzled look, I feel equally confused.

"You don't live on level one?" I ask.

"Level one?"

"Here. The bottom of the city. You don't live here?"

Miaka slowly shakes her head.

"No. I am from Tokyo."

There are some sentences that knock us sideways when we hear them. My first was when my boyfriend said he was dumping me. The second was when my dad said he was leaving us. Of the two, the second is obviously the one which sent me reeling. To be honest, I think the scars his words left will never fade.

Now, I can add a third to the list. It may not have dealt the same kind of emotional damage as the other two, but it certainly scrambled my brain.

"You can't be from Tokyo," I say, reacting almost the same way I did when my boyfriend and my dad hit me with their news. "You just can't."

"Why not?" Miaka replies with a frown.

"Because you can't be! It's impossible."

"Why is it impossible?"

"It's a ghost city! Has been for a hundred years. No one lives there now. Everyone's dead."

"No," she says, shaking her head. "People still live."

"But... what about the walls? Nothing can get past the walls. The government said so."

Miaka moves a little closer to me.

"I got past the walls."

I lean my head back against the cold metal of the cab door.

"You can't be from Sector Thirteen," I whisper. "You can't."

Children are taught only a little about the history of old Japan.

Our studies focus on the glory of Nihon city and its leading position in the world today. When it comes to learning about Sector Thirteen, all classes are led by a member of the DPA and a monk. They briefly tell us about the ghost quake and what had to be done to protect the rest of Nihon. Then they drill into us what could happen if we ever talk about Tokyo and what lives there. It is made crystal clear that if we say anything about Sector Thirteen, we will be in very serious trouble. Not just from ghosts, but from the DPA also.

Then, when we are all scared out of our skins, we are told to forget.

And like the good little citizens we are, we do just that.

It's amazing what fear can do to a person.

I slowly get up from the floor of the cab and slump heavily onto the back seat. Every inch of my body aches. I am sure I will be even worse tomorrow.

"So, you're from Tokyo," I say without looking at her.

"Yes," Miaka replies. "That is true."

"And people still live there."

"Yes. Not many. But some."

"And you got past the walls."

"Yes. It was not easy. It took many years to find a way. Then I had to find my way here. This was also difficult. It took many nights."

"And you came here because…"

"Because I need to find the man who failed."

"Because of the…"

"Blood Daughter. Yes."

I close my eyes and massage the bridge of my nose with my fingers.

"Have you seen her?" I ask. "The Blood Daughter. Have you really seen her?"

"Yes. Once."

The charcoal sketch from Mr. Tanaka's book fills my head.

I cannot imagine this spirit looking any less evil in real life.

I open my eyes so I can banish that terrible image and turn to look at Miaka.

Miaka: the girl from the ghost city.

This is insane.

Everything she has told me is totally and utterly insane.

The craziest thing, though, is I believe her.

"When will we meet your friend?" Miaka asks. "Can it be soon?"

"I don't know," I say. "Maybe, I..."

The cab is suddenly filled with light. I have to shield my eyes against the sudden brightness.

"Citizen Honda. This is Osaka police patrol nine five zero. Please step out of the cab and slowly make your way towards us."

I glance out of the back window to see a patrol car landing behind us. It looks like an angel descending from heaven, what with all the light. I turn to Miaka and take both her hands.

"Listen very carefully. Let me do all the talking. If anyone asks, you are Miaka Honda, my sister. Got it?"

Miaka nods.

"I am Miaka Honda."

"Cool. And whatever you do, don't say anything about Tokyo."

When we are both out of the cab, I take Miaka by the hand and walk slowly towards the waiting police vehicle. Two police officers, dressed in full riot gear, march towards us with pulse guns drawn. As rescues go, this one seems a little hostile.

"You are Kichi Honda?" says one of them, his voice distorted by his helmet.

"Yes," I reply.

"Report says there should be only one passenger. Who is this?"

They both point their weapons at Miaka.

Before I have time to say anything, Miaka steps forward and speaks.

"My name is Miaka Honda. I am her sister. Please take us home."

Both guns are lowered in unison.

"Get in the car," says the police officer. "We need to get you out of here and home before curfew."

I have no doubt that Miaka charmed them the same way she charmed me.

How the hell does she do that?

We are politely pushed into the back of the patrol car. While not as spacious as a hover cab, there is enough room for the both of us and Miaka's enormous backpack. The seats are surprisingly comfortable, considering that citizens who are usually in the back of a patrol car are criminals.

The door closes automatically and I feel the vibrations of the flight engines starting up.

I allow myself a smile. This day may have been ultraweird, but at least my journey home is cool.

There are no windows for us to look out of and only a metal panel in front of us. I am sure the officers flying us home can see us, even if we cannot see them. I reach for Miaka's hand and give it a gentle squeeze, hoping she understands my signal to keep her silence.

"Citizen Honda," comes a voice over the intercom. "I need to ask you some questions regarding your accident."

"OK. Sure."

"We have most of the information we need, but there are few things we would like you to clarify."

"OK..."

"The cab suffered a power failure, is this correct?"

"Yes. There was some kind of explosion and a bright light."

"Did this occur the same time the ghost siren was sounded?"

"Yes."

"I see. Can you tell me how long it was until power was restored to the vehicle?"

"I'm not really sure. A few seconds, maybe."

"I see. One final question. Do you have any idea why the cab took you down to level one?"

"No idea," I say. "The autopilot just said it was going to fly me to the nearest safe zone."

"I see. Interesting."

"Why is it interesting?" I ask.

"There is no safe zone on level one," he replies. "The lowest is on level twenty."

Miaka gives my hand a gentle squeeze.

We arrive at my apartment door with an armed escort.

One of the police officers presses his hand against the door's palm reader. I hear the locks disengage as the apartment security protocols deactivate.

Scary stuff.

He opens my door and gestures for me and Miaka to go inside.

We do as ordered.

"Don't worry," he says. "Once the door is closed, your personal settings will be restored."

"OK."

"Curfew is expected to start soon. For your safety, please stay at home until it is lifted."

"No problem."

The two officers say goodnight and leave. I close the door and activate the locks.

"Good evening, Ms. Kichi," says Perkins. "I detect we have a guest."

"Yep. Her name is Miaka. She's going to stay here for a while."

"Very good, Miss. Saving her bio-scan now and updating security clearance records. Welcome, Miaka."

Miaka stares around the hallway, looking for where the voice is coming from. Her look of bewilderment makes me laugh.

"Don't worry," I say. "That's just the apartment talking."

"This house can talk?"

"Yep."

"I see."

"You ever been in an apartment before?"

"Of course. There are millions of buildings in Tokyo. But they are all empty now. They belong to the dead."

My amusement fades as quickly as it arrived.

I lead Miaka through my apartment, avoiding the living room and Mother, and into the spare bedroom. Aside from a single bed, the room is just four white walls and a faded green carpet. Miaka places her backpack at the foot of the bed and gives me a warm grin.

"I will sleep here?"

"Yeah, that OK for you?"

"Yes. It is perfect. Thank you."

She sits on the edge of the bed and looks around the room. The expression on her face is like she is in the penthouse suite at the Shangri-La.

"Bathroom is outside and to the left," I tell her. I will be in the next room to the right, if you need me."

"Thank you," she says, hugging the pillow to her chest.

"Do you have any other clothes? Pyjamas?"

She shakes her head.

"No problem. I have some old things that may fit you. They may be a little big, but we can fix that. I'll be back in a minute, OK?"

"Yes. That is fine."

I leave my new sister to enjoy her new room and go to check in with Mother.

"Sorry for being late," I say as I enter the living room. "It's been quite a day."

Mother remains as still as a tombstone. Perhaps the world would end should she ever show any signs of acknowledgement to me.

I turn off the TV and unplug her.

"We have a guest," I tell her. "Her name is Miaka. She's going to stay with us for a while. OK?"

Mother stares back at me with the eyes of a corpse. If not for the blinking, most people would think that is what she is.

"See you tomorrow," I say. "It's late. Goodnight."

In an alternative reality, Mother wishes me good-night and tells me that she loves me.

In another reality, I do not turn the lights out on her and leave her to sit in darkness.

When I return to the spare room, I find Miaka in bed and fast asleep. I creep into the room and place the clothes I have collected for her on top of her bag. Before leaving, I stop to look at the strange girl I have invited into my home. Stands of her unkempt hair stick to her youthful face. I want to reach down and gently brush them away, but I am scared of waking her.

As I turn off the lights in this room, I realise I care more about this stranger than the dead thing that is my parent.

At exactly midnight, every light in the apartment turns on and flashes red. Curfew has started.

I turn on my video-window to find my pastoral view has been replaced with instructions to stay indoors until it's safe. I turn off the screen and close the curtains.

My intention was to go and shower, check my head wound, and then go to sleep. My subconscious has better ideas. I find myself taking a leaf out of Miaka's book and climbing into bed fully clothed. The softness of my mattress and the warmth of my covers are far too inviting to resist.

I can shower in the morning.

"Perkins?"

"Yes, Ms. Kichi?"

"Kill the lights."

# ELEVEN

*Good morning, Osaka Sector!*

*It's 6am on Thursday the fourth of December and you're listening to O-zone Radio Three. You're with Taro Yamada, broadcasting live from my kitchen. Yes, that's right, Osaka is still under curfew. But try to look on the bright side, this means you get to spend the day at home and have less chance of being attacked by evil spirits! Now, I know some of you out there are curious about a couple of things that happened yesterday. Well, join the club! I think everyone is worried about why the ghost siren sounded and what that light in the sky was. Obviously, I can't say too much. I mean, I don't want to get taken off the air, again! But I think I speak for everyone when I say some answers would be nice. For a start, what the hell is out there on the streets and are we 'really' safe? The official statement from the DPA says everything is under control and not to worry. Personally, I'll stop worrying once the all clear is given! For now though, all we can do is sit tight and wait. Needless to say, if I get any more information, you will be the first to know. OK, let's take a quick look at other news and then get down to some serious music...*

"Off."

The silence in my room is heavenly.

The dull ache I feel in my head and back is not.

I throw back the covers and slowly maneuver myself into an upright position. This is no easy task and is accompanied by a soundtrack of cracks, pops and sharp intakes of breath. Being thrown around the inside of a cab while it's falling out of the sky does take a toll on one's body.

Perkins turns on the lights. I wince and narrow my eyes to slits.

"Good morning, Ms. Kichi. How are you today?"

"Dreadful," I reply.

"I am sorry to hear that. What is the nature of your discomfort? Do you require medicine? A doctor, perhaps?"

"No, I'll be OK. Just had a rough night."

"I see. Would you care for a mild anesthetic to be added to your shower this morning?"

"Thanks, Perkins. But I think I'll pass."

"As you wish, Miss. How about some breakfast?"

"Let me think. I'll hit the shower first and get back to you."

"Very good, Ms. Kichi. I shall await your orders."

Moving like someone five times my age, I force myself to leave the comfort of my bed and shuffle towards the bathroom. A scalding hot shower will either bring me back to life or kill me.

While both outcomes have their benefits, I would prefer the former as opposed to the latter.

I stand in front of the bathroom mirror and stare into the face of a stranger. The person has the same eyes as me, but hers are ringed with darkness. This makes her pale skin look even more ghostly than usual. Add to this the streaks of blood that cover the left side of her face, and you have a girl who looks more like something that has escaped from Sector Thirteen.

Miaka.

I run from the bathroom, both my pain and shower forgotten.

I arrive at the door to the spare room and push it open. The bed is empty. The covers are thrown back, showing only an impression of where Miaka lay; an afterimage of a girl who, by rights, should not exist.

The bulky backpack she was carrying still sits at the foot of the bed, as do the clothes I left for her.

Temptation beckons me forward, whispering for me to open the bag and find out what is inside. I crouch down next to her bag, my heartbeat accelerating. On closer inspection, I see the backpack is made from a patchwork of different materials that have been crudely stitched together.

I reach out to touch it.

"Ki-chi..." calls Mother from the living room.

"In a minute!" I shout.

"Mi-a-ka..."

Every single inch of skin is now covered with gooseflesh. I feel like someone has just poured a bucket of icewater over my head.

Mother has just expanded her vocabulary.

Mother sits in her usual place, ready to worship at the altar of her deity of choice. Miaka sits, cross-legged, at her feet, gazing up at her with an expression of deep sadness.

"She is lost," she says, as I walk to join their silent vigil.

"What do you mean?"

Miaka closes her eyes and frowns.

"She is so far away. She is lost inside."

"Inside?"

"Yes."

"Inside where?"

"Inside herself. I had to concentrate very hard to find her. Her voice is so quiet. So far away. I had to listen very carefully."

"You can hear her?"

The girl from Sector Thirteen nods.

So, not only can this girl control people with just a smile, she is also telepathic.

Why am I not surprised?

"What's she saying?" I ask, joining her on the floor.

"There are two voices," she replies. "One is very faint. A whisper. It echoes from far away."

"What does it say?"

"She is asking for help. Over and over again. Help me. Please, help me."

"And the other?"

"The other screams. So loud. It is like an animal. It keeps calling your name. It won't stop. Kichi. Kichi. Kichi."

Miaka opens her eyes and looks at me, her frown even deeper than before.

"What does she want to be connected to?"

I slowly rise from the floor and glare at the soulless creature that occupies the sofa. The urge to strangle her with the rTV cables is hard to fight.

"I am so sorry about your mother," says Miaka.

"Don't be," I say. "She did it to herself."

Who would have thought a bathroom could hold such wonder.

Even the simple act of explaining how to use the shower has Miaka staring in wide-eyed amazement. Her reactions are so innocently cute that I almost forget where this odd girl came from and the things she can do.

After she has showered and wrapped herself in a bathrobe, I escort her back to the spare room.

"There's some clothes on top of your bag," I say. "They may be a little big, but at least they're clean and warm."

"Thank you," says Miaka. "I am sure they will be fine."

"Cool. I'll just have a quick shower and change and I'll be right back. When you're dressed, just wait here for me, OK?"

"Yes," she replies with a smile. "I will wait here."

I leave Miaka to it and head back to the bathroom. Once inside, I lock the door and start to get undressed. My body decides this is the perfect time to remind me of the beating it has taken. I look in the mirror, expecting to see my naked flesh covered in purple-black bruises. Surprisingly, my skin remains unblemished. Only my face tells the true story.

I peel off the plaster from above my left eye, roll it into a ball and flick it into the sink. The synth-skin has done a very good job. There is no sign of the deep wound my fingers found the night before.

Leaving my discarded clothes to lie in a heap on the floor, I step into the shower cubicle.

It is time to wash away my pain.

"Perkins?"

"Yes, Ms. Kichi. How can I help you?"

"I've changed my mind about the anesthetic."

I leave the bathroom feeling like ten thousand credits.

It has been a long time since I felt this good. Perhaps this is how Ms. Pang starts her mornings. That would explain why she is always so bright and cheery.

As I walk into my bedroom, Mother starts up her mantra.

"Plug."

Normally, she has me running.

Not today.

I close my door and ask Perkins to play classical selection twenty, volume setting eleven.

"This room only," I add. Not wanting to startle Miaka with the impending cacophony.

Mother's pleading is instantly drowned out by the pounding beats of Melt-Banana.

Today, she can wait.

After putting on a fresh set of underwear, a pair of green combat trousers and a plain black t-shirt, I leisurely dry my hair and clean my teeth. I have half a mind to paint my toenails, extending Mother's wait even further. This thought fills me with a perverse sense of glee. Instead, I slip on my thermo-slippers, wander back to the living room and help Mrs. Honda back to her Nirvana.

Miaka sits at the edge of the bed with her hands on her lap and a satisfied smile on her face. As expected, the clothes I gave her are several sizes too big. Still, she looks far better with turned-up trousers and rolled-up sleeves than in her own clothes. All she needs to do now is fix her hair and she will look like a regular young citizen.

"Are you hungry?" I ask.

"Very," she replies.

I hand her a pair of pink slippers to wear and then take her to the kitchen.

"Have a seat," I say.

Still smiling, Miaka sits.

"Now, what can I get you?"

"I am not sure," she shrugs. "What do you have?"

"Almost everything," I laugh.

Miaka's mouth drops.

"Everything?"

"Yep."

"You have rice and bread?"

"Yep. Is that what you eat for breakfast back home?"

The girl shakes her head, her expression now very serious.

"No. Rice and bread are rare. Usually we eat fruit and vegetables. Sometimes animals, if we are lucky."

"Animals?"

"Yes."

"What kind of animals?"

"Mostly nocturnal birds. Sometimes we would find deer. It was very sad to eat them though. Deer are very beautiful. Frogs and insects are easy to find, but they look ugly."

Although I have no real idea of what her life was like in Tokyo, I am sure it must have been a million different shades of hell.

Even still, I do feel kind of jealous to know she has eaten real meat.

"How does chicken and rice sound?" I ask. "Would that be OK for you?"

"I can have chicken and rice for breakfast?"

The look of joy in her eyes is too cute for words.

"Sure!" I say, not daring to mention that both the chicken and rice are synthetic. "Perkins?"

"Yes, Ms. Kichi? How may I help you?"

"Breakfast, please. One bowl of chicken fried rice, one bowl of inferno noodles and two lemon iced teas, thanks."

"Certainly, your orders are now waiting for you in auto-serve hatches two and three. Enjoy your breakfast."

I take the food from the hatches and place them on the table. After collecting a spoon and a pair of chopsticks from the kitchen drawer, I take a seat opposite Miaka and push the steaming bowl of rice towards her.

"Dive in," I say, offering her the spoon.

Miaka looks at the auto-serve hatches and back at the breakfast I have just given her. I can tell she wants to ask where the food came from and how it was prepared so quickly, but hunger gets the better of her. She snatches the eating utensil from my hand and begins to shovel the piping-hot rice into her mouth. The temperature of her breakfast doesn't slow her down in the slightest. I plunge my chopsticks into my noodles and join in the banquet, both of us indulging in food that is extremely hot, in one form or other.

When both of our bowls and cups are empty, we sit in silence for a few minutes and look at each other. I notice Miaka's forehead is etched with deep lines, as are the corners of her eyes. Someone so young should not be scarred this way. I feel something in my heart break when she smiles at me.

"Don't feel sad for me," she says. "I am one of the lucky ones."

There she goes with her telepathy, again.

"How old are you?" I ask.

"Thirteen. I think."

"You're not sure?"

"It is difficult to keep time with no sun."

"No sun?"

Miaka shakes her head.

"There is no sun in Tokyo. The Blood Daughter forbids it."

I cringe at the mention of Tokyo and a certain evil spirit.

"Just say home," I tell her. "Some words aren't safe here."

"I see."

The girl chews her bottom lip for a few seconds, lost in her thoughts.

"Is it safe to talk to your friend?" she asks.

"Yeah," I say. "Totally safe."

"We must go to him."

"We can't. The whole sector is under curfew. If we go out, we'll be arrested before we get to the lifts. Or killed."

Miaka's shoulders slump. She looks utterly dejected.

"Maybe the curfew will be lifted soon. We'll go as soon as it is. I promise."

The girl from Tokyo solemnly shakes her head.

"It will be too late. It happens tomorrow."

"What happens?"

Miaka does not answer. She simply gets up and leaves the kitchen in silence.

Wonderful.

Take away the psychic abilities, and you are left with just another moody teenager.

I lean back in my chair and let out a very deep sigh.

As I'm about to start clearing the table, Miaka returns carrying a bundle of black rags.

"I have something to show you," she says, placing whatever it is on the table.

She carefully peels back layer after layer of musty-smelling cloth to reveal a corroded metal tin. Before opening it, she closes her eyes and mutters some words under her breath that I am unable to understand.

Was she just praying?

She opens her eyes and, with a trembling hand, takes off the lid.

Although wrapped in a final protective layer of dust-covered plastic, I can clearly see what it is she has to show me.

Photographs.

She unwraps the photos and places them in a small pile before me.

"Please be careful with them," she says. "They are very old."

The first photo has faded to sepia. All four corners look like they have been chewed away by something.

Regardless of this, I can still see what the photo is of.

"This is real?" I ask her, my voice no more than a whisper.

"Yes..."

I cannot take my eyes off the scene of horror Miaka has shown me.

Its monochrome brown does nothing to lessen its impact.

The blood is still easy to see.

As are the corpses.

And there, in the middle of it all is madness and evil incarnate.

The Blood Daughter.

"This is what happens tomorrow."

# TWELVE

There are thirty-one photographs in total.

Thirty-one images, each one more horrific than the last.

Streets and corridors littered with the dead, rooms piled high with bodies.

Men.

Women.

Children.

None were spared.

Then, there are the things that walk and crawl amongst the carnage.

White-faced furies with long black hair and hate-filled eyes.

Creatures that look like children, but are not.

Bizarre hybrids of man, animal and machine.

Nightmares come true.

All pale in comparison to what is on the first and last photos.

The Blood Daughter.

And she is laughing.

That twisted bitch is laughing as she brings on the apocalypse.

Miaka carefully packs the photos away, handling them with a tenderness that seems so wrong, considering their content.

I can feel the beginnings of a headache starting. The anesthetic of my morning shower must be wearing off. I consider asking Perkins to fix me a stiff drink to numb the pain, but decide against it. Now is not the time.

Miaka finishes wrapping the metal container in the strips of black cloth and sits back in her chair. The air between us is thick with anticipation as we both wait for the questions to begin.

I decide to go first.

"So, this is what's going to happen tomorrow?"

"Yes."

"Tomorrow?"

"Yes."

"What, like at midnight?"

Miaka solemnly shakes her head.

"No. It will be at dusk. When the sun sinks, eternal night will come and everything will fall into darkness."

My mouth suddenly feels as if it is stuffed with dry crackers.

"I am so sorry to tell you this," she says, breaking eye contact. "I realise that time is short."

I am unsure how to react to her last sentence. Part of me wants to slam my fists against the table and scream at her for having lousy timing, another part of me wants to cry enough tears to drown myself in before the world ends.

In the end, I do neither.

I just laugh instead.

I laugh and laugh and laugh.

Miaka looks at me as if I have gone insane, and maybe I have.

My hysteria increases as I see the absurdity of it all.

The world is going to end tomorrow, and its only salvation lies in the hands of a thirteen-year-old girl and someone who greets shoppers at a mall.

Oh, and possibly an old man who is good at making tea.

I am so sorry, Osaka Sector, but you are doomed.

It takes me about fifteen minutes to regain composure.

After plunging my face into a sink full of cold water, I ask Perkins for two double espressos and knock them back like shots of tequila. Retaking my seat at the kitchen table, I apologise to Miaka for wasting precious time.

"There is no need to be sorry. I understand."

"So, how do we stop all this from happening?"

"We must find the one who failed," she replies, in her usual matter-of-fact way. "It is very important."

"Any idea where this person is?" I ask, hoping her answer will be positive and not accompanied by a shaking head.

Unfortunately, Miaka kills my hopes dead.

"Perhaps your friend will know. Perhaps he can help us. We must go to see him. Now."

I am about to lecture her again about being under curfew, but stop when I see the serious look on her face.

She is right, of course. A curfew is the least of our worries.

"Perkins?"

"Yes, Ms. Kichi. What can I do for you?"

"Voice call, please. Friend two. Tanaka."

"Very good, Miss. Connecting now."

There is a brief pause before Mr. Tanaka's growl echoes around the kitchen.

"Kichi Honda, my girl. What can I do for you?"

"I want to ask you a few questions about baking cakes."

"I see. Wait one moment while I fetch my recipe books."

The call falls silent as Mr. Tanaka secures our call. I turn to Miaka and give her a friendly wink.

"Let me talk to him first," I say. "Explain what's going on."

Miaka nods politely, a slight smile playing across her face.

"Right," says the old man. "I'm all ears, as the saying goes."

Cutting a long story as short as possible, I tell Mr. Tanaka of my journey down to level one, meeting Miaka and the history lesson that followed breakfast. There is another moment of silence as my old friend digests the information I have just given him.

"Interesting," he eventually says. "And is Miaka with you now?"

"Yep."

"I see."

The next words he says are in a dialect I do not understand. Miaka sits upright, her eyes wide with excitement. She replies in the same alien tongue, her normal clipped monotone is now animated and filled with emotion. The transformation is quite something.

The two of them talk for about five minutes or so. When they are done, Miaka leans back in her chair and sighs heavily, a sound that is loaded with relief. Mister Tanaka then returns to Nihon common speak.

"Young Kichi," he says. "You must listen very carefully to what I am about to say and try not to ask me too many questions. Now is not the time, my girl. Do you understand?"

"Yes," I reply. "I got it."

"Good. Now, you two are going to be coming to see me. As soon as we have finished this call, I want you to get your coats and leave your apartment..."

"What about the curfew? Security protocols will..."

Mr. Tanaka gives a very loud sigh.

"What did I just tell you about questions?"

"Sorry," I say. "Go on. I'm listening."

"Good girl. As I was saying, I want you to leave your apartment as soon as we're finished talking. When your security system says you can't because of the curfew, just use this password: reikon zero zero thirteen. You'll then be able to open your door without any problems. Once you're out, make your way to the nearest lift and go down to level ten. Don't worry about security cameras spotting you. I'll take care of them. I'll explain how, later. When you arrive at level ten, follow the signs that lead to the old link walkway. When you get there, enter the same password to open the door. All you have to do then is follow the tunnels until you reach the entrance to 8C. I'll be waiting for you there. I severely doubt this will happen, but if you should be stopped by the police or the DPA along the way, just stay calm and give them the same old password. Now, have you got all that?"

My head is spinning.

Am I still speaking to Mr. Tanaka?

Seeing as questions are out of bounds, I say I understand.

"But can I just ask one question?" I add. "It's kind of important."

I can almost hear him smile.

"Very well, young Kichi. Go ahead."

"What if we run into a ghost? Will they accept your password too?"

Mr. Tanaka laughs.

"My dear girl, if only they did!"

The sound of his laughter usually puts a smile on my face. At this moment in time, I find myself immune to its charms.

The old man gives a rattling cough before continuing. "Do you trust me?"

"Yes. I do."

"Good. So believe me when I say you will be perfectly safe. You will not run into any ghosts. This I promise you."

"How can you be so sure?"

"Because I am. Trust me, like you said you do."

"OK. Fine. I trust you."

"I am so glad to hear that," he says. "Right, I'm going to end this call now. You know what you've got to do, so get to it. See you soon, Kichi Honda."

"Yeah, see you soon."

Mr. Tanaka ends the call, the space his voice occupied fills with anticipation.

"We go now?" asks Miaka.

"Yep," I confirm. "We go now."

Miaka refuses my offer of extra clothing, telling me she has extra clothes she can wear in her bag. I do manage to persuade her to take three pairs of socks and a pair of Mother's snow boots, though.

As fast as I can, I get changed into my many layers of thermal attire, a pair of black combat trousers, and a fresh 'PLEASE DON'T KILL ME, RED RAKU' t-shirt, this time in black. I grab a small backpack and throw in two new cans of riot-mist, a wrist torch and a fresh pack of synth-skin plasters. As I put on my parka, I watch the cows on my video-window chowing down on an endless supply of fresh grass. The nearest one raises its head and silently moos at me. Either she is wishing me good luck or saying goodbye.

I choose to believe the former.

Miaka waits for me in the hallway. Her backpack makes mine look like a vanity case for eyeliner and collagen gloss.

"Boots fit OK?" I ask as I put on my own heavy footwear.

"Yes. Thank you."

"Cool."

I finish tying my laces and get to my feet. From the living room comes the faint sound of Mother 'enjoying' herself.

"Miaka, can I ask you a question?"

She nods.

"What are the chances of us stopping her? The Blood Daughter, I mean. Can we really do this?"

The girl casts her gaze to the floor for a moment. This makes my heart sink. When she lifts her head though, I see a grim look of determination in her eyes.

"Yes. We can do this."

I look back to the living room door.

Should I go say goodbye?

The sound of giggling makes my decision for me.

"Let's go." I say.

As Mr. Tanaka predicted, Perkins is dead set against letting us leave the apartment.

"I am very sorry, Ms. Kichi. But as you know, we are under curfew at the moment. I am afraid I cannot open the door until the all clear has been given. I apologise for any inconvenience caused by this."

"No worries," I say. "Reikon zero zero thirteen."

The thirty-seven locks unbolt as one. The door then slides open.

I take Miaka by the hand and give her a smile.

"OK. Let's do this."

We step out into the corridor. The apartment door closes and locks behind us as soon as we are clear. Even though it would be so easy to reopen the door, I know there can be no going back. Not now.

Turning to Miaka, I hold a finger up to my lips. The girl nods her understanding. I guess she is used to being quiet, considering where she is from.

We make our way to the lifts without incident. The corridors are the quietest I have ever heard them, eerily so. The lack of noise only seems to emphasise the stink of the place, making me wish I had brought some face-masks with me.

At the lifts, I press all of the buttons to go down, praying they are still active. It would be a nightmare if we had to use the stairs, not to mention time-consuming. Thankfully, two lifts arrive within seconds of each other. If only everyday was like this. I lead Miaka into the nearest one and press the button for floor ten. The doors close swiftly, and our descent begins.

We stand facing the door. Neither of us turns to look back to notice the vast emptiness behind us. On any other day, I would be the happiest girl in the sector to be travelling this way. Today, I just want to get to level ten and leave this cold metal tomb as soon as possible.

Miaka squeezes my hand tightly.

"Do not worry," she says. "There is nothing here. Only us."

My imagination makes me ignore her words of comfort and fills the void behind us with all the horrors that will walk the streets of Osaka Sector, should we fail. They stagger and crawl their way towards me with outstretched arms and fingers that twitch and claw at the air between us...

The lift stops and the doors open.

We have arrived at level ten.

I tumble out into a dimly lit corridor, dragging Miaka after me.

Quickly scanning the wall in front of us, I see an arrow pointing left for the link walkway.

"This way," I whisper.

We set off down the corridor at a much faster pace than before.

It is not fear that fuels my footsteps, but anger. Anger at myself.

How can I help save Osaka Sector, when my own subconscious can scare me to death?

# THIRTEEN

The corridors of level ten are exactly as I thought they would be.

However bad I thought the stench of level seventy-seven was, ten is in a totally different league. On top of the cloying aromas of food, piss and incense, a heavy layer of dust permeates the corridors. I've never felt the urge to sneeze as much as I do right now. But there is something else, an unrecognisable odour, which burns both my eyes and throat.

Amazingly, Miaka remains unfazed. She may as well be taking a stroll through an eco-dome.

We continue, at a hectic pace, through the darkened corridors; dark due to every other strip light being smashed or broken. Here and there, the walls are adorned with splashes of graffiti; mostly gangs marking their territory or adverts for prostitutes. Several pieces mention Red Raku, either in support of or pleading for her to leave the residents of this floor be. Although I firmly believe Red Raku to be crazy, she would have to be totally out of her mind to even contemplate looking for victims in this hellhole.

When I spot the door we are looking for, I lift my eyes to the filth-covered ceiling and utter prayers of gratitude that we have made it this far without incident.

Once again, Mr. Tanaka is right; the entrance to the link walkway is well and truly locked. A cracked screen above its window flashes a message in red type that flickers manically, rendering it unreadable. This makes ignoring its warning or instructions a whole lot easier. The keypad to enter emergency access codes has also seen better days. Most of its keys are blank, the letters once printed on them have long since faded away. I punch in the password, hoping the pad has a standard layout. Happily, it does.

The door slides open with a hideous shriek, a sound that sets my body on edge.

"Come on," I say to Miaka.

We step over the airlock lip and into the walkway tunnel, the entrance door screeches shut as soon as we are clear.

Why does it feel like every closing door is laughing at us?

I know for a fact that the tunnels we now walk along follow the same routes as the walkways up on level one hundred. This means we could make the rendezvous with Mr. Tanaka in around fifty minutes, if we took our time. At the speed we are going though, it could be more like thirty-five. This is good.

Aside from the curved walls, the link walkway feels very much the same as the corridors of my apartment block. The colour scheme is the same lifeless grey lit by the harsh glow of strip lights. Instead of doorways leading into citizens' homes, there are small portholes that show charming views of metal and concrete for as far as the eye can see. Occasionally, there are vending machines, offering nico-gum or cans of chilled beverages. Most of them are empty and have been so for a decade or more. From the ceiling comes the gentle whir of fans and air-con units. Although the air pumped into here is recycled and stale, at least it is breathable and doesn't make me want to decorate the floor with my breakfast. This is good, too.

Just like the corridors of level ten, parts of the grey tunnel walls have been 'enhanced' by the skills of graffiti artists. Under a very visible security camera is scrawled a sentence that makes me shiver.

'RED RAKU WAS HERE.'

If this was true, I certainly hope she has since vacated the area.

Bumping into her would most certainly not be good.

We arrive at level ten's equivalent of P7, a circular room with walls of tinted grey glass. It reminds me a little of my one and only visit to the Osaka Sector aquarium, but instead of multi-coloured fish and ghost-like rays, all there is to see here are the bottom levels of apartment blocks and towers. How could anyone appreciate this? It would be like staring at the trunk of a peach tree and never looking up to see the fruit. Even if I had the time, I doubt I would stop to look through those windows. I quickly scan the room, find the exit we need and motion for Miaka to follow me. We move onto the final leg of our journey without a door closing after us.

We have been walking for around five minutes when Miaka stops dead.

"What's wrong?" I ask.

The girl lifts a finger to her lips and then cups her left ear, her eyes darting from left to right. She remains in this comical position for what must be close to a minute. I am about to repeat my question when she suddenly snaps to attention, standing like her spine has fused together into one solid bone.

"Someone is coming," she whispers, her eyes wide and filled with panic. "Behind us. Coming this way. Very fast."

Looking back in the direction we have just come from, all I see are those tired-looking walls and a dead vending machine.

"Are you sure?" I ask, lowering my voice.

Miaka does not answer.

The singing answers for her.

A childish melody drifts its way down the corridors and tickles my ears. The words are not clear, but it kind of reminds me of a lullaby Mother used to sing to me when I was a young girl.

One thing is for certain though: whoever, or whatever, is singing does not want to soothe me to sleep.

I grab Miaka's hand and start running.

The singing morphs into laughter, a young woman's laughter, bright and cheery. My treacherous imagination seizes its chance to amplify the terror that is already making my heartbeat frenzied. In my mind's eye, the Blood Daughter glides her way down the tunnels after us. Her long black robes are slick with blood, leaving a trail of red behind her. The laughter I can hear grows louder as she throws back her head with psychotic glee.

This only makes me run harder.

The tunnel turns sharply to the right. I hurtle around the corner, half-dragging Miaka after me. Ahead of us lies another endless corridor with no discerning features and a definite lack of an exit. I feel like we are running aimlessly around the insides of some giant mecha. If only we were. A kickass mecha would be really useful right now.

Halfway along the corridor, Miaka and I change positions. She sprints forward, pulling me away from the eerie giggling that echoes after us. I chance a look over my shoulder and see nothing but strip-lights and metal.

As I turn back, I see something on the wall that replaces my panic with euphoric relief. I immediately let go of Miaka's hand and skid to a stop. The girl from Tokyo spins round and runs back to me.

"What is it?" she asks.

"Help," I reply. "Possibly. I hope."

On the wall is a small vid-screen. Above that, a sign that reads:

"EMERGENCY FORCE BARRIER."

Under that, in tiny script, are numerous clauses and conditions for operation. Ignoring them, I touch the screen with a shaking finger, hoping the black glass will fill with colour and life. It does.

"Greetings, Citizen," says a recording of a woman who sounds like she has serious nasal congestion. "Please state the nature of your emergency."

I butt in with good old Mr. Tanaka's code.

"Force barrier activated," says the whining voice. "Be safe and have a nice day."

Although I have been told the barrier is on, I heard and saw nothing to confirm this; there was no audible fizz or crackle of electricity, nor was there any sign of anything in front of me. I tentatively reach out my hand and recoil when my fingertips are suddenly filled with a pain that reminds me of when I was stung by a hunter wasp.

I stick two of my throbbing fingers in my mouth. Even though I know this will do little to take away the sting, at least it stops me from swearing.

Miaka and I stand and stare through the invisible force field, back to where we have just come from. Apart from an occasional flicker from a strip light, we see nothing out of the ordinary.

"We are safe," says Miaka.

"Mmmpphh," I reply, my fingertips still in my mouth.

"Good. They are very close now."

I stop sucking on my digits and squint ahead of us.

"Are you sure?"

"Yes," she nods. "Very close."

"I can't see..."

My words trail off as that eerie song starts up once more.

Then, the lights go off.

Something starts pulling at my backpack. I am seconds away from screaming my lungs out when Miaka clicks my torch on.

"It is all right," she whispers. "It is me."

I take several deep breaths and try to calm my hammering heart.

Miaka points the torch in the direction of our pursuer. The yellowish beam cuts through the darkness, sending shadows dancing up the wall. Whoever is following us remains invisible.

"Are you sure someone's there?" I ask, keeping my voice as low as possible.

Miaka nods.

"They are in front of us."

The thought that someone is standing just inches away from us is enough to give my goosebumps goose pimples.

"They are laughing at us."

"I can't hear anything," I say, noting the lack of sound.

"In their heart," says Miaka. "Their heart is full of laughter. She is mocking us."

"She?"

Miaka turns to face me, her eyes wide and serious.

"We should go."

I do not need to be told twice.

We turn from the wall of energy and continue running. Even though I'm a billion percent sure that nothing can possibly get through a force barrier, I don't fancy being in here a second longer than I need to.

Walking is a luxury I will enjoy a little later, I hope.

After five minutes or so, we reach a crossroads. The left corridor beckons us with a small neon sign that promises it can take us to our destination.

We take the corridor and, true to the sign's word, we see that it ends at a door.

The entrance to 8C is finally within sight.

We pound our way towards it at a speed I'm sure neither of us have ever run before. The only sound we can hear now is that of our stamping feet. Still, we continue to run. The metal door steadily grows bigger and bigger, its definitions becoming more defined and real as we draw closer. It dawns on me that if we do not begin to slow down soon, we will plough straight into it. As if preempting this, the entrance to 8C promptly shoots open. Hand in hand, we leap over the lip of the door and into safety, or what we hope will be. It is at this point where our agility fails us and we both crash to the floor in a heap of flailing limbs and heavy backpacks.

I hear the door hiss shut and lock. Any moment now, we will hear the mysterious singer beating their fists against the window, as they curse us for escaping. Either that or the entrance will simply open again, allowing them to walk into the corridors of 8C and kill us where we lie.

Neither happens.

Seconds pass, turning into minutes.

Still nothing.

Then, the laughter starts.

Not some fiend from hell, but my own.

I'm unable to control myself. This laughter is born of sheer relief and demands to be released. I could not hold it in if I was paid a billion credits to try. Much to my amazement, Miaka joins in. Our entangled bodies slide into a warm hug, as the pair of us laugh like there is no tomorrow. The irony of this thought is not lost on me and makes me hold Miaka even tighter.

Eventually, our mirth subsides. I pull a pack of tissues from my parka and use one to wipe away Miaka's tears and then my own.

"We made it," I say.

"Yes," says Mr. Tanaka. "You most certainly did."

We swivel our heads round to see the old man standing to the left of the door we have just fallen through, a wry smile upon his wrinkled face.

"How long have you been standing there?" I ask.

"Long enough," he replies. "I saw you through the window, so thought I'd open the door. Save you a bit of time. I didn't expect you to come leaping through it like a couple of salmon."

"Someone was following us," I say, getting to my feet. "We could hear them singing and laughing. I activated a force barrier before it could get to us."

"Really? How curious..."

The old man moves to the door and squints through its glass panel.

When he turns to face us, I see he is wearing a worried expression.

"Do you think it was a ghost?" I ask.

"No. Of that much, I'm certain. Whoever was following you was definitely a 'who' and not a 'what'."

"So, who was it?"

"No idea," he replies with a shrug. His look of concern vanishes as his grin slides back in place. "No matter, you're here now and you're safe. That's the most important thing."

With that, he turns his back on us and slowly heads off down the corridors of 8C.

"Come along," he says. "There's tea waiting at my apartment."

I would be a complete and utter idiot to think the threat of Armageddon would stop Mr. Tanaka from making tea.

"It helps me think," he says, pouring us all a cup. "And I feel there will be a lot to think about this morning."

The three of us settle into our respective seats, each cradling our beverages as if they were the most precious of objects. I glance at the scanner, wondering if it is switched on or not.

"Don't worry, Kichi," says my old friend. "It's on. Has been since you called me earlier."

"OK," I say.

The atmosphere between us could be cut with a katana. It feels like we are in some kind of game where everyone has to speak, but the first one who does is out.

I watch Mr. Tanaka as I drink my tea. His eyes flit between me and Miaka, as if he is choosing who to start with. Finally, he fixes his gaze upon Miaka and gives her one of his warmest smiles.

"So, you are Miaka."

"Yes," she replies politely. "It is nice to meet you, Mr. Tanaka."

"The pleasure's all mine. Such a pity about the circumstances though."

"Yes. I am so sorry to be the bearer of such terrible news."

The girl bows her head and stares into her tea cup.

"Not your fault, dear child," he says, waving a hand in dismissal. "You're just the messenger. Can't blame you if the news is bad, can I?"

Miaka smiles.

"You are very kind. I do hope you can help me, Mr. Tanaka."

"So do I!" he says with a snort of laughter. "So do I."

He finishes his tea and pours himself another. Then, he turns his attention to me.

"So, young Kichi, I suppose you have many questions for me. Am I right?"

"Yes," I say. "You're right."

His grin grows wider.

"I guess you are wondering how an old man like me can hack into Osaka Sector security and take control of all their cameras, and how I have a special password that can open any door, even during a curfew lockdown. Am I correct?"

"Correct."

Mr. Tanaka jerks his head towards the scanner.

"Do you remember me telling you how I got that?"

I look at the blank screen on the wall and nod.

"Yeah, you said you had friends in low places."

"So I did," he says with a mischievous wink. "Very low places, the lowest in fact."

"You mean from level one?"

He slowly shakes his head.

"Lower still."

He drains his second cup of tea and leans forward in his chair.

"The government."

My jaw hits my chest.

"The government?"

"Correct."

"You have connections in the government?" I splutter. "How?"

My old friend leans back in his chair, smiles broadly and delivers a line that makes my jaw drop.

"I'm Chief Historian for the Department of Paranormal Activity," he says. "Or to put it simply, I am Agent Tanaka, DPA."

# FOURTEEN

Even though we live our whole lives in fear of encountering a ghost, many citizens secretly harbor the hope that, one day, they will have the chance to see one with their own eyes. Just a glimpse would be enough to satisfy our curiosity, as anything more than that would most probably lead to a horrific death.

This desire to witness the evil that keeps our city on the edge of a knife is a little strange, considering the high risk of fatality. What is the point of achieving our dream if it costs us our life?

Another thing to consider is the fact that if we do manage to catch a glimpse of a hellish shade and survive, we could never ever tell anyone. Although the word 'ghost' is common enough in everyday conversation and on the news and all that, talking about specific details is very, very dangerous.

Not only that, it is illegal.

There are a number of reasons why 'spook chat' is banned, one of them being that ghosts are attracted to certain words, especially their names or descriptions of their appearance. The last thing citizens want is a chat about things that go bump in the night and have one of them turn up at their door, looking for a party of pain.

I guess I am very lucky to have the chance to talk about this kind of stuff under the protective gaze of Mr. Tanaka's scanner.

Except it is not 'Mr.' Tanaka.

The scanner belongs to 'Agent' Tanaka of the DPA.

I stare at the stranger that wears my old friend's face.

At this precise moment in time, there is nothing else I can do. Words have failed me, and the part of my brain that controls movement has switched off. Staring is all I have.

Agent Tanaka shakes his head and chuckles.

"I can see this news comes as something of a surprise. You should see the look on your face, it really is quite amusing."

He finishes his third cup of tea and pours himself a fourth. The smile on his face grows wider, the sparkle in his eyes brighter. While he may be enjoying himself, I am most definitely not.

Miaka shifts position, moving along the sofa until she is practically leaning against me. Either she is wondering what the hell is going on or she has read my fear-filled mind. Agent Tanaka relaxes back in his comfortable chair and clears his throat.

"I suppose you may now be thinking this has all been a lure, yes? That I've tricked you into illegal spook chat and you're now going to be arrested and taken in for interrogation, perhaps even exorcised."

"I don't know," I mumble. "Maybe."

The old man adopts an expression of mock-horror.

"Kichi Honda! I'm most hurt you think that way!"

He then starts quietly laughing to himself, only stopping when he is seized by a coughing fit. When he has regained composure, he looks directly at me. Suddenly, the stranger has gone and I am once more sitting opposite the old man who saved my life.

"I'm sorry, Kichi," he says. "Perhaps I was a little over-dramatic when it came to revealing my 'secret identity'. I should've made certain things a lot clearer, but chose to pretend to be James Bond instead. I hope you can forgive an old man's foolishness."

"James Bond?"

"Before your time. Never mind. The point is, while I may be an agent of the Department of Paranormal Activity, I am simply an historian. There are some perks that come with the job, such as codes to bypass lockdowns and a scanner. But apart from that, I am merely an old man who keeps records of ghosts and spirits. To be brutally honest, it's been about three years since anyone from the department contacted me to make use of my knowledge. You know, I sometimes think they've forgotten I work for them!"

Mr. Tanaka drains his cup and smiles. This time, I smile back.

"So, I'm not in trouble?" I ask.

"Of course not!" he replies. "Well, not unless you decide to hand yourself in and damn me in the process! Do you realise just how many laws I've broken, filling your head with the complete history of haunted Nihon?"

I do not reply. There is no need. Every citizen knows the punishment for illegal spook chat. I think back to all the stories of people being dragged out of their apartment blocks in the dead of night, never to be seen again.

And then there was poor Ryuu, the boy I hardly knew; drowned during an exorcism.

I shudder to think what the DPA would do to me and Mr. Tanaka, should the scanner ever fail to keep our conversations secret.

"Why did you tell me?" I ask.

"I'm sorry?" Mr. Tanaka says, puzzled at my sudden question.

"The stories of ghosts and what happened to Tokyo. I mean, I love to hear them, you know I do. But why tell me if it's so dangerous?"

My old friend gives one of his warmest smiles.

"Because I trust you," he says. "And because some stories are meant to be shared."

Satisfied that everything is OK between us, Mr. Tanaka turns his attention to Miaka, asking to see the photos she had shown me earlier. Although I do not relish seeing those pictures again, I stay put on the sofa. Something inside tells me I need to get used to those images, no matter how much they terrify me. Miaka follows the same careful ritual as she did at breakfast, slowly taking the photos from out of their protective wrappings and displaying them on the table before us. Mr. Tanaka leans forward and starts his perusal of possible events to come. His gaze lingers over the first and last photos. It comes as no surprise to learn we are both drawn to the darkest of horrors.

"I have a question," he says, still staring at those two pictures.

"What is it?" asks Miaka.

"Not that it really matters, but who took these? Do you know?"

"Yes. His name was Takeo Abe."

Miaka gets up from the sofa and walks over to her backpack. She searches inside and pulls out two more cloth-wrapped bundles, one large and the other the size of a pack of nico-gum. She places them both on the table, sits back on the sofa and starts to unwrap the larger item first. As the layers of rags are stripped away, it becomes obvious what the object is.

It may be bulky and ancient, but there is no mistaking a camera when I see one.

"Takeo Abe took the photographs with this," she says. "It is called a Polaroid."

Mr. Tanaka is now on the edge of his seat. I have never seen him look so excited.

"Oh my. I haven't seen one of these in decades."

"There is this also," says Miaka, unwrapping the smaller package. "It is said to contain moving images. My great-great-grandfather saw them when he was a young boy. The generations after him were unable to view them. The means to do so was taken away from us."

Sitting in a small pile of black cloth, sits the tiniest of plastic boxes. Miaka carefully clicks it open, revealing what is inside.

Mr. Tanaka gasps.

"Yet another blast from the past!"

Again, it may be old and outdated, but it is clearly some kind of memory card. An ancient one, too.

"You've never seen what's on this?" asks the old man.

Miaka shakes her head.

"No, never. But I know all the stories. I know what history this relic holds."

Mr. Tanaka slowly rises from his chair and rubs the small of his back.

"Some stories need to be shared," he says. "And others need to be watched."

"What do you mean?" I ask. "Are you saying we can watch what's on there?"

"Oh yes," he confirms, the mischief returning to his eyes. "Most definitely."

Half an hour later, Mr. Tanaka is ready to show us whatever is stored on the memory card. A multitude of different coloured wires and leads now trail from the scanner, connecting to a battered old computer tablet that sits on his lap.

"You see, the problem with modern technology," he says, tapping at the tablet's screen. "Is that it becomes antiquated. One can buy the latest in comm-phones today and find the next-generation already in the shops tomorrow. And what do we do with all these gadgets that work perfectly but are no longer new? We throw them away and upgrade as fast as we possibly can!"

The old man shakes his head in disbelief.

"And people wonder why I stay away from cybernetic implants!"

Mr. Tanaka then pulls a small white box from his shirt pocket and slots it into the side of the tablet. Without looking up from the device, he holds a hand out towards Miaka.

"Could you pass me the memory card, please?"

Holding the card like it was made of the most fragile of materials, she passes it to him. He takes it from her, handling it with equal delicacy and slots it into one side of the white box.

"Kichi, my girl. Please press channel four on the scanner remote."

I take the control from off the table and do as instructed. There is a sudden hum of power as the blank screen suddenly turns a deep shade of blue.

"I'm running a program to clean up the files and see if they are still viewable," he says with a grin. "Shouldn't take too long."

Before I can point out he had earlier used the words 'most definitely', when asked if we were going to be able to see whatever is on the memory card, the old man points at the screen.

"Ha! Make that no time at all!"

The screen now displays twelve folders, each with an icon indicating it contains a film clip. Mr. Tanaka looks back at his tablet, rubbing a hand over his white stubbled chin.

"The program is saying that these files should play, but the quality may be of a very poor level. Clips three and four should have both been around five minutes in length. Sadly, we will only be able to see six seconds of three and eight and a half of four. Oh, and ten and eleven will be without sound. Apart from that..."

His words trail off, the sentence hanging unfinished in the air above us.

He stares at the scanner for a moment, lost in his thoughts. When he finally turns to me and Miaka, I see something in his eyes other than excitement, something hiding in plain view.

Fear.

"Are you ready?" he asks.

"Yes," replies Miaka. "I am ready."

"And you, Kichi?"

I take Miaka's hand and nod.

"Yep. I'm good."

The old man gives a small, nervous cough and types something on his computer tablet. When he is finished, he looks up at the scanner and the dozen folders it displays.

"Play all files."

# FIFTEEN

We sit and watch as the scanner's screen fades to black.

For a moment, it looks as if nothing is going to happen and we will just have to make do with Miaka telling us about the clips instead. As I try to decide whether the feeling inside of me is one of relief or disappointment, clip one begins to play.

Although Mr. Tanaka warned us that the quality of the recordings may be poor, what we are watching is surprisingly clear. This is even more amazing when you consider how long ago it was filmed. Another plus is that the person filming seems to have a steady hand, at least for now. This is good, as hand-held footage usually makes me feel dizzy, which then leads to possible puk-ing.

The first clip shows us a busy Tokyo street at ground level. The thing that strikes me straight away is how small the buildings were back then. Compared to those of modern-day Nihon, the neon-covered towers that line the crowded street look unfinished. The next thing I notice is the early-evening sky and the fact it is easily visible. If only this were possible here in Osaka Sector. Perhaps then, the citizens who live on level one would have a different kind of life.

It is only when the audio track kicks in that I remember what we are watching and why.

The person holding the camera or phone, presumably the Abe guy Miaka mentioned, is talking in an alien dialect as he films people crossing the street and filing in and out of those stunted skyscrapers. I turn to Mr. Tanaka and shake my head, politely letting him know I have no idea what is being said. Before he can say a word, Miaka starts to translate. Her tone is monosyllabic, devoid of feeling. The words that spill from her mouth as dead as the city she comes from.

"So here we are. Our first night in Tokyo. We have just left our hotel and walked to Shinjuku. Have you ever seen so many people? Still, isn't it something? What do you think?"

The camera pans to the left to show a young woman in a red parka. She tucks a strand of hair behind her left ear and smiles at the camera.

Miaka continues with her soulless narration.

"Say Hi, Yuki. Hi. Isn't it cool here? Yes. It's amazing. I love it. Can we move here? Really? You want to move here? Yes. Can we? Tell you what. If you can find me a good job, we will move here tomorrow. Does that sound OK?"

Miaka pauses as Yuki laughs. The sound is loaded with so much emotion it makes her next translation seem even deader.

"OK. Deal. Can we go for dinner first, though? I'm starving."

Yuki and Shinjuku suddenly disappear from the screen, replaced by lines of red and silver and blinding flashes of white.

The screen turns black.

The first clip is over.

Clip two shows us the same view of Shinjuku, but with one difference.

Everyone on the street has frozen.

People are streaming out of buildings, only to become statues as soon as their feet touch the sidewalk. Everyone stands silently, looking at something further down the street and out of view. I want to shout at the screen and tell Abe to show us what everyone is looking at. Frustratingly, the camera remains fixed on Yuki as she stares wide-eyed at whatever it is that has captured all but Abe's attention.

She slowly turns her face to the screen and starts to speak. At first, she looks scared but this turns to confusion as she continues.

Miaka's overdubs enlighten me.

"What is that? Can you see it? Hey. Are you OK? What? What are you looking at?"

Yuki turns and looks in the direction the camera is pointing.

I almost leap out of my chair when I see it.

Amongst all those paralyzed onlookers, there stands a person who is not looking in the same direction as everyone else; a woman with dark blue hair and a complexion as white as the dress she is wearing stares into the camera.

The forbidden words Mr. Tanaka taught me spill out of my mouth.

"Yurei. Onryo."

As if she has heard me, the creature smiles and slowly starts making her way through the crowds, towards the person filming her. Her movements are awkward. Every step is accompanied by a violent twitching of her arms and shoulders. The smile on her face grows wider and more sinister as she shuffles forward.

Yuki screams. The sound breaks the spell that has fallen over the people on the street. Some then notice what walks amongst them. The screams multiply.

Something blurs past the camera.

There then follows a shot of a darkening sky.

And after that, nothing.

The silence in Mr. Tanaka's living room is as loud as bombs.

The next thing we watch is several seconds of people flooding into some kind of building, possibly a mall or hotel, judging by its size. The soundtrack of fear and panic that accompanies it is so uncomfortable, I am glad it is over quickly.

After that, we see a stairwell filled with people. The camera is pointed at a door, through which a never-ending stream of citizens come running like a spooked pack of wolf-rats. Some of them lose their footing and fall to the floor. No one stops to help them up.

The fifth piece of film shows us the same stairwell, now carpeted with either the dead or unconscious. A young woman stumbles through the open door way. Her green coat is ripped in places and her left sleeve is missing from the shoulder down, the same half of her face is covered with blood. She looks at the camera and starts to sob.

"Help me. Help me."

Behind her, something part human, part shadow reaches out for her with long, spindly arms.

"Oh my god! Behind you! No," say Yuki and Miaka.

The girl is swiftly pulled back by her hair and out of sight.

The sixth clip starts to play and pauses after only a few seconds, the screen frozen on a blurred and grainy image of a closed door. Mr. Tanaka curses under his breath and starts jabbing his computer tablet's screen with his gnarled fingers. The image changes a few times, making us unable to tell what we are looking at. After a few more swear words and some rapid typing, Mr. Tanaka succeeds in getting the file to play again.

We are looking at a close up of Yuki's face. The lighting is poor, the picture devoid of any other colour but grey. Still, it is clear enough to see she is crying. At first, the words she speaks are nothing more than whispers. But as she continues, her fear and anger rise and the final moments of this piece of footage are filled with desperate screams.

In a bizarre kind of way, Miaka's robotic translation emphasizes Yuki's desperation.

"Please. Why are you filming this? Just stop. We need to get away! Please! Stop! Are you listening to me? What is wrong with you? Turn the fucking camera off! Stop filming! Stop it! Stop it!"

I have to agree with Yuki there. If I had been her, I would have taken his camera or whatever, thrown it to the floor, stamped it into smithereens and dragged him the hell out of there. So sad to see the curse of the zombie voyeur was alive and kicking, even back then. Still, no matter how screwed up it may be, these people do play an important part in recording history. Sometimes.

All I know is, should tomorrow be the end of everything, I will not be taking any photos. I will be running for my life, if I'm able to.

File seven refuses to play ball, as do file eight and nine.

Miaka silently sits and watches as Mr. Tanaka's anger rises, scared to move in case we become a target for his wrath. After around ten minutes of fiddling with his antique computer, he looks about ready to hurl it across the room. Somehow, he manages to control his frustration and only throws hissed insults at the machine instead.

"Shall we just skip to the next one that will play?" I suggest, in an attempt to pacify him. The old man stops what he is doing and sighs, nodding his head in defeat. The redness of his face fades a little and I mentally congratulate myself for putting out the flames.

"I guess we'll have to. Sadly, the program I ran didn't work as well as I first thought, damned thing. I'm afraid we'll have to go straight to file ten. Sorry about that."

"Not your fault. I mean, the files are really old. I'm not surprised some of them won't play."

He lifts his head and stares with contempt at the scanner's blue screen for a moment, before turning back to us and attempting a smile.

"You're right, of course. I think we can count ourselves extremely lucky to have viewed the first six. If 'lucky' is really the right word, all things considered."

He puts a hand to his mouth and coughs, before turning to Miaka.

"Miaka, my dear girl. What happens after Yuki tells him to stop filming?"

"She dies," she says. "An Onryo takes her."

The nonchalance of her reply takes my breath away.

The fact that Yuki died in such a grisly manner brings a lump to my throat.

Of course she is dead. They all are. It should come as no big surprise to learn the girl who was so excited to be in Tokyo has long since left this world. Even so, her death hits me hard. Miaka takes my hand.

"I am sorry."

I do not reply. I am not sure how to.

Before we skip to the tenth clip, Mr. Tanaka reminds us there will be no sound, for either this or the next piece of footage.

The silence is not a blessing.

The screen shows us a view from a window, looking down at Shinjuku. Night has fallen, the glow of neon illuminates the dead that litter the street. The corpses are bathed with gold, green and red as they gaze up at the blackened sky with unseeing eyes. Amongst the piles of bodies crawl things that look like women but have the necks of snakes. One of the creatures looks up in the direction of the window. The clip ends there.

Eleven shows a hotel corridor. Some of the doors are closed, others open wide. A few have been ripped clean off their hinges. The dead lie scattered here and there, their bodies twisted and broken, those facing the camera show only hollow sockets instead of eyes.

Standing halfway down the corridor, with her back towards us, is a naked and blood-splattered girl. She is painfully thin, more like a skin-covered skeleton than a person. Her hair is long and moves as if it is alive.

As if this is not scary enough, the girl is not standing amongst the corpses.

She stands above them.

Her bare feet are planted firmly on the ceiling.

Tendrils of long black hair reach down from her head to caress the bodies on the corridor floor.

The screen turns black before she can turn to face us. I mentally thank Buddha and all the Bodhisattvas for sparing us from seeing her face. I cannot imagine it would have been a pretty sight.

The twelfth and final clip shows us another view from a window, this time from a much higher level. The snake-necked women that crawl through the carnage below have increased in number, their ranks swelled even further by other hell-sent things that defy both description and belief. As Abe films, all that can be heard is the sound of his quiet sobbing. Amazingly enough, his camera hand remains perfectly steady.

The view changes as he moves the camera away from the street and focuses instead on the stygian sky. In the near distance, we can see something flying through the air. Abe zooms in and the screen is filled with an image of some kind of flying craft. This machine is not of supernatural origin. It's an early form of copter.

Abe zooms out a little and reveals there are three of them, flying in close formation. Hanging by ropes or wires from these vehicles are huge rectangular slabs of metal.

Mr. Tanaka rises from his chair, shaking a finger at the screen.

"Stop. Pause clip."

Moving faster than I have ever seen him, he goes to stand directly in front of the scanner, inspecting the image at close quarters.

"No. It can't be…"

"What is it?" I ask. "What's wrong?"

The old man spins round and stares at Miaka with wide eyes. The look on his face makes me shrink back in my seat.

"When were these files recorded?" he snaps. "How much time passed between each clip? Do you know?"

"Yes, I know," she timidly replies. "The story says that this all took place in less than one hour."

Upon delivering her answer, Mr. Tanaka's face drains of colour. His eyes mist over as they fill with tears.

"They lied," he whispers. "They lied to everyone."

I do not know how to act or what to do. I have no idea what he is referring to and to see him crying breaks my heart. Indecision turns me into a pathetic excuse for a friend.

Miaka stands and moves to his side. She holds the old man's hand and looks up at him with an equal amount of sorrow.

"You understand now, don't you?"

Mr. Tanaka nods.

"You know what happened."

"Yes," he replies, his voice breaking with emotion. "I know."

I stumble to my feet, mostly because I feel like the odd one out just sitting there. The only thing I can think of saying is the same old dumb question.

"What happened?"

"They knew," he croaks. "They knew the ghost quake was coming. They knew…"

He pauses to wipe his tears away with the back of his sleeve. After taking a deep breath, he looks at me with eyes that burn with anger.

"Those copters were carrying sections of the wall that sealed Tokyo off from the rest of the world. There's no way on earth something that size and so complex could have been designed and constructed in less than one hour. No way. The government knew the ghost quake was coming! They knew it was going to happen. They built the wall long before that day. They were prepared and ready for it. But they didn't make it public. The government knew what was going to happen and chose to say nothing! All those people! Men, women, children..." Mr. Tanaka continues, his expression as grave as his words.

"They killed them. The government killed everyone in Tokyo."

# SIXTEEN

I now know three different versions of Sector Thirteen's history.

The first version is the one we were told as children: a vague account that mentions the ghost quake, the walls being put up, the great sacrifice made that day to ensure Nihon's safety and the warning to never ever go looking for any further information.

The second is what I have learned from Mr. Tanaka. In all honesty, his story still lacks certain details, but does go on to tell the public's reaction to the day Tokyo fell and the general apathy that followed.

The Tanaka version also includes ghosts. Lots of them.

The latest look at what happened reveals the government knew the ghost quake was coming and decided to keep silent about it.

Instead of saving everyone, they damned the whole city to hell.

A government lying to its citizens is neither new nor shocking.

The fact that our government secretly decided to kill an entire city is just plain sick.

Every single Nihon citizen lives their life under the impression the government did all they could for those in Tokyo and that the walls were a desperate final option. The DPA even taught us to applaud the scientists and military of that time for constructing the barriers so quickly, thus saving countless lives.

*'The genius of those brave men and women must forever be remembered. For without them, there would be no Nihon today.'*

This may be right, but it is also very wrong.

Truth is, even though Miaka has helped shed some light on the truth, we will never fully know what happened that day. Those who made the decisions back then are long gone, and the leaders who followed them have done everything possible to keep its citizens in the dark.

And by filling the hearts of every last man, woman and child with fear, they succeeded in doing just that.

Fact of the matter is, the lie spread around the entire world and was believed. It must have been. How else could genocide on that scale take place without an international outcry?

How did things get so screwed up?

Mr. Tanaka has been in his bedroom for around fifteen minutes now. Occasionally, Miaka and I hear an outburst of muffled shouting, followed by something heavy hitting the wall. My guess would be he is throwing his books across the room, his anger stripping them of their value. The thought of this saddens me greatly. I want to go to him and tell him that I still think he is awesome, but the noise coming from his room tells me to stay seated and to let him vent.

Poor Mr. Tanaka. He was just as in the dark as everyone else.

I reach over for my parka, which lies balled up at the end of the sofa, and start searching my pockets for nicogum. As well as my gum, I also find Ms. Pang's contact card. I never did call her to fix that lunch appointment. If we don't succeed in tomorrow's impossible mission, I doubt I'll ever have the chance.

I pop two pieces of synthetic nicotine substitute into my mouth and start to chew. Another loud crash emanates from my old friends room, the shouting that comes after is his loudest yet. I turn to Miaka and give her a feeble smile.

"He is very angry," says Miaka.

"Yep," I nod. "He is."

Under her fringe of matted hair, a heavy frown appears.

"I did not mean to make him so angry."

"Not your fault," I say, patting her knee. "You didn't make him angry."

I nod my head towards the scanner and the frozen image of the copters and their terrible cargo.

"That's what pissed him off."

The girl from Sector Thirteen stares silently at the screen for several minutes. I glance down at the contact card in my hand and start to think of what food I would have ordered for lunch. An image of thick white noodles in a bowl of red chili broth pops into my head. It looks so real that it makes my stomach growl its approval. My hunger turns to horror as the noodles morph into writhing worms squirming in congealing blood. I shake this nauseous thought from my head and shove Ms. Pang's card into a side pocket of my combat trousers.

"What happened next?" I ask Miaka. "I mean, after those films were taken. What happened?"

The girl turns to face me and smiles.

"We survived."

"How? How did people stand a chance against those... things?"

"Everything has its weakness," she replies. "Theirs was faith."

"Faith?"

"Yes. Belief is something Hell cannot win against."

She stops for a moment and tugs at a length of her tangled hair, rolling it between her slender fingers. What I would give to work on that mess with some industrial-strength shampoo and a pair of scissors. Oblivious to my grooming desires, Miaka continues.

"As soon as the walls went up, the Blood Daughter and her kin made their way to the barriers. They realised Tokyo had become a prison for both its citizens and them. The survivors of those first hours watched them go. They waited until the streets were safe and then they ran to the city's temples. Under Buddha's gaze, they prayed to be rescued. After some time, they realised they had been forgotten and prayed for a quick death instead. It is not known how long they stayed in the temples, waiting for Hell to come for them. Perhaps it was days. Our history is not clear on this. But, we know that when the ghosts did return, they did not enter the temple grounds. The survivors soon learned it was because they could not."

Miaka leans into me, her smile both childish and full of wisdom

"Balance still existed. Even if just a little."

Before I can ask what she means, Mr. Tanaka storms back into the living room. Both of his fists clutch sheets of yellowed papers.

"It was her, wasn't it?" he hisses, his eyes fixed on Miaka. "The Blood Daughter. It was her."

The girl from Tokyo slowly rises to her feet and nods.

"Yes," she says. "It was her."

"The ritual... They stopped it..."

My old friend stumbles to his favorite chair and slumps down into it. The papers he carries fall to the floor as he buries his face in his hands. Miaka walks over to him and kneels at his feet.

"Yes. They stopped it. One man's love for his child damned all of Tokyo."

Mr. Tanaka lets his hands fall to his lap. The frown he wears adds years to his confused face.

"Who was it?" he whispers. "Who could do something so..."

Miaka stands up and looks towards the scanner and the sinister slice of history it still shows.

"Kazuo Shimizu," she says, "The man who failed."

All the jigsaw pieces of weird and terrifying information I have inside my head suddenly snap together. Judging by the look on Mr. Tanaka's face, it is obvious he has just completed his own puzzle. Chances are he will be nearer to the truth than me, but I still feel pleased with myself for putting two and two together and getting something that's close to four. Before either Miaka or Mr. Tanaka can say another word, I decide it is my turn to drive the conversation, mostly to see how wrong or right I am.

"OK. So a hundred years ago, an ancient ritual to keep a psychotic supernatural killing machine from slaughtering everyone on earth failed. Because of this, the Blood Daughter was set free from Hell, as well as a multitude of her closest and creepiest friends. Yes?"

The old man and the girl look at me with mouths open like hungry koi. Perhaps my sudden explosion of enthusiasm has shocked them. I decide to take their reaction as a sign I am on the right track. Filled with confidence, I continue painting my picture.

"So, as soon as she arrives in town, her and her friends get the party started. While it's in full swing, the government, who knew this was going to happen, starts sealing off the city with walls they prepared earlier, right?"

My two companions nod in unison. So far, it seems I've been spot on with my theory of events.

Now comes the grey area.

"So, putting what little I know about the Blood Daughter together with what Miaka has now told us, the ritual to keep her happily locked up in Hell is something real nasty. My guess is it involved a sacrifice, a human one."

A look from Mr. Tanaka says I'm right again.

I suppress a satisfied smile and go on.

"The government knew this was going to happen. The question is how? How did they know?"

I gesture towards Miaka

"Am I right in guessing the sacrifice had something to do with Kazuo Shimizu?"

"Yes," says Miaka. "Kazuo Shimizu was supposed to sacrifice his daughter..."

Her sentence trails off, unfinished. She looks down at her hands, which are balled tightly into white-knuckled fists.

"... but he did not. One man's love for his child was worth more than a whole city."

Kazuo Shimizu is regarded as Nihon's foremost leader.

We were told as children of how Shimizu's quick thinking saved Nihon, even though its salvation came at a terrible price.

*'If not for President Shimizu, Nihon City would not exist. The place we call home would be one of darkness and eternal suffering. Never forget that President Shimizu saved us from Hell.'*

If Miaka is right, President Shimizu is now worthy of joining the ranks of the world's most evil men and women. In my opinion, the guy goes straight to the number one slot.

Forgetting Shimizu's crimes for a moment, I press on to discuss the final piece of the jigsaw.

"Miaka, when we first met, you said you needed to find the man who failed."

"Yes," she replies. "That is true."

"You said it was very important."

"Yes it is."

"And just now, you said Kazuo Shimizu was the man who failed."

"Yes."

"So the person you are looking for, the one who has a major part in stopping the Blood Daughter from killing every last citizen in Osaka, is Kazuo Shimizu?"

"Yes."

I start laughing. I cannot hold it back. Not a chance.

"Why is this funny?" asks Miaka.

Her innocent question only makes me laugh harder. Tears fill my eyes, stream down my face and drip onto my anti-Red Raku shirt.

Mr. Tanaka gives a sorrowful groan and buries his head in his hands.

He knows what I will say, once I've got control of myself. Oddly enough, he makes no effort to stop me. Perhaps it needs to be said.

After wiping my eyes on the back of my sleeve, I take several deep breaths before delivering the punch line to the cruelest joke ever.

"Kazuo Shimizu's been dead for eighty two years."

I shouldn't feel smug, but I do. The sentence that has just spilled out of my smiling mouth was neither funny nor cool. The words I've just spoken have made it absolutely clear that we are all, well and truly, dead.

Perhaps the satisfaction I felt telling Miaka we're doomed is a kind of weird self-defense mechanism. After all, the information about Shimizu's death could have quite easily been delivered with me hyperventilating and sobbing my eyes out. In all honesty, I'm totally amazed the latter didn't happen.

But all the same, I shouldn't feel smug.

Mr. Tanaka comes to stand next to me and takes my hand.

"I'm sorry, Miaka," he says. "But Kichi is right. Kazuo Shimizu died a long time ago. I'm afraid he'll be unable to help us."

Miaka slowly gets to her feet and looks at the pair of us, her eyes dark and serious.

"He is not dead," she calmly tells us. "He lied to you all again. Shimizu is only sleeping."

My smugness instantly disappears. Mr. Tanaka squeezes my hand so tightly that I fear he may break my fingers.

"What do you mean?" he splutters. "Miaka, tell me! What are you saying?"

Miaka doesn't answer. Her entire body stiffens, her eyes open so wide I worry they may pop out of her skull.

"Outside," she whispers. "There are many people outside."

Before anyone can say another word, there comes the sound of a small explosion from the hallway.

The clang of metal that follows is Mr. Tanaka's security door being blown off its hinges.

"I think we may have company," I say.

# SEVENTEEN

Back when I first started hanging out with Mr. Tanaka, he told me the emergency procedures for if we were caught talking about ghost stuff and paid a surprise visit from the DPA.

"Not that it's going to happen," he had said. "My scrambler is easily the most sophisticated in all of Nihon. I'd stake my life on its integrity."

I then pointed out that every time we had chatted about ghosts and such, we had done exactly that.

"Indeed," he replied. "And no one has ever come bashing down the door to arrest us, have they?"

So far, today has not been a good day for him.

I spring into action. Leaping across the room, I slam my hand hard against one of the seven concealed panels the old man had shown me. The one I choose is to the left of the scanner that has failed to keep us safe from eavesdroppers.

A second later, there comes a whooshing noise, followed by a loud thud. A smile of relief forms on my face when I see the corridor that leads from the living room to the hallway no longer exists. Now there is only a wall of reinforced titanium.

"That should give us some time," says Mr. Tanaka. "Quickly! Move on to stage two!"

I take Miaka by the hand and drag her after Mr. Tanaka. We follow the old man as he runs down the corridor, past the kitchen and bathroom and on to the master bedroom. The old man flings the door open and disappears inside. We follow suit. The master bedroom is totally bare, a windowless rectangle of cold grey.

Mr. Tanaka leans against the wall, his breath coming in wheezing gasps, exhausted from his sudden burst of physical activity.

From the living room comes the sound of a second explosion. The old man gestures urgently at the floor with a shaking hand.

"Exit," he splutters. "Activate it."

I dash to the centre of the room, fall to my knees and press my left hand against the bare plasticrete floor. There is a slight tremble as a thin line of white light rapidly forms a square around me.

The hidden trapdoor is revealed.

I scrabble to my feet and wave Miaka to come and stand with me on the square of floor that will take us out of this mess.

Before she can move a step, the bedroom door is kicked open and a figure in black combat armour speeds into the room. He grabs Miaka by her tangled hair, lifting her clean off her feet. More intruders follow. One of them stabs some kind of hypo-gun into Miaka's arm. She passes out instantly. A third slams the butt of his rifle into Mr. Tanaka's stomach. He collapses to the floor and lies motionless at his assailant's booted feet. A fourth and a fifth aim their weapons at me.

"Niagara," I say.

The room and all its occupants and guns blur out of existence as the trapdoor slides open and I plunge down into the dummy apartment below.

The next thing I know, I'm lying on my back on something very soft and extremely bouncy. It reminds me a little of when my father used to take me anti-grav swimming. I shake that thought from my head and half roll, half struggle from off the air-ball that has saved me from breaking my legs or back. Glancing up, I am relieved to see the trapdoor has closed again.

Doubting its integrity, and knowing for sure that time is a luxury I do not have, I get to my feet and race out of the room and through Mr. Tanaka's empty second home.

Lights come on automatically as I run through the naked apartment. I do not slow down. I pound down the corridor towards the front door. As the way out draws closer, I shout out the password that will open the door.

"Adios."

The barrier between me and the escape shoots upwards and I run out of the apartment like a person being chased by a swarm of blood moths, out into the corridor and smack right into the opposite wall. Searing white pain shoots up my right arm, my lungs feel about ready to collapse. I peel myself off the wall, point myself eastwards and continue running.

Down the corridors I run. With every corner I turn, my heart accelerates at the thought of running into more of the people who I am currently fleeing from.

The people who like to make an explosive entrance and carry big guns.

The people I have just left my two friends with.

But this does not happen. Each new section of the corridor I meet is empty and silent.

I run on and on, until I reach the evac point.

Every residential and commercial building has evac-points, but they are seldom used.

This is due to two reasons.

The first is because improper use of an evac-point can lead to a very long stint in prison. What actually constitutes correct use is so vague that citizens would rather avoid using them than face the rest of their lives confined in solitary.

I heard a story once about a fire in an apartment complex in Okinawa Sector a few years back. Apparently, citizens who used the evac-point to escape being burned to death were rounded up by the police and taken away, never to be seen again. I am not sure I believe that to be true, but it would not surprise me.

The second reason for not using an evac-point is the one that does bother me, the one that I am hoping is not true.

Word is, evac-points have a habit of not working correctly.

And when an evac-point fails to do its job, there is only one result.

People become pizza.

The airlock to the evac-point opens with Mr. Tanaka's magic password. I enter a strip lit room about a quarter of the size of a regular elevator. Along the walls to my left and right are rows of people-sized tubes. They look a little like suspended animation chambers from old movies, except these babies are designed to transport you out of trouble, not keep you preserved for x-amount of years. I choose a random evac-pod along the left wall and press my hand against the control pad on its surface. The tube hums into life and glows a ghoulish shade of green.

Nice.

An automated voice starts up with its welcome spiel, but I cut it dead with the ever-trusted Tanaka password. The plasti-glass cover of the tube slides back and I step in and hold the handrail in front of me. I hear the cover hiss shut behind me, locking me in.

I close my eyes and exhale deeply. My mind starts projecting images of Miaka being injected and Mr. Tanaka falling to the floor.

"I'm sorry," I say and pull the hand rail I am holding sharply towards me.

"Evac-pod descending," says a recorded female voice. "Have a safe trip, citizen."

And then, for the second time in my life, I am falling.

I clutch the handrail for all I am worth. My eyes are screwed up so tightly that I fear I may never be able to open them again. My internal cinema of guilt continues to play the movie where I leave a girl and an old man in the hands of...

In the hands of who?

Who were those people?

I feel the evac-pod speed up.

How long until it reaches level ten?

Will it stop at level ten?

Perhaps it will continue down to level one, getting faster and faster and faster, only stopping when it hits the ground and splatters me dead.

Then the replay of Mr. Tanaka being beaten fades and is replaced by a memory from back when I first started to visit him. The old man is sitting in his favourite chair, sipping his tea.

'And what if we are paid a surprise visit from unsavoury guests and I am captured?' he asks. 'What must you do then?'

"I must get out" I say, both in the memory and out loud. "I must save myself and live to fight another day."

The old man laughs.

'Just live is all I ask, young Kichi. Get out as fast as you can and then go live your life. Don't you worry about me. I'm old and ugly enough to take care of myself.'

My friend winks mischievously at me and takes another sip of tea.

'But like I said,' he continues. 'The chance of anyone ever disturbing us is extremely unlikely...'

I snap my eyes open. Directly in front of me is a screen with pulsing green digits. After several seconds, my vision comes back into enough focus for me to see I am moments away from either reaching level ten or dying horribly.

"I want to live," I say. "I want to live and fight another day."

The evac-pod starts to slow. The racing digits follow suit.

Seventeen.

Sixteen.

"I want to live,"

Twelve.

Eleven.

Ten.

The evac-pod stops with a sudden jerk. My head jolts forward and hits the screen with a dull thud. Behind me, I hear the pod open.

I slowly turn around, rubbing my surely bruised and aching forehead.

Standing in front of me is a vision from my worst nightmares.

A girl, dressed totally in black.

A girl with a manic smile and the eyes of a lunatic.

A girl with hair the colour of blood.

"Goodnight," says Red Raku in a sweet voice, and then punches me square in the face.

The force of her blow instantly transports me to a land of pure and utter darkness.

# EIGHTEEN

I am standing in a field of red and white flowers. A light summer breeze swirls around me, passing easily through the thin fabric of the white dress I am wearing to caress my skin. Although the sensation is a little cold, it is not entirely unpleasant. I look up to see a sky so blue, it is breathtaking.

"Awesome," I say, actually using the word in its truest sense.

"Yes," says a voice. "It is very pretty here."

I turn my eyes away from the cloudless blue above to see Miaka standing directly in front of me. She too is wearing a flimsy summer dress. Her hair is untangled and shines in the sun, a deep black with occasional flashes of iridescent green.

She holds up a bunch of brightly-coloured flowers.

"Here," she says. "Smell these."

I bend down a little to take a sniff of the fragrant bouquet she is offering me.

"These will wake you up,"

I inhale deeply.

The pain of my broken nose snaps me back to reality. My eyes open, but a blinding white light makes me wince and close them again. Even without the sense of sight, I know for sure I am naked and tied down to something cold and metallic. There are thick straps around my ankles, wrists and neck. They feel thick and heavy against my naked flesh.

I swallow painfully. There is a slightly bitter chemical taste in my mouth and a fading dullness to my senses which is something other than the result of physical injury. I am also not as cold as I really should be, considering my lack of clothing.

Have I been drugged?

How long have I been out?

I open my eyes again, blinking away the pain of the white light in a fit of panic.

How much time is left until...

Until what?

Until I die?

It seems to me that dying very soon is something I am going to have to accept. The only thing I should now be concerned about is by which method.

My eyes grow accustomed to the glare of the six long strip-lights that hang from the ceiling high above me. From my position, I can only ascertain I am in a very long room with grey stone walls, kind of similar to the lifts in my apartment complex, only much longer. The metal thing I am now strapped to is at such an angle that it allows me to see down the room to a point where there is no lighting, only a darkness that crouches on the horizon, waiting.

From somewhere in that darkness, I can hear the echo of dripping water.

At least, I guess it is water.

I am just able to turn my head enough to see that about six feet to the left of me is a door. It may as well be a million miles.

I crane my neck to the right.

What I see makes my blood run cold.

A few feet away from me is an altar, of sorts; a crude fashioning of blackened wood and rusting metal. On top of it sits a collection of black wax candles, most of which are now nothing more than melted stubs that sit amongst the dust of burned incense sticks. Hanging from hooks on either side of this worship point are two knives. One of them has a blade almost as long as my arm. Neither of them are things of beauty. Their silver blades may be all clean and shiny, but I know for damn sure they have been red with blood on multiple occasions.

Above the altar is the thing that scares me beyond measure.

An image of something I saw not so long ago; a picture, scrawled on the wall in black and red, an image of madness and the purest evil.

The same picture Mr. Tanaka showed me.

The Blood Daughter.

I turn away from her eyes and glare up at the light directly above me. I stare until tears start streaming down both sides of my face.

Behind me, I hear the hiss of a door opening and someone entering the room, the sound of their footsteps bouncing around the cavernous room until it sounds as if I am being approached by an army of giants.

The footsteps stop abruptly behind me. Suddenly, there is the whirring sound of motors and the table I am on moves slowly into an upright position and then swivels round, coming to a stop when I am face to face with lunacy incarnate.

"Hello there," says Red Raku, with a smile. "Are you ready for the fun to begin?"

Even though I have been casually following the exploits of the infamous Raku Nakamura for some time, seeing her live and in the flesh is an entirely different matter.

The level of insanity in her eyes is a lot clearer and a billion times scarier when they are fixed solely on you.

Looking into those eyes, you know they belong to a person whose life went very wrong somewhere. You know their humanity has been diminished to almost nothing, a tiny speck of light in an eternity of darkness.

I want to close my eyes so badly, but I am so scared of what her reaction would be.

She tilts her head to one side, allowing her long red hair to fall down in such a way that it looks like blood pouring out from a massive head wound. Then she grins like a five-year-old girl who has been given a mountain of soy-candy.

As well as wearing a pair of heavy-duty boots, black fishnets and a pair of black shorts, she is also proudly sporting my 'PLEASE DON'T KILL ME' shirt.

"I like your t-shirt," she says, as if realising I have just noticed.

I remain silent. I mean, what the hell should I say? Do I need to thank her for the compliment?

"Seriously though," she continues, casting her gaze up to the ceiling. "Did you really think this would work?"

I give her an honest answer and say no. Raku, still focused on something maybe only she can see, grins even wider.

"I remember watching a really old movie about a serial killer, one of the classics from what was once America. Anyway, there was this part of the movie where the serial killer was being taunted by the police about how people would forget him and his work in the future, about how unimportant he would be in the annals of history."

Raku returns her attention to me, her eyes burn with an intense and twisted glee.

"Do you know what they said to him?"

"No," I reply meekly.

"They told him he'd be a t-shirt at best."

And with that, she starts to laugh.

I recognise the laughter from back on the link walkway.

Suddenly, I feel very cold indeed.

Red Raku walks over to the altar of horror and takes the smaller of the two knives that hang there. She then moves back to me, holding the weapon in both hands, just like it was a bunch of artificial flowers.

"You know, your death is going to be something rather special," she says in that sickly-sweet tone of hers. "You really ought to be thrilled. I mean, you're about to be my one-hundredth kill!"

With that, she starts doing little jumps of joy on the spot. I can imagine that if she wasn't holding a knife, she would be clapping her hands.

One-hundredth kill?

Raku notices the frown that has formed on my face and stops her display of joy. She frowns back at me and pouts.

"What's wrong, baby? Did I say something bad?"

Seeing as my doom is certainly very nigh, I decide to answer her question, but I tread as carefully as possible.

"The news reports, they say the total number of your victims..."

Raku shakes her head and waves a finger at me.

"Nihon News is not given the full facts, dear. That info is strictly on a need-to-know kind of basis. And they don't need it."

"What do you mean?"

"I mean that they don't need to know!" She shakes her head and rolls her eyes in mock disgust. "Wow. Just how stupid are you?"

Nihon's most prolific female serial killer then gives me her best 'you are so going to die soon' smile.

"Stupid or not, you are gonna be the one-hundredth sacrifice."

I turn my head away from Red Raku Nakamura and look at the drawing of pure evil above the altar.

The Blood Daughter stares back at me. Her gaze tears through my flesh and bones, boring into my heart, into my soul.

"Why?" I ask, not entirely sure who my question is aimed at.

"Why what?" comes Raku's reply.

I snap my head back to look at her. Words start to spill from my mouth in a tumble of fear, hate and confusion.

I can't stop them.

"Why do you worship that bitch? Don't you know she's coming? I've seen what she can do, what she's going to do! She's going to kill every single person in Osaka Sector, possibly the whole of Nihon! You really think she's gonna thank you for all this? You think she's gonna spare you? Fuck! Just how stupid are *you*?"

Red Raku moves so fast it is almost inhuman. The point of her knife now gently digs into the skin under my right eye. All she has to do is increase the pressure, just a little, and that cold blade of hers will slice into my flesh and into my eye, popping it like gum.

"Have you quite finished?" she asks. The twisted smile she was wearing has gone. Her expression is now deadly serious.

"One more uninvited comment from you, and I promise your death will be the slowest, most painful anyone has ever suffered in the whole of Nihon. I'll make sure every single second of agony lasts for an eternity. You got that? Are we crystal fucking clear?"

"Yes," I croak.

We are totally crystal.

Red Raku turns away from me and walks slowly towards the door through which she entered.

"I get a lot of screamers," she says to me and the empty room. "Some beg. Some promise me stuff. But mostly, I get screamers. Scream and scream and scream. I did consider listening to music while I did my thing, but..."

She slowly pirouettes round on the tips of her bulky boots to face me again. Her trademark smile is now firmly back in place.

"Where is the fun in that?"

She then starts walking in a circle around the table I am strapped to. Her manner is like that of someone taking a leisurely evening stroll through one of the sector's eco-domes.

In reality, she is the predator, circling her prey.

"You know, when I saw you and that little girl on the walkway, I truly thought my luck was in. I mean, what with the curfew and all that, the chances of finding my one-hundredth were looking pretty slim. And believe me when I say I was not happy about that. Nope, I was not happy about that at all. Time was running out on me, for everyone, and I only had one more to go. When the ghost siren sounded, I was like 'Oh shit, what the hell am I gonna do now?' But then I saw you and I knew you were the one. Just knew it. So, I followed you to that old guy's house and I waited outside for a while. And then this woman and all these guys turn up. Wow, what was all that about? Anyway, I had a feeling you would make a run for it. Don't ask me, but I had this feeling you'd escape and head down to a safer level somehow. So, down I went and waited for you. Sure enough, you turn up! Like I said, I knew you were the one to end it all."

She stops walking somewhere behind me.

"Are you a screamer?"

I close my eyes and clench my lower lip between my teeth.

"You are invited to reply," she chuckles.

I ignore the invitation. Raku continues ambling around me, giggling as she goes.

"Well, we'll find out soon enough. Personally, I don't really care. You can go scream all you like. But, just to let you know in advance, you have nothing, and I do mean nothing, that you could use for bargaining. So please, don't waste your breath."

She sighs and stops her strolling, this time some-where to the left of me.

"You know what today is?" she asks.

I shake my head. My eyes and mouth remain glued shut.

Raku's next words are whispered directly into my left ear.

"It's Friday."

As she laughs merrily to herself, two facts are clarified for me.

First is that I have definitely been drugged. Raku's punch could not have knocked me out for that long. I was last conscious sometime in the afternoon on Thursday.

The second is that today is the last day.

Not just my last day, but everyone's.

And then something Red Raku said comes back to me.

'Time was running out on me, for everyone...'

What did she mean by that?

I open my eyes and stare straight into hers. She is, quite literally, in my face, the tip of her nose touches mine.

"You said you've seen what she's done. You said she's coming. Explain. Now."

Although her words are delivered with a slow men-ace, I can detect a small amount of confusion. I start explaining, as ordered.

"The girl you saw me with. She's from Tokyo."

"How?"

"She never really said how. Just that she got out."

"The Blood Daughter, you saw what she can do? How?"

"The girl, Miaka, had photos and old video footage of what really happened in Tokyo that day. She showed them to me."

"And she's coming? The Blood Daughter is coming?"

"Yes. That's what Miaka said. Today. At sunset."

Red Raku slowly moves back and away from me. Her retreat does not stop until her back meets the wall behind her.

She almost looks frightened.

Bizarrely enough, I feel a little confidence returning. It may be microscopic in size, but it is confidence all the same.

"What's wrong?" I ask. "Doesn't that make you happy?"

Raku narrows her eyes. Her brow furrows.

I realise I may have just earned the slow, painful death she promised.

Whatever.

If these are to be my last words, let them be ones worth dying over.

"Congratulations! You win! Got a bottle of synth-champagne we can open? Should we order a pizza? Grab ourselves a celebratory Wasabi-dog? Come on! Surely it's time for a party, right? I mean, isn't this what you've always wanted?"

Red Raku slowly shakes her head.

"No," she says, her voice a trembling whisper of barely controlled anger. "No. It is not."

Now it is my turn to be confused.

"What do you mean?"

"I mean it is *not* what I wanted."

She lifts the knife she is still holding and looks at it with a quizzical expression on her face. It is like she has forgotten why she has the weapon and what she is supposed to do with it.

She slowly starts to slide down the wall until she is crouched on the floor, hugging the lethal blade to her chest like it is a child's toy.

At first, it sounds like she is crying, but I quickly realise she is laughing. She sounds like a young schoolgirl, sniggering at a private joke.

"She's getting ready," she says, just loud enough so I can hear. "She thinks we're gonna fail."

The girl with the blood-red hair nimbly leaps to her feet. The grin she wears is more maniacal than ever, her level of lunacy increases by a thousand as she approaches me, pretending that she is anti-grav skiing, complete with whooshing noises.

When she comes to a stop, we are nose to nose once more.

"Thing is," she says, nodding her head toward the altar. "I don't worship that bitch, as you call her. Yes, I make sacrifices to her, but I don't do it in her name."

My poor brain is now totally and utterly sick of all these riddles. Perhaps Raku can see this in my eyes, she is sure close enough.

"I kill people to keep her locked in Tokyo."

# NINETEEN

Red Raku, Nihon's most infamous daughter, calmly sits down on the floor, places her knife in front of her and assumes the lotus position. I half expect her to start chanting a nu-Zen mantra or slip into quiet meditation. Instead, she simply sighs and slowly shakes her head. Her smile now displays a certain amount of genuine humour but remains that of a demented killer.

"You Osaka lot have got me all wrong, you know. The whole of Nihon has got me wrong. You all think I'm crazy!"

She genuinely sounds surprised by this. Thankfully, I am not invited to share my opinion. Raku speaks for me instead.

"Well, yes. I am kind of crazy. My parents first told me that when I crippled my brother on his sixth birthday. Then the teachers said the same when little Mika had that accident with the skipping rope during Phys-Ed class…"

Her sentence trails off. Her eyes glaze over as she becomes lost in her cruel memories.

"Children like to break things," she says to the air. "I liked to break people. I still do."

Her attention falls to the knife before her, the instrument she will use to end my life. She stares quizzically at the cruel steel blade for several moments before speaking again.

"How much do you know about her?" she asks without looking up. "The Blood Daughter, I mean."

"I know she used to be a girl called Ai." I reply. "She murdered a lot of people a long time ago."

"And then the people of her village killed her."

"Yes."

"Do you know what happened next?" she asks.

"Sort of," I tell her. "She placed some kind of curse on the village. They all died."

"And then?"

Raku is now looking at me with eyes full of anticipation.

"I don't know," I say.

The red-haired girl chuckles at this, raising a hand to her mouth to stifle her mirth.

"You don't know the best bit," she says.

If I were having this conversation with Mr. Tanaka, I would be burning with curiosity, begging him to tell me more while pouring him another cup of tea.

But this history lesson is being taken by a naked girl, strapped to a table, and her teacher is a girl made of horror.

All the same, as she begins to talk, I find myself hanging onto her every word.

Damn my curiosity to Hell.

"You know, Nihon police actually caught me after my first real kill. I was a little bit careless when it came to disposing of the body, basically led the police straight to my front door, what an idiot! Anyway, I thought I was up for the death penalty or a brain-hacking or something, so I was really confused when they took me to this room and got given all this really fucked up info about this girl called Ai who killed all these people way back when, and how she went to Hell and turned into this real mega-bitch who was all set for drowning the world in blood. I must admit though, a part of me thought she was quite cool at the time."

She pauses to glance at the altar to her right.

"Hi there," she says, giving a wave to the macabre image on the wall. "How's it going?"

She sits in silence for a moment and stares at the picture she drew.

"Sometimes, she speaks to me," she says, still focused on her art work. "She whispers in my ear and tells me I'm a wicked girl. Don't you?"

The thing on the wall does not answer, thankfully.

Red Raku shrugs and swivels her head back in my direction.

"Anyway, where was I? Oh yes, I remember! So, I was still clueless as to why they were telling me all these ghost stories and not violently rehabilitating me. I asked them why. I did, I said 'why are you telling me all this crap?' and then this one guy hit me a load of times and told me to shut up. I just laughed. Couldn't help myself. I just started laughing and laughing. There's this big guy with all these muscles and fists as big as my head and he hits like a girl! Anyway, that's when this tall man in a black suit tells them to stop hitting me because I was the perfect candidate for the job. I ask what job. He tells me I'm gonna save the world and I start laughing again. Mister Hit-like-a-girl starts punching me again and so the guy in the suit pulls out a gun and shoots him in the head.”

She stops and mimes pulling the trigger of a gun and then someone’s head exploding.

“So cool,” she beams.

“After they clear away all the blood and brains and bits of skull, Mister Suit and three other government guys take me to this room with a big sofa and a table full of drinks. He tells me to sit down and offers me a real cigarette. So, while I’m drinking real cola and smoking, Mister Suit starts talking about the job offer and how I’d be working for something even more secret than the DPA. Then, he tells me all about this ritual people would do to keep Ai from returning. Turns out killing an entire village wasn’t enough for her and that the only way to keep her content was to kill people in her name every twelve months or so. I asked why it had to be a yearly thing and wasn’t that a bit predictable. Mister Suit told me to stop asking dumb questions and to just listen. So I did.”

She stops once more to look at the macabre image on the wall. For a moment, she looks confused, lost even. But then she smiles, shrugs her shoulders and continues her tale.

“So, for hundreds of years, there was this secret society who would sacrifice young citizens to keep the Blood Daughter happy. Apparently, she would communicate with them, tell them the name of the person they must kill. Once the name was given, they’d go get him or her, pluck their eyes out, cut things into their bodies and then, after they were in real pain, they’d stab them to death. Real nasty stuff, right?”

Her question hangs in the air like an oppressive thundercloud. I do not answer her, I refuse to do so. Red Raku slowly gets to her feet and stretches, her arms reaching up for the ceiling. For the briefest of moments, we are mirror images of each other, only she is dressed and I am very much not.

"Thing is," she continues. "This secret society wasn't just made up of your everyday kind of citizen. No, no, no. It was made up of the rich and powerful, leaders of men. Government. For many years, those wealthy bastards were lucky. Not once was the soul that Ai demanded connected to anyone in their little gang. That's until a hundred years ago, when their luck ran out. The Blood Daughter sent out the message saying the next citizen she wanted hacked to pieces was to be Kazuo Shimizu's daughter."

Even though I knew Shimizu's name would eventually crop up in her story, I still feel shocked and angered at the mention of him. Raku notices this and becomes amused at my reaction.

"So, you knew this bit too?"

"Yes. Kind of," I reply. "I knew he was involved somehow and that he knew what was coming."

Raku laughs at this, a sound filled with scorn.

"He didn't just know what was coming, he made it come!"

She walks over to the metal table I am secured to and places both her hands on my naked shoulders.

"That fucker loved his daughter so much, he refused to kill her. He told his little buddies they could all go to Hell and that he'd never allow his dear daughter to be sacrificed. Of course, this made his friends extremely unhappy and they made it clear to him that refusing to allow his daughter to be sliced and diced wasn't an option. So, he went and killed them all. Actually, he had them killed, he wasn't brave enough to do the job himself, you see. After that, he made contact with the Blood Daughter and promised to do anything she asked, just as long as his darling daughter was taken off the menu."

Raku leans right into me. Her smile now takes up the majority of her face.

"The Blood Daughter asked for Tokyo, so Shimizu gave it to her."

So, now Raku has clarified why Kazuo Shimizu damned the whole of Tokyo to Hell.

He did it all for his daughter .

Have to say, as a show of paternal love, his sure takes some beating.

My own father could not even find the time to say goodbye before he disappeared off into the sunset.

Shimizu's daughter must have really been something special.

So many lives were given to save hers.

She must have been the most amazing person to have ever lived.

Raku Nakamura walks back to where she was sitting and crouches down to pick up her knife.

I know her story will come to an end soon.

And when it does...

She picks up the bladed instrument and stands with her back towards me.

"After Tokyo was all sealed off, Shimizu used the fear and horror of the citizens to control them. He set up the DPA and banned any mention of ghosts and creepy shit. As the years went by, he became known as the savior of Nihon. The guy became a legend, where he should have been a monster. What a bastard, right? But he was real clever, too. He knew that Ai would get him when he died."

Raku turns her head and peers at me over her left shoulder.

"Guess what he did."

"He didn't die?" I offer.

"Clever girl," she replies before turning her head away from me. "He got himself plugged into this machine that keeps him alive. The guy's a vegetable, can't move, speak or anything, but he's still alive. The crazy old fool prefers a virtual Hell to an actual one."

I watch as Red Raku ambles towards the altar, kicking at imaginary stones as she goes.

"Thing is, he kind of fucked up. Yes, he saved his daughter, at the cost of millions of innocent lives, but he forgot about the ritual. He presumed that giving all of Tokyo to Ai would keep her happy forever, but he was wrong."

She stops at the altar and pulls a lighter out of her back pocket. One by one, the black candles are lit,

"The whole Tokyo thing was only for the life of his daughter. The yearly ritual thing still stood. Perhaps Shimizu knew this, maybe he didn't. Could be that he just didn't care. The Blood Daughter was trapped in Tokyo, after all. What harm could she do? Anyway, whatever he thought or didn't, a hundred years passed without a single offering being made."

She returns the lighter to her pocket and then quickly claps her hands together twice.

The lights go out.

Once again, Raku starts circling me. As she goes, the candle's flames dance and flicker, sending twisted shadows scurrying up the walls.

I close my eyes and make a resolution to never open them again, no matter what.

"Then the messages started coming. People in high-up places had this dream about you-know-who and how she was totally pissed and wanted what she was owed. Then the government guys started saying weird stuff in the middle of a normal conversation. Like they were talking about which sushi place to go to and then one of them suddenly started on about how she's coming and she wants her blood and that. So the DPA looked into this and made contact with her. And yes, she wasn't happy at all. She told them that the walls of Tokyo wouldn't hold her forever and that a hundred years of missed sacrifices must be given to her, or else. The DPA called her bluff and pointed out she's trapped in sector thirteen and they don't owe her anything. She says that isn't true and she'll soon be able to break out and will kill anyone she comes across. Unless she gets what she's owed, then she may show mercy."

By the sound of her voice, I can tell she has stopped somewhere in front of me.

The storm is coming, I can feel it.

Lightning is going to strike.

I know it is going to hurt.

"So, that's where I come in. Mister Suit informs me they need someone to go out and kill a hundred people. They need someone to sacrifice one-hundred citizens to the Blood Daughter, before she escapes and goes mental. Nihon needs a serial killer to save the world! I say sure, but what's in it for me? I mean, after the hundred sacrifices are all done, what happens then? Mister Suit shares his plan with me. To the masses, I will be this screwed-up murderer. I'll be someone to fear, someone that keeps citizens indoors and careful about walking home alone late at night. I laughed at this, I really did. As if ghosts and all that wasn't enough to scare people to death, they need me, too? Anyway, in return for completing a century of missed ritualistic slayings and being made public enemy number one, I'd secretly have complete government protection and immunity from arrest. They'd give me a chameleon suit so I could stalk my victims without them knowing and a cool pad where I could kill them at my leisure. After each sacrifice, I had to tell Mister Suit where I'd dumped the body and he'd then decide whether to make it public knowledge or not. He said he wanted to avoid the whole hundred victims thing, just in case a clever citizen put two and two together. No skin off of my nose. Even in the edited records, I'm still someone Nihon will remember forever. So..."

I hear her step slowly towards me.

My eyes are so tightly shut, it hurts.

"This is where you come in. Number one-hundred."

I flinch when her fingers softly caress my left cheek.

"You know, Mister Suit isn't so happy with me today. He said I am cutting things too fine. I said it was kind of cool for my last kill to be just before the deadline."

Her fingers move from my face and trace an invisible line down my neck and towards my left breast.

Dear Buddha, please let this be quick.

"After I kill you, Red Raku will die. The news will report that police cornered her here and shot her to pieces. The whole of Nihon will breathe a silent sigh of relief. In reality, Raku Nakamura will go to a private hospital and have face-change surgery."

She gently squeezes my left breast.

"I may even get a pair like these, too."

She slowly removes her hand.

My breath comes in shudders of blind fear and revulsion.

"In my opinion, the whole of Nihon should thank me," she says. "After all, if not for me, tonight would be the city's last. But I reckon they should also thank you. I really mean it. The whole of Nihon should go outside tonight and shout their thanks to the sky! They need to thank you for dying, because your death is the one that's going to save the world!"

Her next words are whispered into my left ear.

"Kichi Honda, thank you for being awesome, but I'm afraid I'm going to have to kill you now."

She then kisses me lightly on the forehead and with-draws, giggling. I do not know whether I should cry or vomit.

Is she right?
Will my death save Nihon?
Should I accept my fate as saviour of millions?

From the direction of the altar, Raku starts muttering in a language I cannot understand. I guess it to be the same dialect Miaka spoke in with Mr. Tanaka.
Then, very clearly, she says words I do understand.
"Daughter of blood, do you accept this sacrifice?"
The temperature in the room suddenly plummets.
It is so cold now.
Every breath I take is a lungful of ice.
And then comes a voice, a surreal mix of something both ancient and childlike that answers Red Raku with a single word; a word that echoes around the room and the insides of my skull, growing louder and louder until it becomes a deafening scream.
"NO."
The straps that hold me to the metal table suddenly slacken and undo themselves. I fall to the cold concrete floor with a heavy thud. From the altar, I hear Red Raku shouting in that strange dialect. Although I am not able to understand her, the desperation in her voice is obvi-ous. I try to move, to crawl away from the sound of her growing hysteria, but my limbs are numb and refuse to

follow orders. I lie on the freezing floor, wracked by spasms of cold and terror.

The voice comes again, but now I can hear two clear and different vocalisations, merged together in madness.

They mutter words that slither into my ears and slice at my brain with razors.

"We still have much to do...

...the game has just begun...

...She must stand and watch everything end...

...blood and tears and death and suffering...

...This girl must bear witness to my rising, as I mock her failure...

...I will see her in Hell."

The next thing I hear is someone screaming.

At first, the sound is one filled with pure horror, but it quickly changes to something born out of agony.

And then...

Silence.

# TWENTY

Time passes.

How much time exactly is hard to say. It could be a handful of minutes, it could be longer. I really do not know.

The only thing I am sure of is that the temperature of the room I am lying naked in has raised enough to stop my teeth from chattering and my body convulsing.

The room I am in has become filled with a silence louder than any bomb. The nothingness weighs heavily around me.

And then I notice the smell.

Burnt meat and corroded metal.

I break my resolution and open my eyes a fraction.

The entire room has been painted the deepest shade of black known to man.

No matter how long I blink or stare, my eyes cannot get accustomed to this darkness.

I raise a hand up in front of me. I know it is there, but it is like I am blind. I do take some small comfort in knowing I am back in control of my limbs, though. I raise my other hand into the air and slowly bring my palms together. After scrunching up my eyes, I clap my hands together twice in quick succession.

Following this mini round of applause, I hear the re-assuring hum of electricity from somewhere above me.

Let there be light.

Gingerly, I open my eyes again, just a fraction at first so as to save my retinas from any pain.

Also, because I am absolutely terrified of what I may see.

The strip-lights above me flicker on and off in a slow hypnotic pulse which instantly brings on a dull throb at the base of my skull. I peel myself off the floor and force myself into an upright position. This is no easy task. My legs and knees threaten to give way from under me at any minute. Still, after several minutes of standing, I feel a certain amount of strength returning to them.

In front of me is the door Red Raku entered through. The sensible part of my brain starts telling me to walk to that door, open it, and get out of this room as quickly as possible without looking back.

The curious part of me is stronger, though, and pulls my head sharply to the left, demanding that I take one last look at the altar of the Blood Daughter.

My breath catches in my throat.

The image on the wall has grown. Changed.

As the lights continue to strobe in slow-motion, I take note of the picture's transformation.

The Blood Daughter no longer leers out from the wall. Instead, she now looks down at the explosion of red she is cradling in her twisted and spindly arms.

In that mess of crimson is a face.

Not a drawing of a face, but a real one.

And an arm.

Raku Nakamura reaches out from the hideous mural she created with one blood-stained arm, her fingers clutching at air, seeking help that will never come. Her eyes have lost all their emotion, she stares out blindly from between the Blood Daughter's arms with orbs of the purest white, her mouth open wide in a frozen scream.

I turn away from the wall and shuffle towards the door on my zombie limbs.

I have to get out of here.

Pulling open the door, I manage to stumble into the room before my knees buckle and I fall painfully to the floor. I let loose a string of expletives at my clumsiness, anger being preferable to self-pity.

Tears are not going to help me, not one bit.

Once I am back on my feet, I take a look at the room I am now in.

At first, it is a little hard to believe what I am actually seeing. Then again, knowing Red Raku, this is perfectly logical.

The door in the torture chamber leads to a small bedroom, the walls of which are painted the most vomit-inducing shade of pink ever. A double-bed occupies most of this compact sleeping chamber. On top of a bright pink duvet sit countless fluffy toys of all shapes and sizes. My eyes widen as I notice an antique Hello Kitty plush doll. That item alone must be worth millions.

I guess her job paid well.

To the right of this creepy display of cuteness is another door from which hangs a full-length mirror. To the left stands a tall white wardrobe, its doors ajar, forced open by the sheer number of clothes that have been stuffed inside. I notice the arm of a familiar black combat parka, poking out from between the open doors. I walk over and tug at the coat's sleeve, pulling it free. This action is enough to throw the wardrobe's doors open, making the mountain of clothes tumble out onto the floor.

I hug my parka to my naked chest.

Hello, old friend.

After searching through the clothes, I manage to find everything I was wearing before Red Raku stripped me for her grisly execution. All except for my t-shirt, that is.

No matter. Its function is well and truly redundant.

I find a long-sleeved black top that has a line of yellow smiley-faces across its chest. I know full well this shirt belonged to either Raku or one of her many victims, but I pull it on regardless. Now is not the time to worry about the garment's previous owner.

After sliding into my parka and zipping it up to my chin, I walk to the door on the left, surveying myself in the mirror.

I look awful.

My face has become one massive purple-blue bruise. Both my eyes are blood-shot and ringed with black. My nose looks as if it may be broken.

I smile at my battered reflection. At least I can face the end of the world with perfect teeth.

Once I am out of the bedroom, I find myself in a narrow corridor that is lined with doors on both sides. Thankfully, the corridor's colour scheme is a little more tolerable than the bedroom, changing from vile pink to a soothing shade of pale blue. I pull open one of the doors to my right and find a small bathroom. I go inside and use the toilet, wash my hands, and splash a little cold water on my face.

Next to the bathroom mirror is a small cabinet, which I slide open. Inside are numerous bottles of tablets of different descriptions, a box of toothpicks, red hair dye, a vibro-toothbrush, tooth gel and a can of heal-mist. Shaking the can reveals it is about half full. I stuff it into my parka's left pocket. I then check the rest of my pockets and find only my nico-gum and Ms. Pang's name card.

Knowing that none of these three objects will help me defeat the powers of evil, I leave the bathroom and start opening other doors.

Three doors later, I find Red Raku's armoury.

Most citizens in Nihon would kill for a DPA issue pulse weapon, the Exorcist 6613, especially.

Should anyone ever come face to face with anything non-corporeal and from beyond the grave, the 6613 will send them back to whatever dark place they crawled out from. Not only that, but they are also extremely effective when it comes to living targets.

Red Raku's armoury has three of them.

I cannot help but be impressed by how many weapons of death and destruction the girl managed to cram into one tiny room. For a serial killer who used knives, she sure owned quite a few guns. In all seriousness, she could have taken on an army and won with what she had stowed away. Still, it is the 6613's that grab my eye.

Then I notice the E-4's, all the power of the 6613, but packed into a hand-held pistol.

I tuck one into the belt of my combats and another into my parka. There are several DPA issue backpacks also on display. I take one and fill it with power packs.

Just as I am about to leave, I decided to also take a pulse rifle, just for good measure. Considering its size, it is surprisingly light. This is a good thing, as I still feel as weak as a new-born clone-kitten.

Fully kitted-out, I head back out into the corridor, in search of a way out.

Red Raku's lair consists of one corridor of doors after another. As soon as I reach the end of one, I turn either left or right into another. I open each door, hoping to find a lift or a stairwell, sadly finding anything but. One door leads to a sterile kitchen, another to an empty walk-in wardrobe. On three occasions, I find tiny rooms filled from floor to ceiling with creepy-looking dolls with long-hair and dressed in red kimonos.

Just as I am about to give up hope of ever leaving Raku's house of horrors, I turn right onto a much shorter corridor, at the end of which is a large metal door.

At long last, a lift.

With a smile on my face, I run the short distance towards, what I sincerely hope, will be freedom.

The lift door has a small panel to its left, with one sole green button to press. I do so, three times and with urgency. The door silently slides upwards, allowing me entrance. I walk into a small metallic space, just big enough for about two or three people. I lean against the back wall and watch the door close. A glowing green arrow icon above the door begins to flash on and off as the small cubicle starts its ascent. It moves smoothly and without sound, vastly different to the public lifts of my apartment block. It is a little hard to believe it is moving at all.

As I am being carried upwards, I think about what to do next.

Yes, I have some big guns now, but I lack a plan.

How long do I have left to save Osaka from the Blood Daughter?

Hours? Minutes? Also, just how do I save Osaka? And when did it become my responsibility?

I shake all these questions from my head. I know full well what must be done next.

I have to find Mr. Tanaka and Miaka.

My friends.

A few short moments later and the lift's doors open. My senses are assaulted by a sudden dual attack from the brightness of the sun and the freezing cold temperature of winter.

I walk out onto a small platform, a tenth of the size of P7. After walking to its edge, I stop and wipe tears from my sun-dazzled eyes. My breath comes steaming from my mouth, forming miniature clouds that drift off into the perfect blue sky above.

Never in all of my life did I think I would see this view.

Far below me is Osaka Sector, a sea of metal and neon that stretches on into the horizon.

I do not need to turn around to know what is behind me.

I know exactly where I am.

I'm right on top of the buildings in which Nihon's government resides.

As I stare out at the glittering metropolis below, my mind returns to what it is I should be doing. Now I have the extra dilemma of how to get down to where all the action is going to take place.

That's when I see it.

A hovercar, rising out of the twisted jungle of tall buildings and walkways.

I watch as it glides upwards and then starts to fly in my direction.

Retreating is not an option. For a start, where is there to go? Should I head back to Raku's luxury pad?

No way.

I move back to the centre of the platform, my finger finding the trigger button of my 6613.

Should this car start firing weapons at me, or its occupants prove to be anything less than friendly, I will not hesitate to open fire and blow them off the face of the earth.

The hovercar draws nearer. A sleek purple vehicle, now travelling at a steady speed.

I aim my rifle at its flight path. Not too obviously, but enough for me to be ready to fire, should I need to.

The car gently glides to the edge of the platform and comes to a stop. The energy barrier around the platform shimmers for an instant, allowing the vehicle to dock successfully.

This is no taxi drop-off point, so whoever is in the cab must have high-level clearance,

A door slides open.

My grip on the gun tightens.

From out of the purple vehicle climbs a woman, dressed from head to toe in the same colour as her mode of transportation.

She too is holding a gun. Not as big as the one I am clutching in my icy fingers, but more than capable of doing some serious damage.

With elegant steps, she walks towards me and smiles.

"Good afternoon, Kichi," says Ms. Pang, in her usual cheery way. "I really think we should have lunch and share some gossip, don't you think?"

# TWENTY-ONE

High above Osaka Sector, on a small platform at the top of the government buildings, two women stand with guns aimed directly at the other.

One of them is a vision in purple, with a smug expression and a mischievous look in her perfectly made-up eyes. The other, a decade or so younger and holding a far bigger gun, wants to smack that self-satisfied look clean off the purple woman's face, preferably with the butt of her rifle.

"So?" asks Ms. Pang. "Aren't you going to ask me anything?"

I can tell she is on the verge of laughter. I bite down on my lower lip in an attempt to stem my anger.

"Really?" she asks. "Not one question? You're not even wondering how I found you up here?"

She has a very good point there. How did she know where to find me?

My curiosity piqued, I decide to play along, for the time being.

"Go on then," I say. "Tell me how you knew I was up here."

Ms. Pang's eyes flash with glee.

"Remember the card I gave you? It was coated with a thin layer of nano-trackers. The very instant you touched it, millions of tiny little nano-bugs activated and stuck to your skin like perma-glue. I've been able to monitor your movements around Osaka ever since. Not only that, I've been able to hear you. Every single word."

If I wasn't currently holding a large pulse rifle, I would be rubbing my contaminated hand on the leg of my combat trousers for sure. Instead, I tighten my grip on the rifle and raise my aim a little.

Ms. Pang follows suit and levels her gun at my head.

"Now, now," she says. "Let's not get all upset and do something we'll regret. We have many things to do, you and I."

"Like what?" I ask.

She jerks her head back towards the purple hover-car she arrived in.

"How about we go and discuss things elsewhere? Although the shielding around this platform keeps out the wind, I think it's a little on the cold side out here, don't you?"

Again, she has a point. However, I would rather stick my head in the mouth of a hungry gator-lizard than get into a car with her.

I tell her as much.

"Oh, Kichi," she laughs. "That's what I like most about you. You always speak your mind."

She slowly lowers her gun to her side and backs away a step.

"I know what you're thinking," she tells me. "I really do, and I understand. You think something bad will happen should you choose to get in my car. Perhaps someone is waiting inside, ready to subdue you and take away your gun. I'd be thinking the same thing too, if I was in your position. But I promise that won't happen. You'll be quite safe with me."

"I'm not thinking that," I lie.

Ms. Pang smiles a purple grin.

"Oh, but you are! There's no use denying it. I know exactly what you're thinking, I've always known. I'm a telepath, you see, and you can never lie to one of us."

Shortly after our first ghost story, Mr. Tanaka warned me about DPA telepaths.

'Always make sure you keep a clear mind, Kichi,' he had said. 'Don't go letting that little head of yours get all filled up with forbidden information, especially when you're outside. Keeping your mouth tightly shut is important for your safety, but keeping your mind quiet is even more so. You never know who may be eavesdropping on your inner-most thoughts! DPA telepaths would hear what you're thinking as clearly as if you were shouting it out at the top of your lungs!'

I guess I didn't keep my head as empty as Mr. Tanaka instructed.

"No, you didn't," confirms Ms. Pang, wagging a slim finger at me. "That first time I met you, all I could hear was yurei this and onryo that. You were quite the hive of illegal knowledge. I must give you credit though, after that, you did become a lot quieter. But it was too late by then. You had me intrigued."

"So why didn't you arrest me there and then?" I ask. "Why drag this out for so long?"

She throws back her head and laughs into the sky. My trigger finger twitches. She is so close to being smeared across the energy barrier that surrounds us.

"Dear Kichi," she says, wiping a tear from her eye. "Where would have been the fun in that?"

Her last sentence is too much for me. I truly have had enough for one day, if not a lifetime.

"What do you mean?" I scream. "Tell me who the fuck you are, right now. Or…"

"Or what?" snaps Ms. Pang, her mocking expression replaced with one of cold-hearted conviction . "You'll shoot me?"

She raises both of her arms wide, standing before me like she has been crucified.

"Go ahead then. Do it!"

I raise my E6613, trying to calm my trembling hands.

"Come on then!" she goads. "Shoot me! What's stopping you?"

I suck in a lungful of air through clenched teeth. Tears of anger are welling at the corners of my blackened eyes.

"But I promise you one thing," says the telepath in a calm, steady voice. "Kill me, and you'll never see the old man and the girl again."

Ms. Pang is true to her word. I climb into her hovercar and take a seat without being set upon by masked men with bludgeoning tools or tranq-darts. Neither am I gassed or electrocuted. The inside of her car is more spacious than I expected. Not surprisingly, the colour of the interior of her vehicle is the same as an aubergine.

Ms. Pang takes a seat opposite me, crosses her purple-stockinged legs and places her sidearm on the seat next to her. After giving me a sweet smile, she orders the auto-pilot to take off.

The hovercar's door slides shut and I feel the craft smoothly undock from the platform and fly off towards the city below us.

Yes, she has kept her word. All the same, I refuse to let go of my gun. The only reason why I am sitting across from her now is that she has promised to take me to my friends, to show me that they are both alive and unharmed.

Buddha help her if this promise is broken.

Five or so minutes of silence pass.

Ms. Pang smiles at me. I glare back.

"You look awful," she says, sounding almost as if she cares.

"Thanks," I reply, not meaning it at all.

The woman I used to think of as a kind of friend shrugs and turns to look out of the car's window.

"You know what may happen soon," she says. It is not a question.

"Yes'" I tell her. "The Blood Daughter's going to kill everyone in the city."

Ms. Pang looks back to me, her left eyebrow raised into an arch.

"You sound so certain. May I ask why?"

"You've been listening all this time," I say, holding up my bugged palm. "And you can read minds. You should know."

She sniggers at this.

"Quite right. I should and do know. Stupid of me to ask. Call it a failure of my pretending to be a normal citizen."

She lowers her eyes to her lap and inspects her slender manicured fingers.

"You have had quite a time, Kichi," she says. "You make friends with one of the DPA's top historians, get a visit from an urban legend, meet a girl who shouldn't exist, and then end up being caught by Red Raku!"

"You missed the part where we got busted by guys in black armour," I tell her. "And how the bitch from Hell screwed Raku."

Ms. Pang nods her head at this.

"Yes, what happened to her is puzzling. It seems you-know-who has numerous cards up her sleeves and is trying as many ways possible to get circumstances to swing in her favour. Considering the fact she's a being who demands her rules and rituals are followed to the letter, she had no qualms about stepping in and making sure Raku failed. Interesting, isn't it?"

"Interesting isn't how I'd describe it." I say.

I turn away from her and stare out of the hovercar's window. The city blurs past us, all metal and glass that sparkles and shines. But the longer I look, the shine begins to dull. Gleaming silver turns to a lifeless grey, revealing Osaka for what it truly is.

Cold and dead.

Our journey continues, down to the lower levels of the sector.

"How much longer?" I ask Ms. Pang. "Are we there yet?"

"We'll be there soon," comes her clipped reply.

"Have I got time for a couple of questions?" I ask.

"Sure," she smiles. "Feel free to ask. But you don't really need to." She stops to tap a finger lightly against her temple. "I already know what you want to say, remember?"

"So tell me," I say. "Show me how good you are. Impress me."

Ms. Pang raises a hand to her purple lips and clears her throat.

"OK," she says, elongating the 'k'. "Ms. Pang *is* my real name. That much is true. I work for a subdivision of the DPA, known as Radical 194. In a way, we are a little similar to the people that employed Red Raku, the difference being we focus on practical ways of preventing a second ghost quake, instead of just relying on ancient rituals."

She pauses for a moment to flick an imaginary speck of dust from her purple skirt.

"Yes," she continues, "I was fully aware of what was happening to you and that Red Raku was going to sacrifice you, too. And yes, I could have come for you earlier, but..."

She trails off and looks away from me.

"But what?" I ask. "You couldn't be bothered?"

Her head snaps back in my direction, her eyes wide and full of fire.

"The Blood Daughter is making every effort to escape from her prison. You know what will happen if she succeeds, you've seen it. The girl, Miaka, showed you the photographs, you even watched recordings."

I nod. An image of the girl walking across the ceiling pops back into my head, causing me to shudder. Ms. Pang grins.

"The image that's now in your head is of just one of the ghosts that will flood into Osaka Sector, should Ai escape from Tokyo. That one creature alone is capable of causing so much carnage."

Ms. Pang's hands are clenched tightly into fists. I can almost see her beating them against her thighs in anger. But she does not.

"So, you were hoping Raku would kill me?"

The woman across from me makes direct eye-contact and nods an affirmative to my question.

"Yes," she replies, her honesty evident. "If your death saved Osaka, saved Nihon..."

"But I didn't die," I interrupt. "Ai saved me."

Ms. Pang tilts her head to one side.

"Did she?"

"Yeah. She dragged Raku through a wall. Stopped her from slicing me up like sashimi."

My reply is met with a soft and mocking laugh.

"The way I see it, you weren't saved. You were spared," offers Ms. Pang.

"Same difference," I quip.

"Like I said," she continues. "The Blood Daughter is looking for a way to get past the walls that confine her. And you," she says, pointing a long finger in my direction, "are somehow connected to this. The question is, how?"

"You're the psychic," I tell her. "You tell me."

The hovercar banks slightly to the left. I glance out of the window to see we are about to collide into the side of a tower block. I flinch back from the window, a reaction Ms. Pang, who remains sitting calmly, finds most amusing. When I look again, I see the exterior of the building shimmer and blur. Its façade fades away, revealing a hanger door which is slowly opening like the mouth of some giant, hungry mecha.

"We're here," Ms. Pang informs me.

"I kind of guessed that," I say. "Mind telling me where here is?"

I get flashed another one of her smug smiles.

"All will be revealed soon," is all the information I am given.

We fly into the building and come to a soft landing. Both of the vehicle's doors slide open. Ms. Pang picks up her gun and then nimbly climbs out of her car. I follow suit, although a little more clumsily. I do have a rather large hand-cannon to carry, after all.

Once out of the vehicle, I do a quick scan of the area around us.

We are standing in a large parking area, empty aside from the Pang-mobile. The walls, floor and ceiling are dull-grey concrete. Much like Red Raku's pleasure-palace, the place is lit by hanging strip-lights. The entrance we have just arrived through is now almost closed. I watch as the metal door finally meets the floor with an echoing thud.

"This way," says Ms. Pang, gesturing towards a door to the east.

She then walks off, her high heels clicking as she goes. I follow her, my pulse rifle at the ready.

Arriving at the door, Ms. Pang places her left palm flat against the featureless metal and pushes. An outline of green briefly shimmers around her hand and then disappears. A second later, the door slides up, allowing us inside. Ms. Pang walks forward. Once more, I follow in her shadow.

We walk down a short corridor and into an open lift. Once inside, its door closes and I feel the lift smoothly start to descend.

"Won't be long," says Ms. Pang.

"Fine," I reply.

The compartment we are in is made of metal and utterly featureless. There is not even a health and safety notice to read. I sigh.

"Yes," says my companion. "As lifts go, this one is frightfully dull. I did ask for some muzak to be played, but I got told that was a stupid request."

"I hate muzak," I say. "It's totally soulless."

"I agree with you there, Kichi. Music must have feeling. Without emotion of some sort, all that you're left with is hollow, empty noise. Tell me, what kind of music do you like?"

I look up at Ms. Pang, one eye-brow raised.

"Seriously? We're having this conversation?"

She shrugs and casts her eyes up to the lift's ceiling.

"I guess not," she mumbles.

I smile to myself, happy to have finally knocked the smugness out of her.

The lift finally reaches its designated floor and its door opens. Standing directly before us are four men in black armour, just like the ones who stormed Mr. Tanaka's apartment. The barrels of four 6613's are pointed straight at me.

"Lower your weapons," growls Ms. Pang. "Go back to your positions. That's an order."

The black-clad figures do as ordered, retreating out of sight.

"This way," she says, as she strides out into the room before us. I stomp off after her.

The room we are now in is filled with desks, behind which people in white coats sit and puzzle over information on holo-screens or tap away at keyboards and touch-pads. Occasionally, one of them will look up from their work and give a polite nod to Ms. Pang as we pass. For the most part, she ignores them. I notice many of the holo-screens show an x-ray image of a human body, with flashing green numbers and pop-up screens of techno-babble hovering over certain vital areas.

We reach the end of the room and go through a door that hisses open as we approach. Beyond is a short sterile-white corridor, ending at a bulky airlock. Ms. Pang slows her pace as we walk towards it.

"Most of the citizens in Nihon think of ghosts, from time to time. It's no surprise, considering the history, and most of the thoughts are harmless, nothing worth the DPA issuing an arrest warrant."

She stops walking and spins round to face me. I almost walk into her.

"But the things in your head, well..."

"Well, what?" I ask.

"You were damn lucky the DPA didn't kick down your door and drag you screaming into the night."

"But they didn't," I reply. "You did."

"Yes," she says, her expression changing to something resembling regret. "And I must apologise for the way that was handled. Not what I intended at all, but time was of the essence..."

"What do you mean?"

"Best I show you."

And with that, she turns away and walks down to the end of the corridor. She places her hand on a palm scanner to the right of the door. As I come to a stop behind her, I hear the door's mechanisms grinding into action,

all the locks and bolts releasing. A red light above us begins to flash on and off. Ms. Pang sees this and removes
her hand from the scanner. I hear her sigh. She sounds
tired.

"How do you think Miaka escaped from sector thirteen?"

I shrug, even though she is not looking at me.

"I don't know," I reply. "She never said."

Ms. Pang presses a green button above the palm
scanner. A thin green light horizontally bisects the door.
With a dramatic hiss of released pressure, the two sides
slide apart, revealing a small room bathed in red light.

The woman in front of me does not move.

"Agents from R194 checked the walls," she says.
"There was no sign of any breach."

I ask what she means, but she answers with another
question.

"What do you know about Shimizu's daughter?"

"Not a lot," I say. "Just he was meant to kill her."

"Yes. He failed."

Ms. Pang shakes her head and sighs once more.

"Follow me," she says, and enters the red room.

We walk through a room and into yet another corridor. The walls, floor and ceiling are made of metal; all
the lights are crimson in colour. It's like we're in some
crazy old sci-fi movie, the kind where people get minia-
turised and injected into the bloodstream of someone, in
the hope of performing some sort of weird medical procedure.

We turn left, then right, then left again. We enter a
corridor flanked by rows of featureless doors. Ms. Pang
stops at one to her right and motions for me to join her.
I do so, standing to her left.

She reaches out to touch the blank door's surface. The
second her fingertips make contact, a rectangular viewing window appears.

"Take a look," she says, stepping aside for me. "Tell
me what you see."

I move into position, stand on tip-toes and squint through into the room behind the door.

The room I am looking into is small. Taking up most of the area is a coffin-shaped construction made of green glass. A multitude of different coloured wires and leads trail into and from the transparent sarcophagus, disappearing off into walls of blinking lights. Lying inside, submerged in some unknown liquid, is Miaka.

"Miaka!"

They have cut off her hair.

I am milliseconds away from pushing my pulse rifle into Ms. Pang's face when she calmly tells me to look again.

For some reason, her soothing tones persuade me to do as she says.

"That's not Miaka," she says.

Ms. Pang is right. The girl lying in the green glass box is a little taller, a little older than the escapee from Sector Thirteen.

But her face...

They could almost be the same person.

"Interesting thought," says Ms. Pang. "But not *could* be."

She walks off down the corridor and opens a viewing window on another door.

"Now take a peek through here."

I sprint the short distance down to where Ms. Pang is waiting. My head is a bubbling soup of confusion and anticipation.

Peering through the second window, my heart leaps when I see Mr. Tanaka alive and kicking.

It almost stops when I see Miaka.

The girl from Tokyo lies motionless in a green glass tube. Unlike her older, balder double, Miaka is not being pickled. Instead, she is secured by thick leather straps and metal clamps. On both her forehead and naked chest are what looks to be ancient acupuncture needles. Connected to the ends of these needles are thick wires that undulate as if they're alive. They trail from Miaka, out of the tube and into the walls, much like in the first room. Mr. Tanaka stands with a touch-pad device, observing the flashing lights around him and occasionally stopping to take notes of whatever information the lights are conveying.

"*This* is Miaka," says Ms. Pang. "The first girl you saw was Akane Shimizu. Poor girl's been dead for a very long time now…"

"So Miaka's related to that girl?" I ask.

Ms. Pang chuckles.

"Not related," she says. "They're the same person."

Inside her tube, Miaka opens her eyes and looks straight at me.

Ms. Pang puts her arm around me and gives my shoulder a friendly squeeze.

"Reincarnation is such an interesting concept, don't you think?"

# TWENTY-TWO

I am sitting in a small white room at a small white table, cradling a cup of green tea. The sterility of the room makes me uncomfortable. Memories of childhood trips to the dental office come to mind. I shudder as I recall root-canal surgery and having wisdom teeth removed.

On Ms. Pang's instructions, my small arsenal of weapons have had their settings messed with and locked by one of her tech-guys. Now they are only effective against targets of a ghostly nature. Ms. Pang smiled as both of my E-4's were rendered useless against the living and dumped in my backpack. Still, if push came to shove, I reckon a smack to the face with the butt of my pulse rifle would bring almost anyone to their knees.

I take a sip of my cooling beverage. As I do, the door to the room slides open and a familiar figure enters.

"I bet that tea isn't as good as mine ," says Mr. Tanaka.

I slam my cup down and am out of my seat in a heartbeat. The old man chuckles as I fling my arms around him, hugging him for all I am worth.

"Careful now," he says. "Don't go breaking my ribs!"

Remembering him being beaten by Ms. Pang's armed thugs, I immediately let go and take a step back.

"Are you OK?" I ask.

The old man gives a warm smile and points at the black and blue mess that I call my face.

"I was about to ask you the same thing!"

This makes me laugh. I ignore the pain that goes with it.

Mr. Tanaka takes a seat at the white table and asks me to join him. I sit on the opposite side of him and take a long hard look at my old friend. He looks exhausted, his eyes are bloodshot and ringed with black. His smile is genuine, though, and calms me immediately .

"It's good to see you," he says.

"Likewise."

A silence falls between us and the old man looks down to his hands. I can tell he wants to say something and I have a feeling I know what it is.

"Just say it," I tell him. "It's OK."

Mr. Tanaka looks up at me, his eyes wet with tears.

"When you were with Red Raku... I, I mean we..."

I reach across the table and take both of his rough hands in mine.

"The nano-bugs on your hands. We could hear everything."

A single tear falls from his right eye and runs down his lined face.

"I asked her," he says, his voice thick with emotion. "I begged her to go and rescue you. To stop Raku from..."

I let go of Mr. Tanaka's hands and stand up.

"I'm so sorry," he weeps.

I walk around to my old friend and wrap my arms around him.

He continues to apologise as he sobs into my parka.

"It's OK," I tell him. "It's OK."

A little while later, and after two fresh cups of tea have been delivered by two of Ms. Pang's henchmen, Mr. Tanaka gets me up to speed with the current situation.

"There've been some developments," he says. "Situations have changed. Not all of it is good news, I'm afraid."

I tell him I am not surprised to hear that. The old man smiles at this.

"Nice to see, that despite all you've been through, you're still the same old Kichi."

He leans back in his chair and sighs heavily.

"Before I start, I feel I must apologise to you again. I should never have told you all those ghost stories. Filling your head with illegal information was highly irresponsible of me. I should have known better and thought of your safety. It's because of me and my foolishness that you are here now."

I am about to reply when he cuts in with a scowl and a wagging finger.

"And don't go mentioning that day on the platform, young lady. You know full well what I mean."

I stick out my bottom lip and shrug. My friend continues.

"Thanks to me, Ms. Pang and her team at R194 took an interest in you. Thanks to her little trick with the business card, they were able to listen in on our conversations. They even hacked into my scanner so they could watch us!"

Mr. Tanaka's face turns an angry shade of red at this. Then again, it could be embarrassment.

"It was when they saw Miaka that they decided to crash our little history lesson."

"Did you know about Shimizu's daughter?" I ask.

"No," he replies, shaking his head. "Well, I knew she had died, but I had no idea what she looked like, or that her body was being kept in suspension by R194. Remember, my role in the DPA was merely that of a historian. My knowledge of what goes on within its ranks is limited, to say the least, and when it comes to matters concerning Shimizu, I can only quote from rumour. Radical 194, for example. I'd only heard about them in whispers before they blew my front door off its hinges!"

He stops to take a sip of his tea, wincing as he swallows. I can't help but smile at his comical expression of disgust. He swipes his free hand across the table's surface. A holo-screen pops up between us.

The screen shows Miaka, lying in her glass prison.

"When you met Miaka, R194 sent agents to check the wall around Sector Thirteen. They reported back, saying they could find no visible signs of a breach."

"Yeah, I heard."

"That's why they didn't come for her sooner," he says, stopping to sip again at his substandard tea. "They had her pinned as a lunatic or a liar, possibly both. Still, they continued eavesdropping until the pair of you arrived at my house, just to make sure. They accessed my scanner so they could take a look at this crazy girl who claimed she'd escaped from Tokyo."

"And they saw she was a dead ringer for Shimizu's daughter."

"Correct," says Mr. Tanaka. "That's when they became really interested."

On the screen, Miaka remains motionless.

"They put her in there for testing," says my friend, nodding to the screen. "It turns out she has exactly the same DNA as Akane Shimizu."

"Yeah, Ms. Pang told me." I say.

"Did she now?" His tone is dripping with sarcasm and spite. "And did she go on to enlighten you further?"

"Nope, I just got dumped in here and given a cup of tea."

The old man smiles mischievously.

"Then allow me to do so..."

"The girl we know as Miaka is, to all extents and purposes, Akane Shimizu. The idea of her being a clone has been completely ruled out, as the only people with access to her DNA are R194, and there's no way on earth the cloning process could be carried out within the walls of Sector Thirteen. The only logical explanation is that of reincarnation."

"How's that logical?" I ask.

I am politely told to keep quiet and just listen.

"Akane Shimizu was meant to die a hundred years ago. Instead, her father sacrificed the whole of Tokyo to keep her alive. According to Ms. Pang, Akane died shortly after the ghost quake. Poor girl found out what had happened and took her own life. The guilt was too much for her to bear."

"So, do you think it's possible Miaka's here to honour a century-old debt?" I ask. "She told us she was looking for the man who failed. That could be Shimizu! And Red Raku told me he's still alive. Well, kind of. Is Miaka here so Shimizu can kill her, like he was meant to do all those years ago? Is that why she's here? Dear Buddha! Is she really...?"

I trail off as Mr. Tanaka's brow furrows into a scowl. I give a mumbled apology for failing on the whole keeping quiet and listening thing.

The old man relaxes his expression and smiles.

"Not to worry, young Kichi. "What you say is quite possible. Even though we're dealing with just theory at the moment, it's one that certainly holds water. The results of all the tests they've done show that Miaka and Akane Shimizu are the same person. However impossible that may sound, it is one-hundred percent true."

"Including memories?" I ask.

"Very good question," Mr. Tanaka replies. "The answer to that is no. Miaka has no recollection of having lived before. However, she is fully aware of her physical resemblance to Akane. When it comes to reincarnation, it's my understanding that there are two basic forms. The first is the spirit of a person inhabiting a new body. The second is that of a doppelganger. Miaka appears to be the latter."

He waves his hand across the holo-screen, bringing up a menu of dates, times and icons.

"I really wish I could elaborate further," he says. "But the honest truth is that it would just be supposition. There are many questions that lack answers, but we have no time in which to ask them."

My old friend's expression becomes serious, grave.

"There is, however, something I do know to be true."

He selects a date on the screen and sits back in his chair.

"I just wish it wasn't so."

The live-feed of Miaka changes to a recording of her standing in a room that looks an awful lot like an operating theatre. She is dressed in a plain white gown, her unkempt hair looks more tangled than ever.

I watch as she slowly walks around the room bare-footed. She examines its contents; the bed, the monitoring machines, the tables of surgical equipment. She then ambles back to the centre of the room and looks up to the camera. When she smiles, I automatically smile back.

When her head snaps backwards with an audible and sickening crack, I am out of my chair and on my feet in an instant, sending my chair to the floor with a clatter.

"What the f…"

Back on the screen, Miaka's head has rotated so she is looking into the camera again, only this time her head is upside-down. Her eyes and mouth are both wide-open. For some very bizarre reason, looking at her sparks a memory of how my pet mutefish used to swim before it died.

Thoughts of my dead fish quickly fade when Miaka starts talking.

The main reason being her voice, the sickening tones that ooze out from her gaping mouth are not her own.

More than that, the words being said are ones I re-member.

I go cold to hear them a second time.

"We still have much to do. The game has just begun. She must stand and watch everything end. Blood and tears and death and suffering. This girl must bear wit-ness to my rising, as I mock her failure. I will see her in Hell."

The Blood Daughter.

Mr. Tanaka waves a hand across the holo-screen, pausing the recording.

"When we were… listening in on what was happening to you, we heard the Blood Daughter say those words. At that very same moment, and in perfect synchronization, those exact words came from the mouth of our mysteri-ous young friend here."

"So what does that mean?" I ask.

The old man jabs a finger at the frozen image of Miaka. A selection of icons pop up. After selecting two, the screen displays something that looks like a 3D x-ray with lines upon lines of fluctuating data streaming around it.

"After Miaka's little act of macabre ventriloquism, that Pang woman got all flustered and panicky, ordered Miaka be put into an exorcism chamber."

I shrug to show my old friend I have no idea what he is talking about. Mr. Tanaka scratches the back of his neck, an expression of apology sweeps across his face.

"I must confess to knowing almost as little as you do when it comes to the finer points of this contraption of Pang's," he says. "But from what I can gather, the exorcism chamber will first scan a person for possible high-level possession. Should it detect something nasty, such as a particularly malevolent onryo, the chamber will then go on to purge the spirit from the host's body."

"And what happens to the host afterwards?"

"I'm not entirely sure," he replies. "But I've been informed the process is not as lethal as that of an exorcism performed by a DPA operative."

"So how less lethal are we talking?" I ask. "If they find something inside Miaka, what chance does she have of surviving?"

When Mr. Tanaka answers me, a sub-zero shiver dances up and down my spine.

"It's no longer a matter of if," he says. "They found something."

He raises a hand to the screen and touches the centre of the x-ray image with a trembling figure.

A new layer appears over the skeleton and vital organs of the girl from Sector Thirteen, a swirling mass of black, vaguely humanoid in shape.

Thick tendrils extend from its head, moving like the tentacles of an obsidian octopus. Thin spindly fingers twitch and spasm at its side, the crooked slash of a mouth opens and closes as the thing gibbers silently to itself. Two baleful eyes stare out from the screen, dead but burning with hate.

I am unaware that Mr. Tanaka has moved to my side until he holds my hand.

"Miaka is the host for the Blood Daughter."

The sense of panic starts in my heart.

With every beat, the feeling grows.

It is not long until my very being is consumed with dread.

I can feel it in the pit of my nauseated stomach, in the weakening of my knees, the sweat on my palms, the tears welling up behind my eyes.

Then comes the anger.

The tears I am trying to hold back run down my face as rivers of rage.

"What is Miaka's chance of survival?"

My question comes out as almost a whisper. Mr. Tanaka does not reply.

I shout, "What chances has she got?"

This time, my words are delivered at such a volume, and with such vitriol, I find it hard to believe I am the person who said them.

"Fifty percent, maybe seventy," comes my answer.

"Then do it," I say. My voice is calmer now, more deliberate. "Purge the chamber. Kill the Blood Daughter."

"We tried," says a voice behind me.

I let go of Mr. Tanaka's hand and turn to face Ms. Pang.

She stands in the now open doorway, still in purple and still just as smug. Both of my hands are balled into tight fists, Adrenaline courses through me. My subconscious screams at me to leap at the purple bitch and pummel her face, until she no longer needs make-up to be colour-coordinated with her clothes.

Ms. Pang smiles.

"I wouldn't do that, if I were you," she says. "The consequences could be quite dire for you."

"As fucked as Miaka's?" I spit.

Mr. Tanaka takes me gently, but firmly by the arm.

"Let her talk, Kichi," he says in calm and somber tones.

"Better than that," says Ms. Pang. "Let me show you. We are now ready for sunset."

We stand in an observation gallery.

Looking through the window and down, we can see the exorcism chamber containing Miaka. She has been moved into a much bigger room. The tube she is in lies in the middle of the room. It's connected to wires leading to computers and monitors that are manned by four lab guys. However, from the top of the exorcism chamber come several thick black cables that trail across the floor to the top of a colossal machine that takes up most of the room's space.

It looks a little like a gigantic metal bell. Dull grey in colour, but covered with glyphs and characters written in ancient Japanese. These words glow and pulse with a vivid red light.

"This," says Ms. Pang, her voice containing a small hint of delight, "is where the Blood Daughter is going to sit out eternity."

I press both hands against the cold glass of the window and peer closer at this ominous-looking object as Ms. Pang goes on to tell us about its function and her plan to save the world.

"Because you're behaving a little... emotionally at the moment, I'll endeavour to keep this short and simple. When we realised the entity within Miaka was none other than the Blood Daughter, we immediately activated the purge protocols. Sadly, our technology was no match for a spirit as vile and ancient as her. Without bombarding you with technical details, the process, if not halted, would have killed the girl inside and amplified Ai a thousand-fold. We had no choice but to stop. It was then that your little friend from Tokyo sent me a psychic message. Just two words, repeated over and over: Wait and Prison."

She looks down at Miaka and smiles.

"So, seeing as all the lore and legends say sunset is the given time, we decided to give Ai that time. And as we can't drive her out of Miaka and send her back to Hell, imprisonment seemed like a good idea to run with"

Ms. Pang taps at the glass, indicating the bell-thing.

"Basically, this is now a prison for ghosts. It's been in storage here for years, a relic from when Shimizu had the walls built. Originally, this was to be a kind of emergency shelter, somewhere for our beloved ex-president to hide, along with his family and friends, should the walls have failed and the ghost quake had not been contained. Now, after a few minor adjustments, this is to become Ai's permanent home."

Ms. Pang gesticulates at the glowing writing upon the object's surface.

"You see all those characters? They're Buddhist mantras of protection, cut into the metal by the most venerable monks and priests of that time. Word has it that every inch of this wondrous structure was blessed over a hundred times. Shimizu had this thing designed to be ten times stronger than the walls around Tokyo."

She pauses for a moment, both hands on her hips and a satisfied smile dancing across her lips.

"What we have done to this already impressive invention is enhance it a little. Firstly, we've added the latest in force-barrier tech, just to be on the safe side. The second is to reverse its basic function."

"What do you mean by that?" asks Mr. Tanaka.

The smile that danced on Ms. Pang's purple lips now breaks into a full-on retro-tango.

"It was supposed to keep ghosts out. Now, it will keep them in. When sunset arrives, and the Blood Daughter is finally ready to emerge from her hiding place, a magnetic pulse will activate. It will lure that bitch straight out of Miaka and into the prison like sharks to a drop of blood. The second she's inside, we'll seal the prison. The girl, Miaka will be free and Ai will be trapped. We all get to live happily ever after. The end."

I turn to look at Mr. Tanaka. He stares into the room below us, suitably impressed.

"Will it work?" I ask.

"Well, I'd like to have a close look at those inscriptions, just to be sure. But, I think it could well do as she says."

"It will work," quips Ms. Pang. "The Blood Daughter has failed."

She runs a manicured finger across the glass of the window, tracing an outline of her beloved creation below.

"We've got her."

# TWENTY-THREE

Sunset is in less than an hour.

Ms. Pang, Mr. Tanaka and I sit in front of two large monitor screens, our attention switching from one to the other with clockwork regularity. Although my heart beats stronger with each passing moment, neither of the screens shows anything happening. We may as well be looking at photographs.

The first monitor shows the sky above Osaka, a vista of brilliant blue. The second shows the motionless Miaka in her glass tank and the vast bulk of what we now call the spirit prison.

The three of us watch and wait.

Soon, the colour of the sky will change, darken.

And when it does…

If Ms. Pang and Mr. Tanaka are right, all we are about to witness is the end of another day.

I pray to Buddha and all the Bodhisattvas that they are right, because if they are wrong, the sun will never rise again.

I swivel my chair around so I am facing away from the screens and their displays of inactivity. My view is now of two sets of people in monochrome. Those in white stare at screens of technical data and complicated equations that would make the head of a maths genius explode. Those in black stand a silent vigil at various locations around the room, their pulse weapons at the ready.

I watch them work and stand for several minutes, before boredom forces me to turn back to the screens.

Bored at the end of the world.

That would make a great t-shirt.

I lean my elbows on the desk before me and cradle my head in my hands. When I exhale loudly, Ms. Pang gives an annoyed tut as response.

On screen one, Miaka remains as still as death.

I feel so sorry for her.

Not only was she born into a world of nightmares, she has the biggest ever nightmare living right inside of her.

That girl spent all of her childhood living in fear, fighting for survival against the most impossible odds, only to be sent on an utterly impossible mission; to offer herself up as sacrifice in order to settle an age-old debt, to be the daughter of a man who should have committed filicide in the name of the Blood Daughter a hundred years back, but chose to opt for genocide instead.

Thing is, how can you expect someone to kill you if they are already dead?

Although Shimizu is apparently still alive, the guy is in suspended animation, a vegetable that is seconds away from death.

How on earth could he take Miaka's life?

The Blood Daughter must have known this.

She has been with Miaka every step of the way, knowing she will fail.

Waiting for today to end, waiting to be set free.

But Miaka and Ai are safely contained, at least for now. And Ms. Pang has assured us that should the Blood Daughter leave Miaka's body, she will be sucked up into a prison she can never ever break free from.

While Ms. Pang's words mean little to me now, Mr. Tanaka has given her plan both thumbs up. If it is good enough for him, if he thinks it will work, then I am happy to put my faith in it.

But then there is poor Miaka.

Should tomorrow be just another regular day, should she be as right as the summer rain, I swear the first thing I will do is take her to the best restaurant in Osaka, so the pair of us can eat until we are ready to burst.

Then, we will go and get her hair fixed.

And after that?

After that, there will be no need for her to live her life in fear.

From tomorrow onwards, I will have a little sister. Miaka Honda.

I close my eyes and let my mind wander, thinking of the possible celebratory feast to come, imagining Miaka filling her face with WasabiDogs.

Dear Buddha, how I would love one of those right now.

Hungry at the end of the world.

When I next open my eyes, the screen showing the sky above Osaka tells me that time has moved on significantly. The fuzziness of my head backs this up.

"Have I been asleep?" I ask.

Mr. Tanaka's smile and Ms. Pang's scowl inform me that I have.

"Just for a short time," says my friend. "Not to worry. You didn't miss anything, except for more of that dreadful excuse for tea."

"How's Miaka? No changes?"

"She's still stable. No sign of you-know-who."

I stand up and stretch my arms and back, then I rummage through my pockets in search of my nico-gum. Instead, I find the can of heal-mist from Red Raku's bathroom. After removing the cans lid, I give it a shake, close my eyes and spray the contents straight into my face.

The healing medicine makes my skin tingle, an odd sensation but quite enjoyable. I turn to Mr. Tanaka and give him my biggest smile.

"How do I look?"

"A lot less like a ravaged Panda," he replies. "You can now face the possible forth-coming apocalypse looking like a normal human being again."

"I look normal?"

"Normal for you," he chuckles.

Ms. Pang gives another tut. I stretch my arms to the ceiling and yawn with gusto.

On the first screen, twilight is slithering its way towards Osaka. The sky is slowly turning from blue to indigo, with patches of red and orange here and there. It really is a beautiful sight to behold.

On the second screen, Miaka remains in her chemically-induced slumber.

But something has changed.

Her left eye is twitching.

Then her left hand suddenly pulls itself into a clenched fist.

I am about to mention this to Mr. Tanaka, when a door at the back of the room slides open and someone hurries in. The sound of his shoes slapping against the floor shatters the silence.

An overweight lab guy, white coat open so it flaps behind him like the cape of a superhero, runs up to Ms. Pang and points at the monitor showing us the sky above.

"Something's happening," he wheezes. "Outside. They're all over the sector. Thousands of them."

"Thousands of what?" snaps Ms. Pang.

"Nil-by-mouths."

Ms. Pang pulls out a control pad from her pocket and points it to an area above the monitors. A large holo-screen activates, showing an aerial view of Osaka.

"Show life signs breaking curfew," she says.

The screen flickers for an instant. Thousands of tiny red lights sparkle and glint before us.

The colour fades from her face.

"They've formed a circle," says the lab guy, his voice rising in pitch so that he sounds like a pleading child. "And this base is at its centre! You can't say that's a coincidence, not with today being what it is and what we're doing here. There's no..."

"Zoom in. Area five," says Ms. Pang, cutting him short. "Show me."

Although her words are clipped and authoritative, I notice a subtle undertone in her voice.

Could it be fear?

There is another momentary flicker before we are shown a group of around fifty nil-by-mouths standing on a walkway.

They stand like statues, thin black silhouettes set against a burning-red sky.

"Closer."

Now we can see them clearly.

Black-clad men and women, white-skinned and vacant-eyed, metal surgical masks nailed to their faces. Not one of them looks like they have more than a day to live. To be honest, half of them already look as if they are dead.

Ms. Pang orders several more views of the city.

The pictures we see are all the same: large groups of nil-by-mouths, standing in groups on walkways and platforms, staring blankly into the distance.

I cannot shake the feeling that they are looking at us. This thought unnerves me. And I am not alone in this. Visibly concerned, Ms. Pang is about to order another camera change when Mr. Tanaka quickly points towards the holo-screen and shouts for her to wait.

"Look there. One of them is writing something on his pad."

My old friend is right. One of the almost-cadavers is tapping away at his pad with ivory fingers.

When he is finished, he turns the pad around so we are able to read what he has written.

Then another does the same.

And another.

One by one, the nil-by-mouths pull out their pads and write upon them. Then they display them for us to see.

"Zoom in," orders Ms. Pang.

We all feel a chill of dread run down our spines.

On each and every pad, written in multiple languages, are the words

BLOOD and RED.

Before I can ask Mr. Tanaka what he thinks the meaning of this message could be, the door at the back of the room is flung open again. But this time, four heavily-armed police troopers march with purpose towards us.

"There's been an incident," says the leader. Although his voice is muffled slightly by the riot mask he wears, it is clear he is in a state of high anxiety.

"What incident?" snaps Ms. Pang.

"Nil-by-mouths. Close to a hundred of them. Nobody knows how, but they just..."

"Just what?"

"They just... appeared in Government tower five, armed to the teeth. Multiple fatalities. They've taken the level belonging to Operative Red."

I swear, just for a millisecond, I see Ms. Pang's knees buckle.

When she speaks, there is a definite quiver to her voice.

"What did you say?'

Before he can answer her, before anyone can say another word, all the screens in the room switch to show static, followed by a deafening scream of white noise. We all wince and cover our ears.

Thankfully, the shrieking only lasts for a few seconds. The static clears, all the monitors now show the same shot, a lone nil-by-mouth, standing in a dimly lit room.

I lower my hands from either side of my head.

My jaw drops.

Not only do I recognise him, I know exactly where he is standing.

It is the nil-by-mouth from the walkway.

The one who felt hunger.

The one I 'saved'.

Words written in basic Nihon speak start scrolling across the bottom of the screens, like subtitles from an old foreign film.

But this is no movie we are watching.

The horror is very fucking real.

We read the coming plot twist in silence.

"WE, THE SILENT MINORITY, ARE AWARE OF YOUR PLANS TO SAVE OSAKA FROM DESCENDING INTO HELL. YOU BELIEVE YOUR ACTIONS TO BE NOBLE AND GOOD. BUT YOU ARE WRONG.

THE BLOOD DAUGHTER SPEAKS TO US.

ONE HUNDRED YEARS AGO, TOKYO WAS GIVEN TO THE BLOOD DAUGHTER.

THIS DEAL WAS MADE SO TO SPARE THE LIFE OF ONE UNWORTHY OF SAVING.

THE CITIZENS OF NIHON HAILED PRESIDENT SHIMIZU AS A SAVIOUR.

THEY THANKED HIM FOR BUILDING THE WALLS THAT SEALED OFF THE CITY.

THEY THANKED HIM FOR KEEPING THEM SAFE.

MILLIONS OF INNOCENT CITIZENS WERE DAMNED TO HELL AS THE WORLD CLAPPED THEIR BLOOD-STAINED HANDS IN RELIEF ."

"That's not true," I blurt out.

My intention was to carry on and tell the skinny freak how some people never forgot. It was just that we were unable to talk out about what happened.

But I do not, reason being the sudden and violent shiver that rocks me from head to toe.

But this is no shiver of impending doom.

This is the shiver of being cold.

The temperature has dropped.

"THE BLOOD DAUGHTER SPEAKS TO US.

SHE TOLD US OF THE MILLIONS OF SOULS SHE HAS TORMENTED AND TWISTED.

SHE LAUGHED AS SHE TOLD US OF THEIR SUFFERING.

SHE ALLOWED US TO HEAR THEM.

WE HEARD THEIR SCREAMS.

WE FELT THEIR ANGER AT BEING FORGOTTEN, THEIR DESIRE FOR REVENGE UPON THOSE WHO DID NOTHING TO DELIVER THEM FROM EVIL.

WE SENSED THEIR RAGE."

My breath now comes out of my mouth in frozen clouds as the room continues to get colder. Mr. Tanaka throws me a worried glance, acknowledging that he feels it too. Ms. Pang seems oblivious to it, though. She glares back in fury at the emotionless face on the screens.

"FOR TOO LONG HAVE THOSE INNOCENTS SUFFERED, FOR TOO LONG HAVE THEY BEEN FORGOTTEN.

BUT THEIR TIME OF VENGEANCE HAS NOW COME.

THE BLOOD DAUGHTER HAS GIVEN US THE MEANS TO MAKE THIS SO.

ON THIS DAY, THE WORLD WILL REMEMBER TOKYO.

ON THIS DAY, THE VOICES OF THOSE DAMNED WILL BE HEARD.

ON THIS DAY, HELL WILL RISE."

The nil-by-mouth moves out of shot.

When he does, it takes every fiber of my being to stop myself from screaming out a tirade of panic-filled expletives.

He was standing in Red Raku's torture chamber. The charcoal image of the Blood Daughter stares out from multiple monitors and holo-screens, her eyes burning with insane glee.

"HAVE A NICE DAY."

As those last words scroll across the screen, I realise what is missing from this picture.

"They're going to use Red Raku."

# TWENTY-FOUR

Back when I was about ten years old, back when Mother was normal and my father took an active role in my life, we went out to the bio-park and zoo with a family we were friends with at the time. They had a daughter who was a year older than I was, but a great deal shorter. This made her appear much younger than she really was. Her parents blamed this on giving her illegal stims to increase her intelligence when she was a baby.

I remember us all having a nice day, up until we sat down on the synthetic grass to have a picnic.

That is when we saw the red-rose spider on the girl's back.

I had read about the red-rose in nature class and knew it was the most dangerous thing to crawl the earth. Just one bite from it was enough to kill a grown man within a matter of minutes.

The spider had somehow escaped from its tank and was happily sitting there in the middle of her back. A strange hybrid of arachnid and flower, both beautiful and deadly.

Me and Mother saw it at the same time. And when we did, we froze.

I remember my father looking puzzled at us, wondering what we were looking at. After walking over to us and seeing for himself, he froze too.

The girl was oblivious to the three statues standing behind her and the killer that was peacefully sitting on her back. She carried on playing her vid-game, happy to just be.

Even when her parents joined us in petrified horror, the girl carried on playing.

Seconds passed , turning into minutes.

All we could do was watch.

When the girl shot to her feet and punched the air in glee, we knew what was going to happen next.

As the girl shouted out her happiness at completing her game, the red-rose spider sunk its fangs through her t-shirt and into her back.

Her shout became a scream of sudden pain, which then morphed into a gurgle as blood filled her mouth and she started to choke.

She was dead before she hit the floor.

I guess that the total amount of time from seeing the spider on her back and her last breath was less than ten minutes.

We all knew how dangerous the spider was.

We all knew what would happen if it bit her.

But none of us did a thing to help her.

Not a finger was lifted, not a word of warning given.

Fear turned us all into idiots.

The image of Red Raku's 'office' has disappeared. All the monitors and holo-screens flick back to their previous channels.

Nothing they display is good.

Nil-by-mouths surrounding us.

A burning-red sun in a sky the colour of a bruise.

Miaka thrashing wildly within her glass box.

Mouths agape like Neanderthals at all this, jaws almost touching the floor, are Ms. Pang and her gang of techs. The stupefaction has also hit the small squad of police troopers. They stand there shivering, looking at each other and shaking their heads. Even Mr. Tanaka seems at a loss for what to do next.

Not me, though.

The end of days may be coming, but I am not going to just stand there and watch it happen.

No way.

I am across the room and out of the door in an instant.

I have to save Miaka.

Out of the room, I take a left and run to the end of the corridor and its lift. A million thoughts are racing through my mind, but I have to stay focused and remember the way to where Miaka is being kept.

I have no time to worry about the ever-decreasing temperature, no time to wonder why the lights are starting to flicker. I get to the lift and push the down button again and again and again, only stopping when the doors open. When they do, I dive inside and punch the button for the lowest level of the complex. The lift's doors close with a shudder that I mimic. I have to grind my teeth together to stop them from chattering.

After a short descent, I rush out of the refrigerated cubicle, straight into Hell on ice.

'Cold' is no longer a suitable adjective to describe how freezing it is on the lowest level of R194's headquarters.

I push myself on, down another damned corridor, turn right onto yet another, then turn left.

I force my aching legs into a sprint when I spy the door I am looking for: a bulky red air-lock, positioned between two large observation windows.

I throw myself to the floor when the nearest window shatters, showering glass shards in all directions. Luckily, I am out of range and am not hit by any of the deadly shrapnel.

Chalk up one small victory for Kichi Honda.

I look up just in time to see the airlock door buckle and fly off its hinges, slamming against the opposite wall with a resonating clang.

The other window is then blown out.

From within the room comes a chuckle I know all too well.

Scrabbling to my feet, I realise my backpack and selection of ghost-killing guns are back in the room with Mr. Tanaka and the dumb brigade.

Way to go, Kichi.

"I know you're out there," says a sing-song voice.

Getting to my feet, I ball my hands into fists. Not much in the way of weaponry, but it is all I have.

"Don't be shy," says the voice. "Come on in and say bye."

My feet do not want to go in the direction I insist upon. They want to turn in the opposite direction and run as far away from this place as they can.

Perhaps the old Kichi would have heard them out and followed their suggestion.

But not this Kichi.

This girl has been through far too much and running away is not an option.

I walk towards where the door used to be and stop in an empty frame.

The room is in a state of total destruction.

Ms. Pang's ghost prison still looks imposing, even though there are great holes torn into its metalwork. Its protective glyphs no longer pulse with energy. Now, they are dull, meaningless characters of a language mostly forgotten.

Lab techs lie scattered around the place like broken dolls, the awkward angles of their limbs telling me their deaths were gruesome.

The glass tube that once held Miaka is now empty, of course.

Miaka now lies in the arms of what used to be Red Raku.

And never has her name been more apt.

Last time I saw her, she was partly sticking out of a wall. Mainly, her face and most of her left arm.

These are the only two parts of her body that are not dripping with blood.

The rest of her skin has been flayed off of her, the clothes she was wearing stained crimson.

"Long time no see," she grins.

"Not really," I reply. "What is it? A few hours?"

"Maybe to you," she replies. "But, where I've been, time moves... differently. Hours becomes years, become eternity."

"Go anywhere nice?" I ask, sarcasm becoming both my defense and method of attack. "Did you have fun?"

Red Raku laughs. It is a sound I have not missed.

"Sure!" she beams. "At first, I wasn't too impressed with the whole Hell idea, but after a while, the place kind of grew on me."

Cradled in Raku's arms, smeared with her blood and gore, Miaka starts twitching violently. Instinct pushes me to take a step forward.

A gurgling hiss of warning comes from the partially-skinned serial killer.

"Not so close, pretty girl."

"What are you going to do with her?" I ask, readying myself for a futile fist-fight.

Raku smiles and looks down lovingly at the girl in her arms.

"She's a gift," she whispers. "I'm gonna take her outside and unwrap her."

Her sentence lights the firecracker inside me.

I launch myself at her; a small girl-shaped missile of limited power, but filled with intentions of mass-destruction.

Sadly, I never hit my target.

Raku raises her head and glares at me with blinding-white eyes.

I am picked up off my feet and hurled back through the doorway. Crashing against the wall, I fall heavily down upon the twisted wreckage of the airlock door.

Rage-induced adrenaline gets me back to my feet, ready for another attack.

But she is not there.

Red Raku has gone, taking Miaka with her.

"Miaka!"

No one answers.

I stagger forward, back through the doorway I have just been flung through and into the room where the end of the world was supposed to be stopped.

Walking past dead bodies and mangled machinery, I make my way into the centre of the room. Once there, I spin round and look up to the ceiling, at the cameras I know are there.

And to the people I know are watching, I say two words:

"We failed."

Sinking to my knees, tears of despair and fury blurring my vision, I wonder how long it will be until Ai declares her victory.

I do not have to wait long.

In a voice that seems to come from everywhere all at once, but also from just inside my head...

The Blood Daughter speaks.

# TWENTY-FIVE

Children of Nihon...
 *...it's time to play...*
 ...Eternal night has fallen...
 *...I promise it will hurt...*
 ...Rejoice the beginning of the end...
 *...screaming and blood and pain and darkness...*
 ...Revere my name and fear me...
 *...I'm coming to find you...*
 ...I reign victorious...
 *...kill and kill and kill and kill...*
 ...Hell is here...
 *...you're all going to die.*

# TWENTY-SIX

Mr. Tanaka, Ms. Pang and an assortment of techs and troopers arrive about ten minutes after Ai's gloat-fest. Poor Mr. Tanaka looks like he has had enough. His breath comes out in the form of wheezing gasps that sound utterly painful. This focuses me somewhat and knocks some composure back into me.

I get to my feet and walk over to my old friend.

"Are you OK?" I ask.

He nods and waves a dismissing hand.

"Don't worry... about me," he says. "I... I will be fine. Just fine."

Of the twenty or so people that stand in this room of failed hope, I am the only not carrying a gun. Ms. Pang gives me a knowing smile and throws me my backpack.

"I gave your rifle to Ono," she says, nodding towards the overweight lab guy. "You'll have to make do with one of your pistols, if you don't mind."

I don't answer her. I open my pack and return one of my E-4's to the belt of my combats and stuff my pockets with power packs. The other pistol finds a new home in my right hand.

There it will stay, until...

"So," I say to the room. "What's the plan?"

"We get out of here," replies Ms. Pang. "There's an emergency tunnel access point on this level. The tunnels will take us all the way out to the coast. If we're lucky, we can get there before the walls go up."

Memories of the video clip from Tokyo start replaying.

Are copters now on their way to this sector?

Has construction on the second wall of Nihon already begun?

Ms. Pang somberly shakes her head.

"This time will be different," she says. "Once the ghost siren sounded, Osaka was sealed off by a level three force-wall. I would guess by now that it's at level six."

"Care to explain a little more clearly?" I ask. "You know, for people who aren't DPA or Radical 194 or whatever."

"I agree," adds Mr. Tanaka. "A small explanation would not go amiss. What exactly are you talking about?"

After a deep nasal exhalation, Ms. Pang starts to explain, doing little to hide the contempt in her voice.

"Following a ghost siren, a force barrier is activated. The potentially affected area is sealed off, until the all clear is given. Seeing as Ai has ascended from Hell, I think it's safe to say we're now in the middle of Nihon's second ghost quake. Most of the power in this sector has already gone down, all com and net signals lost. The force-wall, however, is powered independently from orbiting satellites. Sensors will have detected the ghost quake, pushing its integrity up to level five. This means we've got around ninety minutes before it reaches level ten."

"I see," says Mr. Tanaka, scratching his chin. "So, at lower levels, living beings can pass through the wall unharmed, whereas ghosts would not be able to?"

"Correct. But at level ten, nothing and no one will be able to get through. Osaka Sector will be completely sealed off, just like Tokyo. But, whereas the citizens of Tokyo were given zero chance of escape, at least here, today, the citizens of Osaka have something."

"No they don't."

Ms. Pang and Mr. Tanaka turn to look at me.

Not just them though. It would seem I have everyone's attention now.

"What do you mean?" asks Ms. Pang.

"You said all the power is out. Com and net access has died, right?"

Ms. Pang nods.

"So how will anyone in Osaka know what's happening with the dome? There's been no emergency broadcast telling them anything. They have no idea what's going to happen! And even though they've all just heard the Blood Daughter's genocidal proposal, no one's gonna dream about leaving their home. The DPA's done too good of a job at keeping them scared. The citizens of Osaka will stay at home, where death will visit each and every last one of them!"

It seems my words have struck a chord with those around me.

A palpable silence falls over us.

I start thinking about Mother.

What will she be doing now?

Will she be shouting for me? Asking for me to restore the power, so she can feed her addiction for virtual reality porn?

How long will it be before something makes its way into our apartment and puts an end to her miserable existence?

Although she never once showed me any love or affection after my father left, she is still my mother.

I cannot leave her to die alone.

"Forget her," says Ms. Pang. "She's practically dead anyway."

Her words do more than break my train of thought, they shatter it into a million tiny particles of fury.

I bring my pistol up and smash its barrel hard into the side of her face with a satisfying crunch.

The blow knocks her cold to the floor.

Although she is right about Mother, she can't say whatever she wants.

And while I may say all kinds of bad things about her, Ms. Pang does not have that right.

No one does.

Seeing their superior pistol-whipped, the trooper goons raise their rifles in unison. Mr. Tanaka quickly moves to stand in front of me, waving his hands as he attempts to calm the situation.

"Don't shoot, don't shoot!"

All the lights in the room suddenly go out.

Then we hear the noise.

A groaning, rattling sound echoes around us.

From above us.

We all look up, into the dark. The trooper's shoulder-mounted torches cut through the murk, revealing...

Nothing.

The temperature has dropped even further now. I can hear the overweight lab guy's teeth chattering.

The noise comes again, this time from the back of the room, then from the left of us, then from the right.

Torches follow the noise, but find only dust motes dancing in their beams.

One of the troopers kneels down, picks up Ms. Pang and ungraciously throws her over his shoulder.

"To the emergency tunnels," he says, rising to his feet. "Before..."

His sentence trails off as a lab tech to his right is suddenly dragged screaming upwards. Torches quickly follow her ascent in time to see her kicking feet disappear into the dark.

Her screams stop.

Croaking laughter follows.

The trooper carrying Ms. Pang runs from the room.

"Evacuate the area. Now!"

Grabbing Mr. Tanaka by the hand, I follow after him.

Out in the corridor, we turn left and keep on running. Thankfully, emergency lights are still operating, bathing us in a pale shade of orange.

Despite carrying an unconscious woman, the police trooper certainly can move. I half lead, half drag Mr. Tanaka along with me. I can hear my old friend gasping for breath as he tries to keep up the pace.

Behind me, I hear more screaming.

Pulse rifles are fired, their blasts illuminate the corridor

I do not look back.

We take a sharp right and then left at a crossroads. In a door-lined corridor, the trooper chooses the first on the left and punches the control panel with his gloved-fist. The door slides open and he dives inside. I follow after him, pulling my old friend with me.

We are now on the landing of a stairwell. Mercifully, the temperature is a little warmer in here. I take this as a good sign, even though the lighting is still emergency orange. Mr. Tanaka slips his hand out of mine and slumps to the floor, every breath he takes sounds like it could be his last. I sink to my knees beside him.

I do not ask how he is this time. That would be stupid. The old man nods anyway and gives me a shaking thumbs-up. I know he is lying. Of course he is. The guy is over a hundred now. People his age should not be running for their lives.

A single police trooper and two female lab techs burst onto the landing, followed a few moments later by Ono, the overweight lab guy. Somehow, he has managed to lose my rifle.

"I'm the last," he says, his voice half-choked with tears. "I'm the last."

"Ito, close the door. Lock it," barks the lead trooper.

The trooper does as instructed.

"You two," he says, jabbing a finger at the lab women. "Help the old man up. We have to keep moving."

I glance back to see the two women help Mr. Tanaka back to his feet. His breathing is still ragged, sweat lines his aged brow. I want to tell our self-appointed leader we must rest and give my friend time to recover.

Unfortunately, I know it is out of the question.

We must press on.

Please, Buddha. Give him strength.

Help him make it.

Help us all make it.

As we head down the spiraling staircase to the tunnels below, the fear hits me. Goose pimples rise on my skin, my palms dampen with sweat.

Now is not a good time to confess my phobia of stairs.

Although I do my best to contain it, the feeling of terror intensifies with every step.

Shadows become phantoms that reach out towards me with terrible fingers; every echoing footstep turns to evil mocking laughter.

I swing my gun from left to right, but find nothing to fire at except the wall.

"Not much further," says our self-appointed leader.

After several minutes have passed, I want to ask him to define 'not much further', as the end is nowhere in sight.

The orange emergency lighting now deepens to a dark shade of red.

My imagination paints a vivid picture of us all sliding down the throat of some hideous demonic creature. Instead of escaping, we will all be doomed to a slow, agonising death by digestion.

Behind me, Mr. Tanaka gasps in agony. I stop running and whirl round, only just keeping my balance. Bathed in red light, the sweat that pours from him looks like blood. He clutches at his chest, eyes screwed closed in unsurmountable pain. The lab women start to panic, unsure as to what to do for him. Ono, standing behind the women, looks equally as vacant. Obviously, this situation is way beyond their abilities.

Enter Ito, the hero of the hour.

The police trooper pushes Ono and one of the lab women out of the way, scoops up my old friend in one fluid motion and continues running.

"Come on," he yells at us, as he zips past me. "We're almost there."

I hurry after him, hoping beyond hope that we really are.

When my feet leave the last step and touch solid ground, I am tempted to fling myself to the floor and kiss it.

We gather at the bottom of the stairs. Both police guys put down the human loads they are carrying.

"Adreno-shot," says the leader. "Quickly."

Ito opens a compartment on the utility-belt around his waist, pulling out something that looks like a silver pen. After shaking it twice, he slams the pointed end straight into Mr. Tanaka's chest.

Before I can shout out in shock, my old friend is suddenly sitting bolt-upright, taking in great gasps of air. To my right, I hear a scream as the previously comatose Ms. Pang rejoins the land of the living.

One of these things pleases me immensely.

The other, not so much.

"How are you feeling?" I ask my friend.

"Never better, young Kichi. I feel like I'm eighty again!"

Even in the direst of situations, Mr. Tanaka can still make me smile.

I take a sideways glance at Ms. Pang and smile even more when I see the bruised side of her face. I no longer care if she can read my mind. Truth be told, she is no longer someone to be afraid of.

The lead police guy marches us away from the stairs and through a small archway, on the other side of which is a room not much bigger than my bedroom. Here, the lights are a dim yellow, like the pages of an old book. The only feature in this room is a circular metal door in the north wall.

Behind us comes a shuddering clang. We all turn back to see the archway we entered through has been sealed off.

"Emergency protocols activating," says a recorded voice. "Now scanning for non-corporeal entities. Please remain still."

A pulse of harsh white fills the room, forcing me to shield my eyes.

"Scan complete."

I blink rapidly, trying to dispel the orbs of red and white that dance across my field of vision.

"One non-corporeal detected."

Both police troopers bring up their rifles, aiming first at one person, and then another. Ms. Pang pulls out a pistol and edges back against the wall. When Ito levels me in his sights, I reply in kind.

"Lower your weapon," he screams.

"You first!" I shout back.

"What's happening?" sobs one of the lab women.

It is then that Mr. Tanaka takes a step forward and bellows an order that shocks my socks off.

"Everybody, calm down!"

All eyes turn to look at him. He ignores us all and walks over to the sobbing lab tech.

"My dear child," he says. "I'm sorry to tell you this, but it seems there may be a ghost in here with us."

The woman's eyes widen in fear, as do those of her colleague. Ono covers his face and starts to moan.

"Purge protocols initiating. Please wait," announces the security system.

"Stand against the wall," orders my old friend. "Spread out as best you can."

This stern version of Mr. Tanaka is not one to be trifled with. We all do as we are told.

"You there," says Mr. Tanaka, clicking his fingers at the lead trooper. "Officer..."

"Akiyama."

"Yes, what do you know about these purge protocols?"

"Exorcism pulse energy. Whole room will be flooded. Anything that's not of this world will be shredded."

"But there isn't a ghost in here!" says the crying lab woman. The near hysterical tone to her voice sets me on edge. "There's only us!"

Ono, hands still covering his face, moans again.

"Please wait. Purge protocols initiating. Please wait," repeats the security system.

"There is something in here," I say, raising my gun. "Inside us."

I level the E-4 at Ono's head.

"Inside him."

Cue given, Ono lowers his hands.

Ono is not Ono any longer.

Ono is an onryo.

A naked girl, long dead, takes one twitching step forward. Its skin is pulled tightly over its skeleton. Copious amounts of eerily straight black hair sprout from its head, reaching down to its boney waist. Although its eyes are a sightless white, I am beyond doubt that this damned thing can see.

The onryo opens its wet, black mouth, spilling noxious smelling goo onto the floor. A sound like the screeching of a million forks being dragged between a million sets of teeth fills the room.

The thing is laughing.

"Insufficient power," declares the safety protocols. "Purge failed. Repeat. Purge failed."

And with that, the room explodes into chaos.

Akiyama and Ito open fire.

Two 6613's unleash their deadly ghost-killing loads at the onryo.

They miss.

Where the ghost once stood is now an empty space.

Both the lab women throw themselves into hysteria, one of them collapses to the floor, screaming in terror.

The onryo reappears behind her.

Thin rotten fingers reach down, grabbing handfuls of the woman's hair. With one ghastly tug, the onryo rips the lab tech's head off.

A fountain of blood sprays in a crimson rainbow from the stump of her neck, splattering across the room.

Ito is showered in gore; the shock makes him stumble backwards, making his shot go wild. Akiyama drops to one knee and fires his pulse rifle.

But there is nothing in his sights.

I rush over to Mr. Tanaka, pistol at the ready. Ms. Pang swings her gun around the room with a trembling hand. The remaining lab woman starts to choke and then vomits all over her white shoes.

The onryo's grotesque laughter rings in my ears as she punches her fist straight through the back of the puking woman's head, exiting through her mouth in an explosion of blood and teeth.

Ito, who has just finished wiping his visor clean, is too late to respond to this attack. Akiyama and Ms. Pang are a little quicker on the draw.

While Ms. Pang's shot is a mile off, Akiyama's is on target, hitting the onryo square on the shoulder. The creature shrieks in rage, a sound of blood-chilling agony that will haunt me forever.

This time, the onryo does not disappear. Perhaps the blast from the 6613 has diminished its powers.

The creature glares at us with tofu-white eyes as it shakes its hand free from the head of the lab woman, letting the body drop to the floor with a sickening thud.

Akiyama fires again, hitting the ghost in its chest, the impact knocking it back against the wall. Ito and Ms. Pang score a second and third hit to the onryo's skeletal torso.

More out of luck than anything, my first shot of the battle hits home, right in the ghost's unholy face.

The onryo slides down the wall and onto the floor in a spasm of writhing limbs, before blinking out of existence.

"Room has reached necessary safety levels," announces the room's security system. "Doors are now opening. Please leave the room. Emergency transport will depart in four minutes and thirty-seven seconds."

We leave the blood-soaked room and step straight onto a small train compartment. This comes as a surprise, as I expected our flight for freedom through the emergency tunnels to have been on foot. The off-white compartment with its blackened windows and faded-red seats comes as a welcome relief.

Akiyama orders us to take seats and to strap ourselves in. Me and Mr. Tanaka are way ahead of him, we are already seated and fastening the numerous safety belts before he has finished his sentence.

As soon as the five of us are buckled up, the train violently shudders into life and we are off like a missile. G-force slams us further back into our seats.

"Holy shit!" says someone behind me, possibly Ito.

The front of the carriage is nothing but a dirty white wall and a door with the smallest of porthole windows. I presume there is no need for us to see where we are going, just to reach our end destination is enough.

I close my eyes and wait.

My thoughts drift to what I know must be taking place in the city above us.

A single onryo cut our number of lab techs, troopers and regular citizens down to five in mere minutes.

Buddha only knows how many 'friends' Ai has brought with her.

Perhaps it is already too late for Osaka Sector.

Perhaps we five are now all that remains of a city of millions...

Someone behind me starts screaming.

My eyes snap open. I want to turn round, to see what is happening, but the safety belts and speed of the train keeps me pinned into place. All I can do, all any of us can do, is sit and stare dead ahead.

"Ito!" shouts Akiyama, "Ito, what's happening?"

Ito does not reply. Instead, he manages another scream, and a gurgling choke before falling silent.

To my right, I hear Ms. Pang mumbling an ancient Buddhist mantra.

At the front of the compartment, something vaguely humanoid materialises before us. A translucent figure of a naked boy, twisted in visible agony; all hollow eyes and a mouth that gibbers and twitches silently.

It takes a single step forward...and fades into nothing.

"What the..."

My exclamation trails off as another apparition appears in the central aisle of the train.

Ms. Pang's mantra gets louder and faster, more desperate.

The train banks suddenly to the right, and then to the left, as if trying to shake off its unwelcome passenger. The creature quickly scans the carriage and decides that Kichi Honda is to be its first victim.

Oh, lucky fucking me.

With outstretched arms, the rotting corpse of a long-dead man shambles forward.

It disappears after only three steps.

Thank you, Buddha. Thank you!

"Can't be much further," says Akiyama. "We'll be out of this soon. Everyone just…"

He does not get to finish.

Whatever piece of advice the police trooper was about to impart dies with him.

The yurei standing before us cradles Akiyama's severed head to its chest like a mother holding her newborn.

Although the sight of this ghost fills me with dread, I cannot help but be captivated by it.

Unlike all the stories I have heard from my times at Mr. Tanaka's house, this yurei does not follow the traditional guidelines. Instead of a white kimono and long black hair, this yurei is the opposite, a negative version of her kin. The kimono she wears is jet black, her hair as white as the snow I love so much.

And she is beautiful.

Her skin is ivory-white, lips full and pink. Her eyes hold no trace of evil, more a deep sadness that is so palpable it brings a lump to my throat.

When she drops Akiyama's severed head to her feet, reality kicks in.

This beautiful dead woman is going to kill us all.

She lowers her head and gazes towards her feet.

Steel chains suddenly shoot out from her black robes, punching holes through the left and right sides of the train's compartment, continuing their journey beyond.

The yurei slowly lifts her head. Twenty lengths of slackened metal trail from her robes and out through the sides of the train.

With those beautiful mournful eyes of hers, she looks at me and gives a smile of apology.

The chains instantly go taut.

Tears fall from the yurei's eyes as she rips the train apart.

# TWENTY-SEVEN

I am back in the field of red and white flowers.

Just like before, I am wearing the flimsiest of dresses, as is Miaka, who stands to the right of me.

This time, instead of offering me flowers, she hands me a very large and delicious-looking ice cream.

I take it without hesitation.

"It is nice," she says, between licks.

I have a taste and nod.

It most certainly is.

The two of us stare off into the distance as we enjoy our treats.

I think back to the last time I had an ice cream. It must have been when I was around eight. My parents had taken me on holiday to one of Thailand's floating islands, New Phuket or Samui, I forget which one. I do recall that we had a good time, though.

I think.

A vague memory of riding a clone-elephant through a jungle flashes hazily through my mind.

As I blankly stare ahead, an eight year-old child on the back of a huge beast with ivory tusks materialises into my field of vision. I can hear her chuckle as her steed stomps its way through an invisible jungle.

"Mummy! Mummy! Look at me!"

She sounds so happy.

Everything turns cloudy as my eyes fill with tears.

I drop the remainder of my ice cream and wipe my eyes on my arm.

When I look again, both the child and the elephant have gone.

"You are lucky," says Miaka. "I never knew my mother."

"I've almost forgotten mine," I reply.

"Not entirely. Your memories are just sleeping, that is all. You can wake them up, if you really want to. All you need to do is try."

"What if I don't want to?"

"Then they will sleep until you do."

The girl from Tokyo takes my hand.

"You will have to be careful," she says. "She will use her against you."

I turn to look down at her. Although she is smiling, I see fear burning behind her eyes.

"What do you mean?"

"Love is the strongest weapon. She will use her against you."

A deafening crack of thunder makes me look up to the sky. What was once blue is now dark with rain clouds.

"I am sorry," says Miaka. "It is time for you to wake up."

The blackened clouds release their burden. It only takes seconds for me to be soaked through to the skin. Not that I was really wearing much to protect myself, but still.

When I look back to Miaka, I see only my discarded ice cream being obliterated by the rain.

"...hurt..."

A voice whispers into oblivion, their words search for me.

"...hurt?"

I know that voice.

A good person is talking to me, someone kind, important.

What was their name again?

"... are you hurt?"

A screaming wave of pain suddenly arches through my back, jolting me into an upright position. This action only increases the agony. It feels like someone has stabbed acupuncture needles into the entire length of my spine.

Firm hands take me by the shoulders.

"Stay still," orders Mr. Tanaka. "I'm going to inject you with one of those adreno things."

Another wave of blinding torment assaults me.

The scream that follows sounds like that of a wounded animal, not a girl who works at a mall.

Mr. Tanaka slams the adreno-shot pen into my left arm.

And just like that, all sensation of pain disappears.

My old friend squats before me like a giant frog. The smile on his face is one of his biggest.

"Welcome back, young Kichi Honda."

Ms. Pang, Mr. Tanaka and I stand before what is left of the tunnel train. The yurei did a fine job of totaling our means of escape. All that remains of it is shredded metal and broken glass.

"I can't believe we are walking away from that," I say.

"Neither can I," says Mr. Tanaka. "Thank Buddha the safety foam activated. If not for that..."

I bring my right arm up to my nose and sniff at my sleeve. The chemical stench from the dissolved safety foam still lingers.

"We're not out of trouble yet," says Ms. Pang. "Time is of the essence and we still have to find the nearest exit, that's if we manage to get there..."

"We'll get there," Mr. Tanaka says. His tone is matter-of-fact and deadly serious. "We have to. I'll be damned if I'm going to end my days like a rat in a sewer!"

After the safety foam dissolved, Mr. Tanaka and Ms. Pang carried me from the wreckage of the train. Apparently, a length of the carriage wall had hit the back of my chair before the foam had been released, encasing us like mosquitoes in amber. While my old friend kept watch over me, Ms. Pang went back to what was left of the train and quickly searched for first aid, torches and weapons.

Before we set off on foot down the escape tunnel, Ms. Pang hands me two bright-orange pills.

"Take these," she orders. "They'll repair any muscle damage."

I do not ask how they will do such a job. I simply pop them in my mouth and dry swallow them. If she says they will fix me up, who am I to argue?

The three of us head down the tunnel.

Thankfully, the track's power died the same time the train did. This is very much a positive result for our escape bid.

Above us, dust-covered strip lights flicker on and off, adding to the fear factor.

The torches Mr. Tanaka and I carry are our only true source of illumination. They cut through the dark, sending dust motes spinning and wheeling. Ms. Pang walks behind us, swinging her rifle from left to right and from ceiling to floor as we go. I tighten my grip on my pistol and hope that if I do have to fire, luck will be on my side.

The tunnel is quiet , unnaturally so.

The sound of our fleeing footsteps becomes a soundtrack of hope and freedom, chasing away the silence and the fear it contains.

When Mr. Tanaka sneezes however, I almost have heart failure. The old man apologises for his sudden outburst.

"Stale air. Plays havoc with my sinuses. If only..."

Ms. Pang hushes us to be silent.

I freeze.

From somewhere in the darkness ahead of us, there comes a sound.

We are not alone.

Someone wearing heavy boots is marching towards us.

As far as I am aware, ghosts do not usually wander around wearing shoes. They prefer the silent approach.

All the same, there is no knowing who or what is really approaching. Best play it safe, at least for now.

I think about killing the torches, but plunging us into near-darkness seems like a bad choice. Instead, the three of us stand like statues, ready to blast anything remotely ghostly off the face of the earth.

Time passes.

The booted being continues its march towards us.

In the near distance, the tunnel snakes off to the right. It is from around this bend that our mystery guest star will appear.

We do not have to wait long.

A nil-by-mouth walks directly into our torch beams and stops.

The gangly black-clad creature cocks its head to one side, as if it's listening for something.

Or someone

From this far away, and without enough light, it is hard to tell whether the nil-by-mouth is male or female. One thing I do notice is that they don't have their compad .

This is not good. What happens if we have to communicate? Should we use body language?

"Hungry…"

It takes several seconds for realization to dawn on me.

The nil-by-mouth just spoke, audibly.

Before any of us have time to register, the nil-by-mouth begins running full speed at us, screaming its heart out.

"HUNGRY!"

Ms. Pang does not hesitate to shoot the raging cultist.

Her aim is absolutely true. Two blasts to its skeletal torso send the nil-by-mouth flying backwards down the tunnel.

It crashes to the floor.

A few moments of nerve-wracking silence follows as we wait to see what happens next.

The nil-by-mouth remains motionless.

"Let's go," whispers Ms. Pang. "We need to get out of here."

Albeit a little slowly, the three of us walk to where the nil-by-mouth lies. Ms. Pang sails straight past it, not even bothering to glance down at the body as she passes it.

Me, on the other hand...

I crouch down beside the body and take a good look.

He is certainly dead. No doubt about that. Ms. Pang's E-4 has punched two holes straight through his chest.

If today was a normal day, those wounds would have really grossed me out.

Today is as far from normal as it could get.

The thing that unnerves me is the faceplate.

Instead of it completely covering his mouth, his faceplate has been cut open. A ragged gash stretches diagonally across its length.

The dead nil-by-mouth leers back at me, makeshift metallic jaws glinting in the beam of my torch.

How did he manage to do that?

More importantly, why?

Mr. Tanaka pats me on the shoulder, cutting my investigation short.

"Let's go," he says.

I get to my feet and follow my friend further down the tunnel.

Another ten or so minutes of walking passes by without threat.

My palms are covered with a film of perspiration, my heart beating at twice its normal strength.

How long until we are set upon by something freakish or just plain evil?

And there, around ten feet away from us, we spot it. An exit.

"I told you we'd make it," whispers Mr. Tanaka.

I cannot speak for the others, but a smile of relief manages to find its way onto my previously grave face. The three of us pick up our pace and hurry towards the way out.

The sign on the door informs us that this 'Emergency Grav-lift' will take us all the way up to 'Safe Area Three', wherever that may be.

"Close to the old Osaka Castle Park ruins," says Ms. Pang, eavesdropping in on my thoughts, again. "From there, we can make our way to the bay and past the force wall."

The lift opens, allowing us in. We board without a second thought, the door slithering to a close once we are all inside.

Over the course of the last few days, I have been in a lot of lifts. This one is the smallest of them all. There is barely enough room to contain our unlikely trio. The whole of the compartments' ceiling glows orange. An automated safety announcement kicks in, and falters.

"Scanning... Detect... det... de... de..."

"Fuck."

The expletive I spit is loud and heartfelt. It fills the cramped space we occupy, shocking my companions like a slap to the face.

I do not apologise.

"This is it then?" I say. "We die down here because of..."

"Insufficient pow... pow..."

"Override Pang beta triple-six," shouts Ms. Pang.

The orange light fades to warm, soothing red as the lift hums to life and glides smoothly upwards.

When the lift opens its door, all we see beyond is black.

The darkness here is a living entity, snuffing out our torch beams after just a few meters.

"Walk straight forward," says Ms. Pang. "There's a door at the other end of this room. Follow me."

Even though my subconscious is telling me not to venture out of the lift, I realise we have little choice. Now is not the time to think of what the dark may be concealing, such thoughts can only hinder our escape. We have to keep moving.

Single file, we advance into pitch-black nothingness.

"This should be a manned security post," mutters Ms. Pang. "At least two troopers at all times..."

"I think we can forgive them for abandoning their post," quips Mr. Tanaka. "Today's a rather unusual day, after all."

For the first time in my life, I find myself disagreeing with the old man.

Today is not unusual.

Today is totally fucked.

After several more meters of stumbling blindly forward, Ms. Pang calls us to a halt.

"Door," she says. "Wait."

I hear her tapping at something, presumably a security panel. Then she curses under her breath and sighs.

"Power's out," she informs us. "Have to use the manual lock."

A hideous screeching noise then reverberates around the room. I wince sharply. Partly due the skin-crawling sensation that sweeps over me, but mostly because the noise is damn loud.

Thankfully, the process of unlocking the door is over quickly.

The blackened room turns as quiet as death.

"Are you ready?" Ms. Pang asks.

"Is it too late to say otherwise?" asks Mr. Tanaka.

Without waiting for my answer, the door is slowly pulled open, inch by squeaking inch. Once fully open, we finally say goodbye to our subterranean existence and venture back out into the real world.

And then I see the world has been painted in blood.

We stand before the crumbling walls of the Osaka Castle ruins. History says it was once a fine structure and a major attraction for tourists. Now it is mostly rubble, strangled by dead trees and tentacle-like roots. The moat surrounding has long dried out; a trench filled with debris is all that remains of its defenses. Only the main tower remains intact, standing tall and defiant against the ravages of time.

Behind the ruins lies the metropolis of Osaka Sector, with its towering buildings of silver and its countless walkways and mushroom-shaped viewing platforms.

I can only imagine how wonderful this view would have been before today.

I guess it would have been truly awe-inspiring.

But not anymore.

Not ever again.

The towers of Osaka burn as they claw at an eternal night sky. Devoid of stars, a crimson moon claims the void above the city as its own, gloating at the destruction below.

And even though we are so very far away, we can hear screaming. Millions of voices call out in torment, their agony carried from Osaka on a scalding wind.

And behind that desperate wailing, we hear laughter.

Any remote ideas I had concerning rescuing Mother are snatched from my grasp and crushed into atoms.
Osaka is lost.
The Blood Daughter reigns.

# TWENTY-EIGHT

We follow Ms. Pang away from the castle ruins and onto a path flanked by tall trees. The density of the forest on either side of us leaves me feeling claustrophobic. The light from the red moon does little to dispel this eerie sensation, and after several meters, I become convinced the trees are closing in on us.

"Something's not right."

It is Mr. Tanaka who speaks, beating me to the point by seconds. Ms. Pang stops and whirls around to face us.

"Of course something's not right," she snarls. "Osaka is burning in Hell..."

She then stops abruptly, rolls back her left sleeve and looks at her wrist, as if to check the time.

What makes this action even stranger is that her wrist is definitely watch free.

After a few seconds of staring at her bare arm, I am convinced she smiles.

I am about to question her weird behaviour when a teenage girl wearing a blood-stained white dress emerges from out of the line of trees to our left.

The first thing we do is aim our weapons at the crimson-spattered figure that is stepping out onto the path.

On seeing a trio of guns pointed at her, she raises her hands in a request for mercy.

"They came for me when the sun died," she says. "My parents tried to stop them, but there were too many to fight."

Her voice is light and soft, with a musical quality to it.

"I don't suppose I will see them again."

Lowering my gun, I take a tentative step towards her, but Mr. Tanaka grabs me by the arm and pulls me back.

The girl raises her head and looks at us each in turn. Her short black hair frames her slim, pale face, her fringe sticks to her forehead with sweat. The terror in her eyes is a harrowing thing to witness.

"Are you going to try to kill me, too?"

The question is barely audible, but we all hear it.

The words ring and echo in my eardrums like peals of thunder.

Most surprisingly, it is Ms. Pang who speaks for us.

"No."

Both Mr. Tanaka and I are a little stunned by Pang's sudden display of human kindness.

She smiles at our looks of astonishment and taps a finger against her temple.

"Psychic, remember?"

She walks across to the girl, gun lowered.

"This girl has seen enough horror for one day, if not a lifetime."

The girl nods meekly.

"I have seen the most terrible things," she whimpers. "Horrible, evil things..."

Mr. Tanaka loosens his grip on my arm.

"Yes," he says. "I truly believe she has."

I have to agree with him there. I can clearly see she has been through much worse than we have.

I failed to save Miaka and Mother. The least I can do is help save this girl.

"What's your name?" I ask her.

"Kumori," she replies.

"I'm Kichi, this is Mr. Tanaka and that's Ms. Pang. We're gonna escape from Osaka. You want to tag along?"

Kumori nods.

Ms. Pang looks away from us and back up the forest-straddled path.

Then she checks her naked wrist again.

"We must keep moving," she says. "This way."

And with that, she is off. Pang strides away from us on those heels of hers, leaving us with no option but to chase after her.

And so we do, with Kumori following alongside us.

Deeper into the forest park we go.

A creeping sense of doom grows with every step I take. The sooner we reach the force-barrier, the better.

When Ms. Pang stops to check her non-existent watch for the third time, I decide that I need to know what is going on with her.

"Do you have some kind of weird nervous tic?"

"Sorry?"

"You keep checking the time and forgetting you left your watch at home. What's with that?"

Miss Pang glances up at the sky and then thrusts her wrist forward for me to see.

Just visible, below the skin, something pulses. It is oval in shape and about the size of my thumbnail.

"And that is?"

"Bio-tracker," she says through a broad grin. "Activated shortly after we reached the surface. I did worry perhaps the force-barrier may interrupt its signal. That or Armageddon. Happily, neither did."

"And that's good because?"

Ms. Pang smiles and looks back to the sky.

I follow suit, as does Mr. Tanaka and Kumori.

A sleek, black aircraft quite literally appears out of nowhere. Like a triangular piece of night that has detached itself from the sky, the craft hovers silently above us.

"Transport out of here," says Ms. Pang. "Courtesy of Hong Kong City."

A circle of light appears from the middle of the craft's base, shining down like a spotlight. Ms. Pang steps into it.

"If you ever want to see sunlight again, I suggest you join me. Hong Kong City may be a little different to Osaka, but I assure you it's a lot fucking safer!"

"She's right," says Mr. Tanaka. "Come along, young Kichi."

For a moment, a part of me truly and honestly feels that this is it.

The end.

Young Kichi Honda is going to board an HK stealth craft and fly straight out of Hell.

But then I hear it.

One word.
Two syllables.
"Ki-chi."

I have heard stories of travelers lost in the desert, and how their minds snapped due to lack of food and water.

On the very brink of death, their fevered imaginations conjured up cruel hallucinations of things like a water-filled oasis or imminent rescue. Some saw images of their loved ones, encouraging them to keep crawling towards the inevitable.

While I am neither close to dying of starvation or dehydration, I am in a situation where death could come and take me at any given moment. So if I was to have a nervous breakdown, this would be the perfect time.

Hearing Mother's voice makes me think that time has arrived.

When I see the impossible sight on the path we have just walked down, I believe I have totally lost the plot.

Standing proudly in the wrong space and time is the door to my apartment.

Slightly ajar, I can see into the darkened hallway. From further inside comes the voice of Mother again, her haunting cry for help drifts down the path towards me. The two syllables turn into hands that clutch at my heartstrings and pull with all their might.

"Ki-chi..."

*"Love is the strongest weapon. She will use her against you."*
Miaka's warning.
She knew this would happen.
And here it is.

The last temptation of Kichi Honda.

Thing is, I am not stupid. I know that walking through that door means one just one thing for Kichi Honda.

Death.

"Ki-chi…"

I turn away from the door.

Mr. Tanaka gives me a warm and understanding smile.

"Let's get out of here," he says.

My old friend hobbles as fast he can towards the warm glow of the gravity beam.

I am all set to follow him, but something compels me to glance back towards home one last time.

That is when I notice Kumori.

The girl stands in the now fully-open doorway of my apartment, peering into the dark.

"Hello?" she calls. "Is someone there?"

"Ki-chi…"

On hearing Mother's reply, Kumori slowly turns on the spot to face us.

But there is something different about her now.

Gone is the visage of a victim, of an innocent girl caught up in the horror of a world gone mad.

Now we see someone who exudes confidence, some-one who is fully aware of what is really happening around them and is loving every single minute of it.

"Can't you hear her?" she taunts. "Can't you hear her calling?"

Kumori walks purposely in our direction. The aura of menace around her increases with every bare-footed step she takes.

"How can you ignore her? Don't you love your mummy?"

"Get us out of here!" yells Mr. Tanaka, his voice shak-ing with fear. "Kichi, come on!"

I then hear Ms. Pang jabbering in her native tongue, urgently giving instructions to whoever is in the craft hovering above this scene of insanity.

Next thing I know, she is flying over my head,

She hits the floor head first, the impact smashing her skull into hundreds of gory fragments.

Kumori calmly steps over her corpse.

"I didn't like that woman," she says. "She never played fair, always cheated. Always reading people's minds."

"Kichi!"

Back in the gravity beam, my dear old friend is on his knees. I can see his tears streaming down his weathered face.

"Kichi, the girl..."

The beam containing Mr. Tanaka suddenly becomes an intense pillar of blinding white. I fling my arms up to shield my eyes.

"The girl, she's..."

The warning the old man was about to give me is cut short. Both he and the light containing him disappear.

A rumbling sound fills the air.

Then silence.

The stealth craft has set off on its journey back to Hong Kong City, taking with it the only friend I ever really had.

"Goodbye, Mr. Tanaka," I say to the empty space he once occupied. "I hope you make it to two hundred."

"I am sure he will. And every single day will be one of torment. "

The girl is right behind me now.

Kimura.

"Not one day will pass where he does not think of you, and how he left you behind."

"I know who you really are," I say. "I know."

She laughs at this. It is the same laugh I heard coming from the burning city.

"Of course you know me. I have lived in your hopes and dreams and nightmares. I have danced behind your closed eyes and upon your wagging tongue."

A hand is placed on my left shoulder.

My entire body becomes numb with cold.

I slump to my knees, the gun I am holding falls from my limp hand.

"When the villagers came for me, I never got to say goodbye to my parents. All my mother did was scream and scream and scream."

I fall flat on my face. But I feel no pain. I feel nothing but cold.

"Why don't you want to say goodbye to your mother?" asks the girl once more, her voice both melodic and haunting. "Is it because you think she's already dead? She's not. She's just behind that door. All you need to do is go inside and find her. Then you can say goodbye."

The girl picks me up from the floor with ease. I lie helplessly in her frost-cold arms as she carries me towards the door of my apartment.

"Once you've said goodbye, I'll show you what you've been dreaming of all this time. I'll show you all those things you were forbidden to talk about, all those things you wished you could one day see. All the blood and the tears and the pain and the suffering."

I am swept into the darkness of my home. The door slams shut as soon as we are over the threshold.

"And then," whispers Ai. "Once you've seen everything...

Then you will become one of us."

# TWENTY-NINE

Reality, as I know it, has ceased to exist,
No longer am I lying petrified in the arms of a fiend.
Now I am back in my apartment, shuffling sleepily from
my bedroom towards the living room.

As per usual, Mother sits waiting for me on the sofa.

Of course, she doesn't acknowledge me as I enter. The
only thing she is focusing on is that huge blank TV
screen across from her.

I walk around to the back of the sofa and pick up the
two long cables that trail from the rTV box on the wall. I
fold back the two flaps of prosthetic skin located at the
corner of each of her eyes, exposing two deep hungry-

looking sockets. Then I slide the jacks into place with two sickening clicks.

The screen bursts into life as soon as the connections are made. The spiraling rTV logo fills the wall and a range of menus fly onto the screen, allowing Mother to choose what she wants to watch and who she wants to be.

Only this time is different.

Mother chooses not to select an rPorn star. Instead, she clicks on a new icon sitting at the bottom left corner of the screen.

Honda Family Album.

The screen is filled with multiple images, all of them identical.

Mother sitting on the sofa, calling for me.

Me walking into the living room and plugging her in.

The same sequence of events, repeated over and over again.

My life.

A living Purgatory.

The line between reality and illusion is blurred.

The living room dissolves into spirals of mono-chrome. Wisps of grey dance and whirl around me like a tornado, until shooting off like comets to reform, re-structure. Time and space morph around me...

"Ki...chi."

I close the door to my bedroom.

On some twisted form of auto-pilot, I follow Mother's lamenting cries.

Mother sits waiting for me on the sofa.

Of course, she doesn't acknowledge me as I enter. The only thing she is focusing on is that huge blank TV screen across from her.

I walk around to the back of the sofa and pick up the two long cables that trail from the rTV box on the wall.

Slowly, methodically, I wrap the cables around Mother's skeletal neck.

Then I pull them, tighter and tighter.

Mother gurgles and chokes as I throttle her to death, her skinny arms and legs flailing and flapping uselessly against the sofa.

In her last moments, she shows more signs of life than she has in years.

I release my grip on the cables around ten minutes after Mother stops fighting.

Slumping back against the wall, my breath coming in great gulps, I am shocked by just how easy it was to kill her.

"I should have done this years ago," I say to the back of her dead head.

Mother does not answer.

No huge surprise there.

I mean, why change the habit of a lifetime?

A smile creeps across my face.

I snigger.

Then I crack up.

The sound of my sickened laughter fills the apartment. It reaches into every corner, consuming silence, shadows and space.

Soon, the sound is all that exists...

The void takes me.

I am now in a world where eyes have become a redundant organ, a place where one must embrace the darkness to exist.

Welcome to the kingdom of the blind.

My other senses become accentuated to compensate for my loss of sight. Stale air fills my nostrils, stinging cold bites at any exposed flesh.

Someone inhales sharply somewhere ahead of me.

"Is someone there?"

I shake my head in disgust as soon as the question tumbles out of my mouth.

Not because it is insanely obvious, but because I know exactly who it is and what will be their answer.

"Ki..."

I wait for her to finish.

Come on, Mother. Give me the last syllable.

You can do it.

Say my name.

Please.

"Ki..."

Arms outstretched, I slowly navigate my way towards the living room.

The darkness intensifies.

I begin to wonder if I have actually been struck blind, as my eyes refuse to become accustomed to the stygian environment of my apartment. My memory tries to paint images onto the black canvas to help me find my way.

The door leading to the kitchen.

The painted handprint on the wall from when I was six.

The crack on the ceiling that looks like a centipede.

None of these images stay for more than a moment.

All of them fade into the black.

The living room is beyond cold. Freezing air stings my skin and makes my eyes water. Even breathing hurts.

But this is not the thing that bothers me most.

That dubious honour belongs to the smell.

I am reminded of my old coin collection and of how my hands used to smell metallic after I had examined them over and over.

That and rotting durian fruit.

When the toe of my boot nudges something lying on the floor, I freeze in horror.

I know what it is.

Who it is.

"Ki..."

I crouch down beside Mother.

The stench of blood and rot makes me gag. Somehow, I manage to keep myself together. Perhaps this is due to me not being able to see her.

My lack of vision has become a small mercy.

Part of me wants to reach out to touch her, but I dare not do so. I am scared of what my fingers will find, what information touching her will give me.

"Mother?"

She does not answer.

"Mother. It's me. Kichi."

"Ki..."

Mother's cold fingers suddenly caress the back of my left hand. I automatically flinch and think about pulling away from her.

"...chi."

But I do not.

"Yes. It's me. I'm here."

"Ki...chi."

Mother's reply is nothing more than a whisper. But the sound of my name rings in my ears like temple bells.

"You..."

My heart falters as she begins a new sentence.

How long has it been since she spoke to me?

How long have I waited to hear something other than just my name and that damned plug...

"You... came... back."

I grip Mother's withered hand in mine.

"Yes. I came back. I'm here."

"Kichi."
"Yeah, Mother. It's me."

I sit with her in the cold darkness of our home.
It is all I can do.
I cradle her hand in mine and just sit.
The sound of her breathing grows ever fainter. I move my fingers to her wrist, searching for a pulse. What I find can only be described as feeble, weak.
"It's OK, Mother. Let go. Rest now."
Mother releases a long soft sigh, emptying her lungs of air.
She does not inhale again.
I sit with her in the cold, dark silence of our home.
The tears that stream down my face burn my skin.
"Bye, Mother."

I feel reality shift.
The world around me changes.
Form and location become liquid, melting into rivers of nothing. Then, just as quickly, they reform, solidify, becoming tangible once more. Only the dark remains constant.
A voice, both ancient and evil, echoes towards me.
It comes from everywhere at once and from nowhere, screaming inside my head and whispering into my ears.
The Blood Daughter is here with me.
"Why do you weep, child?"

Her mocking inquisition both numbs and angers me. I bite down on my tongue hard. I can taste blood.

"Why do you weep, child? Why do you shed tears for the mother you despised?"

I want to address her directly, but the surround sound from Hell confuses me. In the end, I give up on trying to pinpoint an exact location and just say the words.

"She was my mother. That's the reason."

"But you hated her. She made you a slave, just as she was."

"Yeah."

"Foolish is the child who laments the passing of the parent they wished to be undead."

The next voice I hear is my own. The Blood Daughter mimics my internal monologue perfectly.

"I wish she was undead. I wish so much."

Those often-thought words come at me like a swarm of agitated honey wasps. Each syllable becomes a sting loaded with venomous spite.

Realisation hits me.

This is my Hell.

Something moves in front of me.

This is not a feeling I have. This is real.

I see it.

A twisting chaos of writhing, twitching limbs that are too numerous to count.

Multiple insect-like arms reach out towards me; long fingers with nails like knives threaten to slice my face into ribbons.

Billowing black robes show glimpses of a female form, but one that has been charred by flame. The creature's skin is a hideous mess of cruel scars and burns with pus leaking from them.

Baleful white eyes bore into me, her gaze shredding my skin and muscle, splintering my bones, setting every nerve on fire.

The Blood Daughter smiles, a rictus of gory happiness that stretches grotesquely wide across her face. A blackened, swollen tongue slithers out of that maw, pushing its way over rows of shark-like teeth to lick at scabbed lips.

"Am I not beautiful to behold?" she asks.

I double-up in intense pain. Nausea rises from the pit of my stomach.

The Blood Daughter laughs as I vomit over my boots.

She is still laughing as I pass out.

Cold.

I am so cold, it hurts.

I can hear the howl of wind as it ravages me, sending violent tremors coursing through me.

Am I outside?

One thing is for sure, I am standing. Last thing I remember is falling to a puke-covered floor.

All I need do is open those eyes of mine and all will be revealed.

But I do not want to.

No way do I want to see her again.

Laughter.

Soft, mocking.

Ai is close by.

Better her than the monstrosity she became.

I open my eyes.

I am standing on platform seven.

Here I am once more, back to the place where my story really began.

Although perpetual night has fallen, I can still see the city clearly.

The neon glow has been replaced with flames.

Flickering shadows are thrown up against the tower blocks, creating illusions of gigantic horrors that could possibly be all too real.

The sound of the city has also changed.

Gone are the sounds of sirens and hover-traffic, the music, the advertisements.

The incessant chatter of millions of citizens has been snuffed out, the soundtrack of life turned off.

A new song now plays.

A song of death.

Ai walks to my side. We are now standing at the edge of the platform.

Much like when the power failed that day...

I do not turn to look at the blood-stained child.

Instead, I stare out across the burning city, listening to the echoes of screams and inhuman laughter that drift along on the sub-zero breeze.

"Do you like it?" asks Ai.

It takes concerted effort to control my chattering teeth and answer her.

"No."

"No?"

I bring my numb but shaking hands up to my face and blow on my fingers in a futile attempt to regain warmth.

Ai continues.

"But this is what you've always wanted. You and the old man spoke of nothing else. You wanted to know what happened to Tokyo all those years ago. Well..."

She pauses and points to the horizon I am glued to.

"Here is your answer."

As if on cue, a tower block in the near distance crumbles silently into rubble.

"Fear is the most powerful emotion," says Ai. "Fear is energy. Every tale told about me, every mention of my name, every life taken to placate my wrath has fed me. Through fear, I have become powerful. Thanks to the terrified minds of millions, I am now able to bring my gift of death to all of Osaka. Thanks to Kazuo Shimizu, to the Silent Minority, the DPA, Ms. Pang, Mr. Tanaka. Thanks to you."

Perhaps it is too cold to cry.

Perhaps all my remaining tears have been frozen in their ducts and it is now impossible for them to be shed.

The urge to wail and sob however, is far too much for me to contain.

All the grief and pain I've been holding in is expelled in a scream that drowns out all other sound. I bellow my rage and fear out across this now dead city. Only when my throat becomes sore do I stop and whirl around to face the girl who bought Hell to Earth.

The words that come out of my mouth hurt, in more ways than one.

"Why? Why did you do this?"

Ai simply shrugs and smiles. Her answer breaks me, sending me once more to the floor.

"Why not?"

She turns away from the wreckage of what was once Kichi Honda and stares out lovingly over her new domain.

After a few moments, she reaches down and ruffles my hair like an affectionate parent.

"It's time," she says. "Time for you to join us."

Somehow, I manage to conjure up enough strength to get back to my feet. Every muscle hurts. Everything hurts.

I walk to the edge of platform seven and stand beside Ai.

Together, we look across the ruins of what was once my home, what was once a place of life and hope and love.

But all of that has gone now.

Nothing exists here except pain.

I turn to Ai and give her my cheeriest smile.

"Fuck you."

I step off the edge of the platform.

# THIRTY

For the briefest of moments, I experience a sense of utter bliss.

Gravity seduces me, pulling me down to my death.
Oddly enough, I have never felt more at peace.
Everything suddenly makes so much sense.
Is this Nirvana?
Have I achieved enlightenment?

A universe of indescribable agony explodes within me as I smash into something, possibly a walkway.
Bones break, limbs twist and snap.
A galaxy of stars go supernova, scorching my eyes.

This is it.
Game over, Kichi Honda.
It's been a blast.

Taste of metal.
Choking,
Spit it out.
Breathe out.
Can't.
Breathe.

Wasabi.
Kichi.
Mother.

# THIRTY-ONE

Is this thing working?
    Is it on?
    Right, thank you.
    Yes, Yes, I remember. Keep it short. I'm not an idiot you know!
    OK.
    OK.
    Here we go then.
    This is a message for Kichi Honda.
    Kichi, it's Mr. Tanaka here.
    I know you are alive.

I want you to know that no matter what it takes, I will save you.

None of those ghosts in that damned city are a match for you, my girl. Use all the knowledge I gave you and stay alive. Use that clever head of yours and stay out of danger.

I'm going to save you, Kichi. I promise.

I will save you.

OK. That's it, I'm done here. Just make sure you broadcast it.

Yes! I realise how slim the chances are!

I'm sorry. I'm sorry. Please, just make sure the message is sent.

Thank you.

Yes, can I get a cup of tea, please?

It's been four years since Osaka fell.

At least, I think it is four. Not easy to keep track of time when every day is just one long night. The marks I've carved into the wooden beams of my room tally up to almost four, so I'll go with that.

My name is Hiro. I used to own a small restaurant that sold wasabi-flavoured hot dogs. Back then, I hated the damn things. Far too spicy for my taste. I never told my customer's that though, it would have been terrible for business.

Right now, I could kill for one.

Although we're safe within the temple grounds, a sense of dread has been growing within me for the last few months.

I have this feeling in my gut that time is finally running out for us, that something awful is about to happen.

I've spoken to the monks here about it, and the two DPA troopers that took refuge with the rest of the survivors. They keep assuring me we're quite safe. So long as we don't stray beyond the walls without protective wards or during true-night.

Only a fool would do that. Or someone suicidal. There have been a few of those over the years.

There are eighty-seven of us in total. eighty-seven assorted citizens of Osaka.

Men, women, children. Monks and DPA troopers. There used to be a lot more.

Survivors of Hell on Earth.

Once the people realised staying in our apartments would only mean death, we headed for the temples. For some reason, we knew we would be safe there.

Strange how we all discovered faith as a collective, but there you go.

Perhaps miracles do happen.

I remember the journey well, even though I've tried to blank out parts of it from my memory. Some of the things I saw on that pilgrimage were beyond horrific, beyond evil.

Creatures of nightmares preying on the living. I saw friends die in untellable agony.

I saw darkness snuff out the light.

Around two hundred of us converged on the nearest temple, an ancient place that had been rebuilt numerous times over the centuries.

I think at one point, the whole place had been relocated, brick by brick.

Luckily for us, the temple had been equipped with a servo-hatch, hooked up to an eterno-generator. Without this, we would have starved to death within months.

Food portions may be limited, but at least we have food. Scouting parties sometimes come back with canned goods and wild animals.

Those are good days.

In the first year, many scouting parties never came back at all.

As the years have gone by, we seem to be left alone for the most part. No longer are we hunted like animals. Instead, we are observed and taunted. Only being picked off when mistakes are made, when we think we are safe.

The laughter when they take one of us chills us to the very bone.

Now we live under the watchful eye of Buddha.

We give thanks each day and pray for his continued protection.

But we also thank another.

After year two had passed, a scouting party returned with some communication equipment. At the time, we had a tech guy amongst our ranks. Sadly, he died several weeks ago. Nice guy. Always smiling.

The ghost of Red Raku carved a permanent smile into his face.

I wish I could remember his name.

It took a while to get the equipment working, and when it was up and running, we discovered to our disappointment that we could only receive transmissions.

Our sadness lifted when we heard broadcasts from other survivors.

It did our souls good to know we were not the last of the citizens of Osaka.

Others still lived, much like us, in places of worship.

In temples and churches, the children of Nihon lived on.

All of them spoke about something called The Honda Transmission.

It didn't take long for our tech guy to find it.

Five words, repeated over and over again.

Kichi.

Honda.

Will.

Save.

You.

I used to know a girl called Kichi. She loved wasabi.

I wondered for a while if it was the same girl. And if so, how could she save us?

But I was alone in my doubts. The monks proclaimed it as a message of hope. Those five words soon became part of our daily mantras and prayers.

Kichi Honda, whoever and wherever you are, I pray those words are true; because the doom that I feel in my heart won't go away.

Please, Kichi. Save us.

The representative from Thailand finishes his report and takes a seat. A halo of sweat clings to his bald head, the occasional bead dripping down to hit the mound of paperwork he holds before him in shaking hands.

"And the walls are holding?" clarifies the Pacifica rep, her voice like sandpaper. The man from Thailand nods silently.

Around the table sit experts from different corners of the globe: Thailand, China, Hong Kong City, Pacifica, Europa, The NUK, United Korea, Sovia, and the American States.

All of them have told the same story.

The walls are holding, no signs of breach.

Four years after the second Nihon ghost quake, a total of seventeen cities went on to suffer the same fate. The most recent being the entire south-west of England.

The death toll worldwide is beyond comprehension.

Every month, these experts meet to discuss the situation.

To discuss a world living in fear, a world on the brink of falling into Hell.

They talk about the integrity of spirit walls, the protests and riots, the possibility of complete social collapse.

No solution is ever found.

The expert from America stands and points at a wall-mounted screen. It promptly switches on with a low hum, displaying various views of the planet from space.

"As you can see, these satellite reports clearly show that supernatural activity has decreased significantly over the last five months." He jabs a pudgy finger in the general direction of the screen. "The red areas are what we now know to be the portals or gates that caused the ghost quakes in each affected area. Activity levels in red areas remain unchanged."

"What of Nihon?" asks a thin man from Pacifica.

"To hell with Nihon," spits the American. "They brought this apocalypse upon us all."

An immediate hush falls over the room, every expert bowing their head in order to avoid the hate-filled gaze of the man speaking.

All except for one.

Rising slowly to his feet, a man ancient in years smiles and shakes his head.

"Every meeting we have, the same conclusion we seem to reach," he says in a mocking tone. "We come up empty handed. No solutions whatsoever. We are as weak as English tea."

Agent Tanaka, the Hong Kong City paranormal expert, is given the floor.

"I was there," he continues. "When Osaka fell. Yes, it is very easy to blame Nihon for what is happening. But what good would it do? More importantly, do you honestly think this is all over? Do you think the last of the cities on earth has fallen? Do you?"

While all eyes are on the old man, no one's mouth moves to rebut his charge.

"The lives I saw lost that day. The horrors I witnessed. You have no right to put blame on a city of innocent people! No right at all!"

Despite his obvious anger, the old man remains calm. Even when his milky eyes begin to fill with tears, he maintains composure.

"I left a friend to die in that place. A good friend, the only friend I ever had. Now, I hear a message I sent to her has become folklore within Osaka Sector. As if that message would ever reach her now."

"You may be wrong about that, Agent Tanaka."

Now it is my turn to speak.

I stand up and give the old man my sincerest smile.

"That message has reached someone for sure. My intel says that your message, The Honda Transmission as it is known, can now be heard in what used to be London and Birmingham."

Tanaka's eyes grow wide at this.

"And what's more, the transmission has been answered."

The room explodes into a cacophony of shocked questions. I wave them calmly down into silence. I then reach into my bag and take out a wad of files, distributing one to each of the people sitting around the polished meeting table.

"My name, ladies and gentlemen, is Jonson Sykes. As well as being the new head of paranormal research in the NUK, I am also in charge of a project that, I firmly believe, will save our planet,"

I direct my next sentence at Agent Tanaka.

"And Kichi Honda."

His mouth drops, tears rolling down his lined face.

"If you could open your files to page one."

The panel of experts do as they're instructed. Attached to the first page is a photograph of a girl. She looks to be about eighteen years old or so, certainly no older than twenty. She frowns in the photo from behind a mess of long, brown hair. Her freckles soften the harshness of her stare.

"Ladies and Gentlemen, allow me to introduce operative Zoey Almost: Armageddonaut."

The story will continue in:
# *KillGhostCity*

# ABOUT THE AUTHOR

Simon Paul Wilson is an English man who traveled to Asia and found a second home. Heavily influenced by his time in China and Thailand, Simon's writing usually features strong, quirky, Asian female protagonists, surreal situations, and ghosts with very long hair. He also likes to include Asian food somewhere in the stories he writes. Some readers have commented they feel hungry while reading his books.

*GhostCityGirl* is the first in a series he is calling *The Ghost Quake Chronicles*. He hopes you will enjoy the crazy ride into the depths of Hell and back, and that you don't have too many nightmares.

When not writing, Simon listens to post and prog rock at a very loud volume. He also plays air-guitar. He thought you may like to know that.

Follow him on twitter @spwzen

# SPECIAL THANKS

Thanks to all the folks who have been waiting for this novel since the days of the Authonomy website.

Huge thanks to the Not A Pipe family, especially Benjamin Gorman, Karen Eisenbrey, Viveca Shearin, and Michaela Thorn.

Special thanks to Justin, Lindsey, Martin, and Tina.

Extra special thanks to Mum, Dad, Jacque, Neal, and Violet.

Huge extra special thanks to Xiuting and Corey.

You guys all rock! Much love to you all.